the murmurings

the mur

murings

CARLY ANNE WEST

simon pulse

NEW YORK   LONDON   TORONTO   SYDNEY   NEW DELHI

SIMON PULSE
An imprint of Simon & Schuster Children's Publishing Division
1230 Avenue of the Americas, New York, NY 10020
First Simon Pulse hardcover edition March 2013
Copyright © 2013 by Carly Anne West
SIMON PULSE and colophon are registered trademarks of
Simon & Schuster, Inc.
For information about special discounts for bulk purchases, please contact
Simon & Schuster Special Sales at 1-866-506-1949
or business@simonandschuster.com.
The Simon & Schuster Speakers Bureau can bring authors to
your live event. For more information or to book an event contact
the Simon & Schuster Speakers Bureau at 1-866-248-3049
or visit our website at www.simonspeakers.com.
Designed by Hilary Zarycky
The text of this book was set in New Baskerville.
Manufactured in the United States of America
2 4 6 8 10 9 7 5 3 1
Library of Congress Cataloging-in-Publication Data
West, Carly Anne.
The murmurings / Carly Anne West. — 1st Simon Pulse hardcover ed.
p. cm.
Summary: After her older sister dies from an apparent suicide and her body
is found hanging upside down by one toe from a tree, sixteen-year-old Sophie
starts to hear the same voices that drove her sister to a psychotic break.
ISBN 978-1-4424-4179-8
[1. Death—Ficton. 2. Supernatural—Fiction. 3. Sisters—Fiction.
4. Psychiatric hospitals—Fiction.] I. Title.
PZ7.W51733Mu 2013
[Fic]—dc23
2012013296
ISBN 978-1-4424-4181-1 (eBook)

For Matt, always

Sun slides through bars, painted stripes of life on slick walls.

Glittering blue and amber eyes track blackness, eyes starved for prey.

I fit like a knife in the pocket of him.

Paper cups overflow with ups and downs.

I feel mostly sideways.

He says it can't all be about what's Taken.

I say there's shelter in the West's wickedest town but it won't last.

He says there's a chance.

I say, What's the point?

He points to me.

1

I'm supposed to wonder why Gregor Samsa is a cockroach. Not how. *Why.* That's the way Mrs. Dodd says we need to think if we're going to analyze *The Metamorphosis.* Otherwise, the *how* gets distracting. Apparently, Franz Kafka didn't want us questioning *how* it's possible that some guy could wake up one morning as a cockroach. We're supposed to focus on *why* he would be a giant, hideous insect, to ask *why* it had to happen to him and nobody else, to wonder *why* his family doesn't care.

It feels pretty familiar, actually: all those *why* questions, that whole family-not-caring thing. Except that my mom probably wouldn't notice if I grew antennae and a couple of extra legs, let alone take notice enough to throw apples at me across the dining room table. As much as I want to listen to what Mrs. Dodd is saying about Gregor Samsa and cockroaches, all I can think about is how I wanted my junior year to feel different. Maybe more like it was happening to me and not someone else. Maybe just . . . quieter. Nell was always the outgoing one. I liked being the sister of someone who was popular. It came with fringe benefits. No one teased me if I sat in a corner at lunch with a book, rather than at a table with friends. After Nell went into the hospital, though, everything changed. All of her so-called friends treated her like a leper. And now, I'm someone to be feared by association.

"And what's the significance of Grete, the sister? Anyone?"

In a way, it's better. Even if someone tapped me on the shoulder—some bland-looking new girl who didn't know anything about Nell, someone who didn't know that my mom drinks like it's her job, that I can't talk to my dad about it because I don't even know who he is and probably never will—and told me she wanted to be my best friend, what would I tell her? That I'm the girl whose sister heard whispers that weren't quite words, and saw things so dark they took away her light? That she was really good at hiding it from everyone but me? That Nell cut herself and ran away from her institution with some orderly named Adam Newfeld, and that no one saw her again until her body was found in Jerome, Arizona? That the police haven't found the orderly—who was probably the last one to see her alive—not that they've been trying very hard? That when I went to Jerome a week later to see where they found Nell's body, I felt like I was being watched the whole time, and when I returned to my car, Nell's journal was lying on the front seat?

"Why does Kafka pay so much attention to the father figure? Come on. Someone knows."

Or best yet, would I tell this pretend friend of mine that I'm starting to hear things too, just like Nell did before she got worse? Would I tell her about the thing in the mirror from that night?

"Sophie? You look deep in thought. Why don't you share what's on your mind?"

"The voice," I say.

I hear shuffling behind me. A chair creaks under shifting weight. Someone snickers. I swear I hear "freak" coughed. It wouldn't be the first time.

"Hmm, can you expand on that a little?" Mrs. Dodd's face is puckered with concern.

She thinks I'm getting at something and wants to get there with me. I swear Mrs. Dodd would take anything I said as gospel. She always gives me credit for understanding more than I do. Why she thinks I've got so much figured out is beyond me.

I take a stab at it. "Er, uh, the voice is important for explaining . . . his anger?" Gregor seems mad enough. I mean, if I woke up tomorrow and I was a giant insect, I'd be a little more than pissed.

Still, I wonder if it's worse to wake up and realize that your sister's dead, or that you'll probably wind up just like her. I wonder if that's not a hundred times worse.

"Okay . . ." Mrs. Dodd seems to chew on my words for a minute, then she swallows. Inspiration arrives. "Yes. Okay, anger. Absolutely. And this is the root of Kafka's imagery. Very good. Now, who can take it from here?"

Sure, why not? Anger's at the root of a lot of things.

That's when a memory grips me like a cramp, taking over my body and making me focus on that one singular pain. It's in reaction to a word: "root."

Every part of me remembers the tree roots bulging from the ground in Jerome. The roots of the tree that held Nell upside down amid its high, sprawling limbs until the elderly sheriff found her. She was in a position so unnatural that I still can't fully believe the report. But what I remember most is the feeling of my foot curving over the root of that goddamned tree.

I shudder, knocking my copy of *Franz Kafka's Collected Works* to the floor with a thud loud enough to attract the attention of the entire classroom. The snickering resumes. I look around, but nobody looks back. Like they're afraid I'll turn them to stone.

"Sorry," I mutter to no one in particular and lean for the book, which is just out of my reach. Mrs. Dodd is talking about Gregor Samsa's violin-playing sister, but all I hear is *sister, sister, sister.*

My head starts to swirl, and I'm so sure I'm going to throw up that I don't even ask Mrs. Dodd for a hall pass. I don't say a word. I just get up and charge to the front of the room.

"Sophie, are you—?"

I'm out the door before she can finish.

My cheeks are tingling by the time I enter the restroom. I push into the nearest stall (I don't even scan to see if I'm alone. There's no time) and promptly lose my breakfast: cottage cheese, cantaloupe, and half of a cinnamon-raisin bagel. I'm sure I'll never eat any of those foods again for as long as I live.

"Oh God," I mumble, shivering as I hear my words echo back to me in the dank bathroom.

I emerge from the stall and nearly jump right back into it when I see my reflection. I look like hell. In this light, my hair is less "chocolate auburn," as the box suggested, and more purple. Which matches the circles under my eyes. My eyes are deep-set as it is, so it sort of looks like my skull has swallowed them. My face is thinner than it used to be. I haven't had much of an appetite since Nell died.

Nell.

Nell is dead.

My sister is dead.

There's a faucet dripping. The rhythm is steady, and soon my heart begins to beat in time with it. Then there is nothing. It's as if all sound is pulled from the bathroom with the intake of a breath.

After a moment, sound returns, focused in my right ear, like a hand cupping the air beside my head.

Murmuring.

The sound is so close, yet I can't make out the words. But it wants to be heard.

"Sophie, what is it? What's the matter?"

Mrs. Dodd stands in the open doorway, her hay-colored hair swishing as the door clangs shut behind her. The murmuring is gone. The faucet is dripping again. A tiny spot on the mirror distorts my reflection—a tiny spot that wasn't there a minute ago.

It happened again.

"It's . . ." I start to say.

If I was going to tell anyone, it would probably be Mrs.

Dodd. She reads Poe and Tolstoy, and understands the poetry of Lord Byron and even Nietzsche. She once told us that when she reads Dostoevsky, she can almost hear the author breathing with her. She also gave me my very own copy of T. S. Eliot's *The Waste Land*—my sister's favorite—after Nell died.

"It's nothing," I say. "I-I'm sorry." I start to leave, but she stops me.

"Easy. It's fine. You know you can always talk to me, Sophie, if you need to."

She's trying to sound casual, but her face is scrunched up with worry.

"I'm fine." My voice comes out a little too loud, echoing in the bathroom like a vocal pinball. "Hey, aren't you supposed to be teaching?"

Her face finally relaxes when I say this. She's the only teacher I feel comfortable talking to like she's not a teacher. Maybe because she's never treated me like just another student.

"I figured it wouldn't take much to get you back in the classroom. I know how much you love Kafka," she says as she pushes the door open for me.

I don't have the heart to tell her I used to love him. Until he and every other author started making me think of Nell.

Back in the classroom, I return to my seat as quickly as

possible and fail to block out the whispers coming from Nell's former friends. I try to tell myself that the murmuring isn't getting louder, more insistent. I tell myself it's not happening more frequently.

And mostly, I tell myself that I didn't see the mirror start to ripple where my face was, like something was behind the glass, trying to get out.

The final bell for fifth period is already ringing as I throw my nearly uneaten lunch away. Now that I just don't give a shit, tardiness is a new habit I've developed. Besides, rushing anywhere in Phoenix's autumn heat only makes you sweat more than usual. The Sweep Monitor will catch me today, like he has every other day since the start of the school year.

"Sophie D.," says a deep voice from behind me. The Sweep Monitor.

Sweep is a holding tank of delinquency where the kids who aren't responsible enough to get to class before the door shuts get sent. Only the unluckiest of teachers, usually the football coach, Mr. Tarza, is assigned to babysit the Sweep room. Usually one of his junior varsity players gets stuck playing glorified dogcatcher. This month it's been Evan Gold, and he's on me like a hawk. A cute hawk, but still.

"Hey, Sophie D."

I don't stop walking. I'm already headed for the Sweep room. I just wish I could get there without having to talk to anyone. It's nothing against Evan. He's a junior too, and he recently transferred here from a private school on the other side of Phoenix. He knows all about Nell, so I can forget about that whole mysterious-new-friend-giving-me-a-fresh-start fantasy. The football players date the popular girls—the girls who used to call themselves Nell's friends—so of course they brought Evan up to speed pretty quickly. She died six months ago, but the rumors live on. They may not talk to me, but they don't whisper very quietly, either.

Evan's never said anything to me about Nell, even if his ear has been soaked with a mouthful of gossip. Instead, he says my name in a cool-cat kind of way, like he believes I might be just as cool as he is. He's in for a world of hurt. I'm nothing like Nell used to be. Not in the ways he'd like.

"Hey, look, I'm not trying to give you a hard time," he says apologetically. I turn around as he trots to catch up. He is easily a foot taller than me (which really isn't saying much since I'm only five foot two). His curly black hair is always messy, and today is no exception. But I never realized until now how pretty his eyes are, some sort of super-light brown, like amber.

"Seriously, I'm . . ." he stammers. Usually, Evan just escorts me to Sweep and makes inane chitchat about how lame school is or how Coach Tarza's riding his ass like a jockey. I hardly know him, but for some reason I think he tries to sound like someone he's not. Or maybe I'm just that desperate for someone to relate to. On this particular trip to Sweep, though, he doesn't sound like he's trying to be cool. His voice is deep, and even though I'm not cold, I have to brush the hairs down on my arms.

"Just doing your job?" I say jokingly, but it comes out angry. It seems like everything irritates me lately. I'm swearing more than I used to, which is quite an accomplishment considering I was already hitting the four-letter words pretty hard before all of this happened. My mom doesn't notice like she used to, but it makes me sound like a shrew around everyone else. So when I see Evan's face fall, I feel like a jerk.

"Nah, you get paid for a job. This is punishment for not making varsity," he says in an easy, self-deprecating way, but something about his wrinkled brow tells me he's actually embarrassed.

I've never seen someone popular look embarrassed. Nell never used to look embarrassed. She was into poetry, which should have exiled her to the Loners' table at lunch with me, but she always just looked entitled. It went beyond confidence, yet somehow she dodged arrogance.

"Only seniors make varsity here," I say, and he smiles a

little. His face is long, and his jawbones stick out like he's clamping his teeth together even when he's not. I can't help but smile back at him. It feels like the first time in six months I've moved my mouth that way, and it hurts.

"So what you're saying is I can't be the guy who scores the winning touchdown, gets the girl, and drives into the sunset in some kick-ass new car like in the movies?"

"I wouldn't know," I laugh. "I mostly stick to the scary stuff. I'm a sucker for horror films, old ones mostly."

It's not really worth mentioning that I've been staying away from that kind of stuff since Nell died. It's only fun when it doesn't feel so . . . real.

Evan's walking next to me now, and it feels like we should be holding hands or something. All at once, I'm desperate to cross my arms over my chest. I'm the only one in the family with big boobs and hips. Nell used to joke that my straight hair was the only flat thing on me. Lately, though, everything is loose and saggy on me.

We reach the Sweep room, and I'm barely used to the feeling of Evan beside me before he's trotting backward down the hallway.

"Try to stay out of trouble, Sophie D."

Then he stumbles a little, catches himself, and practically sprints around the corner. I'm still smiling when I open the door.

"Truancy is nothing to smile about," Coach Tarza says, barely looking up from his month-old *Sports Illustrated.*

I make a quick scan of the room before sitting at the desk closest to the door. It's just me and the stoners today. The earthy smell of marijuana hangs in the air, and I can only hope for a contact high to dull my senses. There are thirty-five more minutes of skull-crushing silence before sixth period. We're not allowed to do homework in Sweep, lest we try to turn our punishment into a study hall. So I'll use this time to pick the split ends of my dyed hair.

When the bell finally jolts me back to consciousness, my heart skips heavily in my chest. I had traveled someplace with Evan Gold, and pretty much no one else for miles and miles. In my imagined existence, I discovered soft lips that traced mine and hands that cupped the small of my back and pulled my hips against his. I would have given anything to stay in that world just a little longer. If I knew what normal felt like, I bet that daydream would have been it.

Nell David

October 11

My wrist doesn't burn anymore. I remember feeling pain, then no pain at all, then pain again. The doctors stitched me up in a hurry, then gave me some time to get settled (that's how they put it) before bringing in some shrink.

The shrink seems to be the top guy around here. He had a concerned look, as if he practiced furrowing his brow. Too small of a crease in his forehead implies he's cold. Too much tells me how crazy I really am. But the right crease says it all: It's not my fault.

Apparently there's not much hope for me, but he's going to give me a chance at getting back to normal. Only he doesn't use the word "I." He says "we." We're going to try this or that. We're going to take this slowly.

I don't remember what day that was. Yesterday maybe. They're letting me keep a journal. I guess they figure it's hard for someone to hurt themselves writing, assuming the pencil is dull enough.

I still hear the murmurs, but like always, I can't make out what the voice is saying. I can't tell if I'm supposed to. The pills don't do much to stop it. None of it really matters though. The voice didn't make me break the glass. The thing in the mirror did. And what's worse is that the doctors and nurses here seem to believe me. Not a single person has denied that what I saw—that what I've been hearing— is real.

2

I KNOW MOM'S PASSED OUT in her bedroom. It's too much to hope she's actually gone back to work, especially since her car is parked in the driveway, same as when I left for school. I give myself a minute on the porch before unlocking the front door. Every time I'm about to go inside, I have a hard time catching my breath. It's like my own house sucks the air straight from my body. But it's still home, so I keep coming back. Where else would I go?

I check the voice mails hoping someone's called Mom about a stylist job or a vacant booth for rent, and that this time, she'll take it.

The stilted robotic voice informs me there are two new messages.

Yes, hi, Ms. David. This is Dr. Jeremy Keller at the Oakside Behavioral Institute. I'm calling to follow up on my previous messages. I understand this is a difficult time. We would like to do everything we can to ease you through this progression. When you can, please call us back at the main number, which I'm sure you still have. We would like very much to return Nell's personal items, bearing in mind we have a policy about retaining such items for a limited time before disposing of them. There's also something I'd like to speak with you about, something I believe is of importance concerning your daughter . . . your younger daughter. All right then. We'll speak with you soon.

The robotic voice returns: *Second—new—message.*

Miri, it's Becca. I left you a message yesterday—about the booth opening at the salon down the street? You haven't called me back. You haven't called me in a while. Just . . . call me back. I need to know how you're doing. Sophie, if you pick this up, have your mom call me. Love you. Love you both.

Aunt Becca is Mom's older sister, but seems younger than Mom. She doesn't have any kids, and she always treated me and Nell like her own in that loose, "fun aunt" way. Mom worked full-time doing hair and raised Nell and me on her own, giving us hell about our grades and nutrition and posture and stuff like that. Now she gives me hell about drinking her gin, but I don't drink and she'd know that if she didn't drink either.

Mom took a leave of absence from the salon after Nell was sent to Oakside Behavioral Institute. She was finally getting ready to go back to work when we got the call from the sheriff's office in Yavapai County. Since then, Aunt Becca's been leaving Mom messages on our voice mail and sticking little notes in the front door, making sure she's okay. A lot of good that's doing. I'm just the go-between.

I save both messages for Mom, knowing she won't listen to them. I wonder if she even remembers the code to access our voice mail. She used to get so mad at Nell and me when we'd forget to check messages.

"What if I'd left you an urgent message?" she used to say in that nervous voice that meant she'd already gotten over her irritation and moved on to exasperation. Never mind that we each had a cell phone. Mom, only got one of her own after Nell was committed and Oakside convinced her that they needed to be able to reach her. The Yavapai County sheriff called Mom's cell when they found Nell's body next to the Museum of Copper Mining. She'd been hanging from a ponderosa pine dangling by her big toe, arms at her side like an upside-down soldier. Mom hasn't touched her phone since then.

I find Mom asleep in her room next to an open bottle of Ambien, her hair still rolled up in a bath towel. She must've showered at some point in the day, but she didn't get much further than that, and she's wearing her terry-cloth bathrobe. Mom used to take really good care of herself. She would wear plum-colored liner around the edges of her green eyes to make them even greener. Her brown hair is wavy, unlike mine, which is thick but straight as a board. She has the deepest laugh lines of anyone I know. They form giant parentheses around her lips. While she sleeps, her mouth turns up at the corners like a cat's. She actually looks happy.

Open your eyes, I think. *Open your eyes and stay smiling.*

I touch her shoulder, and she breathes in with a gasp.

"Mom." I squeeze her shoulder a little.

She makes a kind of growling sound. Her mouth pulls down, puckering her chin.

"Mom, I'm going to get the box at Oakside, okay?"

She reaches a hand out and brushes my wrist clumsily.

"No, no, honey. I'll get that."

It's the first time she's called me anything other than Sophie in a while. I like how "honey" sounds like someone who could fall apart in front of her mom and not worry that she would crumble to pieces too. "Honey" could tell her mother that she's terrified of losing her mind like Nell, that she might already be starting to. But since Nell died, I have to play parent, which means I have to go pick up the box of

Nell's things before the next voice mail message convinces me that my life won't ever be good again. Or convinces her that she has another crazy daughter who could just as easily be tucked away in a loony bin. And because I know Mom won't be the one to pick up the box, and she won't stop me when I do.

"I'm taking the car, okay?" She's drifting off again, so I don't wait for her answer.

I'm just grabbing Mom's keys off the hook by the door when the phone rings. I'd almost forgotten about the other voice mail.

"Hey, Aunt Becca. She's sleeping," I say without the customary hello. I'm not in the mood to answer questions about Mom today.

"Uh, is this Sophie?"

Definitely not Aunt Becca. The voice is deep and familiar, but I can't quite place it. It's not like there've been many calls for me lately.

"I . . . who is this?"

"It's Evan. I didn't have your cell number, but you're . . . I Googled you."

My heart starts thumping the way it did in my Sweep room daydream. But this is a different Evan than in my fantasy. He sounds nervous, way more than he does in school.

"I looked you up in the school directory. You weren't listed, so I went online. I hope that's not weird, Googling you I mean, because, you know, it's not like you gave me your number, and—" he says all in a single breath. "Sorry. I caught you at a bad time."

Neither of us says anything. It sounds like he's getting ready to hang up.

"Wait," I say, then continue, trying not to sound so desperate, "you caught me off guard, but it's okay. What's up?"

"I . . . uh . . ." Now Evan seems really nervous, like he has absolutely no idea what's up, like he's never known what's up.

"I was thinking of . . . what was I saying?"

"I don't . . . ," I start, but I have no idea how to finish. He's never acted this way with me before.

"Can I come over?"

"Actually, I was just on my way out."

"Oh." He sounds genuinely disappointed. Then there's a long pause, like he's waiting for me to say more.

I can't stand the thought of ending this bizarre conversation offending him. "I guess maybe you could—"

"I'll come with you. I'll be right over." He hangs up before I can finish saying that maybe he could come over *after* I get back. The busy signal starts. He's coming over. Right now. To go with me.

"Oh my God."

He can't go to Oakside with me.

"Shit. Shit, shit, shit!" I pace the kitchen floor. Why didn't I stop him? Why didn't I say something? Anything? Now I'm going to have to tell him to leave when he gets here. And I really don't want to tell him to leave. Because even though that was probably the most uncomfortable conversation in history, I already miss the way his voice sounded.

Evan drives up fifteen minutes later in an old white Ford Probe. They don't even make them anymore, but somehow, it still looks sporty. I pull on my denim jacket, which smells like old tomato sauce. I consider leaving it, but it's starting to get chilly in the evenings.

I open the front door just as he's getting out of the car. As embarrassing as this situation is, it would be a thousand times worse if my mom woke up and stumbled to the door, hung over in her bathrobe. Evan's wearing faded jeans and a faded green T-shirt, which accents his broad, square shoulders. Dammit. Why did he have to come over looking so cute?

"So where are we going?" he asks with a smile that makes my stomach sink. My anxiety must register on my face because he ducks his head and shrugs. "Sorry, I'm not so good on the phone."

"You don't say." I can't help but smile back. *God, he's cute.*

We stare at each other for a couple of seconds, and then I remember what it was I was going to say.

"Evan, you can't come with me. It's . . . it's . . . well, it's complicated, and you wouldn't want to. Trust me."

That's a lie. It's me. *I* don't want him to. He's never asked me about Nell, about what's going on with my mom, and it'd be fine by me if he never did.

I feel like a total asshole. I wish I could get excited about a cute guy wanting to hang out with me so much that he'd tag along to Oakside. But I can't because if I want that doctor to stop leaving messages for my mom, I have to go get Nell's things. Then I can pretend that night never happened, that Oakside never happened. That there's no chance Dr. Keller knows how much I'm turning out to be like Nell.

"It's okay. I sort of invited myself along." His hand is still on the open car door. He absently swings it back and forth on its hinge.

"It's not that—I want to hang out with you." Immediately my face gets hot. I almost regret saying that, when he finally looks up, and his lips draw into a broad smile.

"So, what's this mystery errand?" he asks. I figure I have nothing to lose. If he hasn't been freaked out by the rumors about Nell, maybe he doesn't scare easily. And even though

I thought I wanted to be by myself for this, something about his smile makes me wonder if I have to do everything alone.

"Come on," I say, nodding toward my mom's car. "I'll explain on the way."

Nell David

October 21

The hallways never seem to end here. There are about a million of them, and they go on forever. I know there have to be more patients in a place this big, but I never see anyone but the nurses and doctors in white, with their false smiles and their searching eyes. Apparently, there's another ward, but I'm not sure what makes that brand of crazy different from my brand of crazy.

I wonder if they make the people from the other ward go into the room with the wall of mirrors, the one that made my legs collapse with fear the first time they locked me in it. They sent LM there today. Afterward, they brought him into the rec room with MM and me. They sat him at a table and gave him whatever he wanted. They told him he did a great job. But LM didn't look proud. He looked like he'd been robbed of something very precious to him.

Where are you when I need you, T. S. Eliot? I could use your nourishing words right now.

I don't think they're going to let me leave this place any-time soon. At first I thought that's what I wanted. I thought that they could help me. But not anymore.

I don't like the way they look at Sophie when she comes to visit.

3

WE'RE HALFWAY TO OAKSIDE BY the time I gather enough nerve to say why we're going there. We'd sat in dead silence for about an eternity, so now I have to fill the space with something.

"Oakside," he said after I told him. He was only repeating the name, but the way he said it told me I'd sufficiently freaked him out with our trip to a mental ward.

"Yeah," I say now, unable to stop myself. "Nell started hearing things when she was a lot younger, but it got really bad by the time she was seventeen."

"Uh-huh."

"She was committed to Oakside after she cut her wrist on glass she broke from the bathroom mirror," I say, my throat

going dry. "They diagnosed her with schizophrenia. She eventually ran away."

"From Oakside," he says again.

"Right. And they found her in Jerome. Dead."

Evan has nothing to say to this, and really, who could blame him?

"The doctor who treated her at Oakside has been calling our house almost nonstop ever since. He wants to talk to my mom about something."

I have no idea how much of this has already been relayed to him by the kids at school. I neglect to mention that I have some doubts about Nell's schizophrenia, and that the way they found her body completely defies explanation. And that there's something about this guy Adam. I just can't imagine Nell would have run off with a total psycho. But then, why won't he come forward?

I also fail to mention that I'm beginning to hear things too, that I'm afraid the people at Oakside somehow know this, that this is why the doctor wants to talk to my mom. Of all the things I'm not ready to talk about, these have to be the biggest. And a ride to Oakside Behavioral Institute is already pushing the boundaries of an appropriate first date.

The car goes silent again until I drive through the intersection at Canyon Road.

"Shouldn't you make a left?"

"Oh, right. Thanks," I say, glad he's helping but completely aware that our conversation has regressed into driving directions. "How'd you know that?"

A tiny smile finds his lips, but nothing about his face indicates happiness, which is how I know I've blown any chance at being anything to Evan Gold.

We pull into the nearly empty parking lot in front of the one-story, sprawling facility where I last saw my sister. I wonder if this place ever looked modern, even when it was first built. Now its tan exterior and flat roof make it seem tired, like an old dog limping around its yard.

"Would you hate me if I asked you to wait here?" I say it more to the steering wheel than to Evan, but I can feel him looking at me, and my face gets hot all over again.

"Whatever," Evan says, his voice kind but distant. I turn to him, but he's looking out the window. His long legs are scrunched with the passenger seat pushed so far forward. It's usually just me sitting there.

"It's not you," I say, and before I can stop my hand, it's on his shoulder, which I can feel tense up under his shirt.

He takes a deep breath and lets it out slowly. "I can see how you might want to be alone."

I nod and pull the door handle. "It shouldn't take long." But he's already fiddling with the radio.

I turn my attention toward the entrance.

This place is like a disease. They claim to heal people here, but anyone with a soul who visits knows that's not true. I have to fight back a surge of nausea every time I walk up to this building.

There's a welcome mat—an honest-to-God mat with WELCOME on it—in front of the sliding glass door. You're either committed with your heels dragging against the cement, or you're lured by visits with your drugged-up loved ones or by polite phone calls, the same phone calls that remind you to pick up your dead sister's personal effects. After the first sliding door, I wait by a Plexiglas window and shove my driver's license through the slot like I'm at a pawn shop.

The bored-looking orderly behind the window checks my ID and opens the second door, which isn't on an automatic sensor like the first. The second door isn't so "welcome."

"Thanks," I say to the orderly, but there's nothing grateful about my tone. I make sure of that.

Once I'm inside, my eyes fixate on the man in the recreation area to the right of the sliding door. He's pretty hard to miss. Even though he's sitting down at a table, he's taller than I am, and probably twice as wide. His head is shaved and shines like a beacon in the overhead fluorescent light. The man's enormous blue eyes dart everywhere except at the massive tower he's working on. To see a grown man playing with Legos—no, *building* Legos with intensity and purpose— is beyond unsettling.

Before, the few times I could muster the courage to visit Nell, I was afraid of this enormous bald guy and his blocks. Fascinated and afraid. That changed when I read Nell's journal, the one that appeared in my car the day I went to see where Nell had died.

"Help you?"

I'm surprised to see the lady who let me in through the sliding doors emerge from the little room to stand behind the front desk. They must be short staffed today. Normally, they'd have at least two other people hanging around, making jokes in low voices and picking hangnails.

"I'm Sophie David. I'm here to pick up my sister's things."

"Oh. OH! You must be Nell's—yes, uh, let me get Dr. Keller for you. He'll know what to—I mean, he'll be able to help—just give me a sec."

Everything this woman says makes me want to strangle her. Not because she's saying anything in particular. Because there's nothing anyone in this place could say that would make me feel okay about being here. Oakside somehow managed to sidestep any legal responsibility for Nell's death. Something having to do with Nell turning eighteen while she was committed. After Nell's funeral, I stopped trying to understand it. We don't have the money to sue anyone anyway, which I'm sure Oakside knows.

Oakside's shady business practices aren't all that give me the creeps. It's like the moment anyone here looks at me, they can see something I can't. Like they're just waiting to lock me up too.

Footsteps echo from down the hall.

Clicksqueak.

The orderly behind the desk could not look more relieved.

"Here comes Dr. Keller now," she says and hustles away before I can react.

Clicksqueak, clicksqueak.

A handsome, sandy-haired man in his forties rounds the corner, a white lab coat flapping behind him like a cape. This is the first time I've seen Dr. Keller in the flesh, and I wasn't expecting him to be good-looking. This isn't the type of place I'd expect to attract a handsome doctor. His shiny shoes come to a stop in front of me.

"Pleasure to meet you, Sophie, though I wish it was under different circumstances."

Dr. Keller's forehead creases, and his full lips turn down in apology. But I don't believe it, nor do I feel anything of an apology in his hands as they hold mine in greeting, grasping it in midair and squeezing it in lieu of the standard one-two pump of a handshake.

"I've packed your sister's things. There wasn't much, but I'm sure you and your mother will want her belongings."

He tells me all of this while holding my gaze. He never looks down or away. I'm not sure he even blinks. I end up doing all of it, first blinking, then rolling my eyes to look at anything but his gray ones.

I can't think of anything to say in response to that, so I just nod. He's still clasping my hand, and I don't want him touching me anymore.

Finally, he lets go, then stretches out an arm, his other hand behind his back like a maître d'. He nods in the direction he just came from. "Please, after you."

A few doors down, I start to head for one hallway, but he intercepts me quickly.

"*This* way, Ms. David,"

I try to glance down the corridor, but he blocks my view. Soon he's *clicksqueaking* me through a different hallway. We come to a nondescript metal door, and he pulls a card from his pocket and glides it through a reader, releasing a lock. We walk down another hallway. To my right and to my left are smooth gray doors with little rectangular windows, mesh wire netting through the middle of the glass. Every door handle requires a swipe card. Between the doors are bare gray walls, their slick surfaces transitioning almost imperceptibly to the grayish linoleum. For some reason, this really bothers me. I can't see the line where the walls meet the floor. This place is supposed to heal people. It seems like you should be able to see the distinction between things.

Dr. Keller's stride is smooth. I'm suddenly furious that anybody could look so f-ing comfortable in a place where my sister sat in some tiny room with a bed and nothing to stare at but the laces holding the skin on her wrist together and blank walls that look like floors.

I twist the silver ring on my right hand. It's a habit I've developed to cope with memories of Nell. I'm frantic all over again as I remember how they didn't find a matching ring on her finger in Jerome. She wore it every day of her life, just like I do. It was a gift to us from Mom when Nell turned thirteen.

We turn another corner and stop at a door with Dr. Keller's name engraved on a shiny silver plaque. He swipes his card again and the lock slips. He chivalrously holds the door for me and slides out a chair in front of his desk, gesturing for me to sit.

"I can just take the box," I say, not caring that it sounds rude.

As soon as his face creases in that perfect, pitying way, I regret my decision. So he takes a second to register the contradiction as I sink into the chair, then he's back to being pleasant.

There's a lidded box with her name in bold black letters on the desk. I suddenly remember one of my first conversations with Nell after she was committed. We sat in the recreation room while she played with the fraying hem of her cotton pants. She was laughing, telling me that they'd expected a guy at first. They'd gotten her first and last names mixed up on her chart.

It took them two days to stop calling me David, LS!

LS stood for Little Sis, her nickname for me. She was forever giving people nicknames, then abbreviating them. She was playful like that. And she'd told me the story like she would tell me any other story, rolling her eyes and scrunching her nose like everything was a joke. But that time I knew she was faking it. I could tell by the way she kept playing with that pant leg.

Dr. Keller pushes the box toward me.

"I didn't think she was allowed to keep anything here," I challenge, remembering the long list of rules some orderly had given my mom the day she brought Nell here. He smiles sadly, like he's been expecting me to say that.

"Well, as you know, we need to ensure that none of our

guests have any opportunity to cause themselves harm. We must, therefore, be strict about the possessions we allow them to retain while they're here at Oakside."

"Right," I say, this time keeping my eyes fixed on his. "Because their safety is your number one priority."

He pushes the box toward me again, gently but firmly.

I slide my fingers through the holes in either side of the cardboard and stand to go.

The box is even lighter than I thought it would be. I turn my back on Dr. Keller and open the door.

"Ms. David, we're not done just yet."

I turn around to find him leaning back in his chair, his fingers interlocked across his flat stomach.

"There was another matter I was hoping to discuss with you," he says, crossing his legs as his chair emits a tiny groan. His face retains its plastic composure.

"My mom's not available," I say, hoping my voice doesn't quaver with anger at having to make excuses for her.

"It's not your mom I wanted to speak with," he says, his gray eyes staring at me so intensely, I momentarily forget where I am. "It's you. Sophie, Nell shared some conversations with me. Conversations between you and her."

Dr. Keller holds his palms up, as though easing my anger down from a ledge.

"I don't want you to be upset. She told me in a safe space. She felt comfortable talking to me. She said it reminded her of talking to you, actually."

I shift my weight from one foot to the other. I'm feeling sort of achy. Tiny prickles of sweat form around my hairline, like when I have a fever. "She talked about me?"

"She talked a lot about you. I get the sense that you two had a lot in common. That you . . . *saw* things in very much the same way."

"I don't see anything," I say a little too quickly. Nell wouldn't have told him anything. She *couldn't* have. Unless she really was that angry.

"I meant that metaphorically, of course," he says, his tone easy, conversational, as if we've known each other a long time. Suddenly, his familiarity makes my stomach turn over.

This box, this is all I have left of her. These are the last things that Nell touched in this place.

"Nell was the poet, not me. A really good one, too. She wrote about things you didn't even know you were feeling, that you didn't even know *were* feelings until she put names to them," I blurt.

I try to say more, but my words get caught in my throat, and my eyes start welling up, and I can feel my breath stop and start. I want Dr. Keller to know that Nell was more than whatever's been left behind in this weightless box, whatever was or wasn't found hanging from that tree, that she was more special and complicated than he could ever understand. I want him to say he's sorry. But his gray eyes just look concerned, and I let the door close behind me.

By the time I reach the front doors, the sun has set.

The orderly behind the front counter doesn't see me at first, so I snap, "Can I get out of here?"

She jumps at my voice, then lazily makes her way to the little room to open the inner Plexiglas door. The man is still playing with his Legos in the corner. We lock eyes, and for the first time since I got here, I'm scared. Maybe it's because, of all the people here, his gaze is the only one I can't read. Then his eyes shift to the box I'm holding, and I can see my sister's name on his lips as he reads silently. He looks up at me again, his hands shaking above his Lego tower, which is higher than I've ever seen it before.

"We were the last three."

He looks sincere, earnest. His chin quivers, and a single strand of spit closes the gap between his upper and lower lips.

What he says doesn't make any sense, but he looks lucid. I open my mouth to say something in return, but all I can picture are the initials my sister used in her journal to describe him: LM. Then, the Plexiglas swishes open, beckoning me into the antechamber between the first and second doors. The orderly in the button room is waving me along. I take one more look at the man with the bald head before stepping through the doors. He's looking at Nell's box again, his mouth open, lips shaking.

I step toward the second doors, waiting for them to open, and catch a glimpse of my reflection. I look skinnier than I did even a month ago, my shorts sitting lower on my hips. But it's my face that startles me. Because it's not my face anymore.

My eyes are gone, sunken into vast caverns above jagged cheekbones. A mouth moves, forming a circle, then stretching into a thin line. Cracked lips pull over long, flat teeth that look too big for their mouth. The mouth keeps moving, but I can't hear what it's saying.

That's not me.

I step backward, dragging my eyes from the reflection. I look behind me, but there's nothing there.

The annoyed orderly knocks on the window, waving me forward. But I just keep looking at her. I can't scream. I can't even move.

Why isn't she coming in here to help me? Can't she see . . . ?

But then I realize she can't. I turn to the sliding doors. My reflection looks just as it should. Only now there's a hairline crack in the glass just above my head that I swear wasn't there before. I can hear blood pounding in my ears. A voice from some staticky speaker above me says, "You've gotta walk forward." The orderly holds the head of a gooseneck microphone in front of her face. "Walk toward it," she says slowly, as if I'm a child she's sick of babysitting.

I keep expecting my reflection to change back into that hideous thing, but I step toward the door, and it swishes open. The smell of sweet desert air conjures memories of playing beauty parlor with Nell on the porch at night, cicadas hissing as we moved scissor fingers over each other's hair and begged Mom to let us stay up a little longer.

I walk back to the car and gingerly place Nell's box in the trunk before sliding into the driver's seat. Evan stops bobbing his head to the Bob Marley song on the radio, looking embarrassed at being caught.

I make myself laugh and roll my eyes. "Sorry that took so long. Bureaucracies and all."

"Yup, they're the worst."

Something about the way he says this makes me think he wants to say more. It's like he's trying to see if I can read his mind or something. Evan stares at his lap, but every couple of seconds he ventures a look at me.

I keep my hands on the steering wheel, but I'm not ready

to start the car yet. It feels like there's more to say, only I'm not sure who should do the talking.

I want to tell him what just happened. All of it. Part of me thinks he'd listen, maybe believe some of it. But then I remember everyone else. Nell's friends from school, who now call me a freak. Dr. Keller, with his confidence and fake empathy. Even my mom, who had her own daughter locked away. I bet Nell thought all of them would believe her, too.

So I start the car and back out of the parking lot. Neither of us says much on the way home.

4

THERE'S AN OLD YELLOW GEO Metro sitting in my driveway as we round the corner onto my street.

"Wow," Evan says. "I'm impressed. That thing's bordering on vintage."

I smile and silently thank him for acting like everything's normal. I basically ignored him the whole ride home and he doesn't seem to be taking it personally.

"It's my aunt's car. She's had it since, like, the dawn of time."

"Well, she'd be crazy not to keep it. I mean, they don't make 'em like that anymore. What is that, a three-cylinder engine?"

I can feel him smiling at me from the passenger's seat,

and I know my ears are burning red. I just hope my eggplant hair is hiding them. I smile and nod, then roll Mom's old blue Buick into the driveway beside the yellow Geo.

Evan is by his car before I can even close the driver's-side door. So much for everything being normal. He probably had his hand on the handle the entire drive home from Oakside. Not that I could blame him. So I plaster on my best easy-breezy-it's-cool-if-you-don't-want-to-hang-out-with-the-class-freak-anymore look and tuck my hair behind my ear (which I've confirmed in the side mirror is, *indeed*, bright red).

He gives me an awkward wave and swings his door open.

"See you in Sweep," he smiles, but I'm too exhausted to know if he's making fun of me.

"Yup. Same time, same place," I say, waving back.

He's down the street and around the corner before I can get my key in the lock of the front door. I tuck Nell's box under one arm and brace myself for the onslaught of the usual questions from Aunt Becca. I know she's concerned about Mom, but I just don't feel up to dealing with her on top of all that's happened today.

When I open the door, the smell of garlic and basil practically knocks me over. I can hear the kitchen faucet running and something clanging against one of our big cast-iron pots. I hover in the kitchen doorway and watch as Aunt Becca—

clad in Mom's *Nosh Now, Kvetch Later* apron—brushes fat brown curls from her shiny face and maneuvers a wooden spoon around a steaming pot of what smells like lentil soup. Our cutting board, which I haven't seen in months, is covered with green stems and onion skins. A tight knot of guilt wrenches my stomach. She's cooking for us. Mom and I haven't made an actual home-cooked meal since Nell died.

Aunt Becca turns toward me and jumps backward, splattering soup on Mom's apron.

"Jeez, Sophie, you scared me! I didn't hear you come in. What'd'ya have there?"

I'd forgotten about the box. "It's not important. Aunt Becca, you didn't have to do all this."

"It's nothing. Your mom's asleep." The look on her face is worried, and I can tell she wants to ask me about my mom's drinking, my mom's job (or lack thereof), my mom's depression. But I keep quiet and wash the cutting board instead.

"It smells good," I say, not bothering to keep my voice down. I'm not concerned with waking up Mom.

"Lentil soup, garlic bread, fruit." She lists the menu like it's a roll call, sounding pleased with herself. She's not the greatest cook, but I'm dying for something besides pizza or Chinese.

"I could try to get Mom," I offer, even though I don't mean it.

Aunt Becca looks like she might venture down the hall-way. Her body leans in that direction. But at the last second, she changes her mind. "No, let her sleep."

When we sit down at the breakfast bar, just the two of us, Aunt Becca chews quietly while I stare down at my bowl and slurp my soup. That's the thing about my aunt. I feel like I can be myself around her, like I don't need to try to be any-thing special. At least I used to feel that way, before Mom started going downhill. Now it's like Aunt Becca expects me to be the parent.

The day rushes over me. The murmuring in my ear at school. The random phone call from Evan. Dr. Keller's awful smile. My reflection in the sliding doors. It feels impossible that this could be what my life has become.

Aunt Becca tugs my earlobe. She's done it for as long as I can remember. It's what she does instead of saying "I love you." If I didn't think it would make her worry even more, I'd lean against her right now and cry. But I just twirl my spoon in my bowl instead.

After Aunt Becca leaves, I grab Nell's box and head back to my room. I pass Mom's room on the way and am surprised to see her door open. I almost don't stop, but I'm startled to find her awake and sitting on the edge of her bed, staring at something off in the distance, her eyes glazed like she's daydreaming. The towel that was wrapped around her head is in her lap now, and her hair is lank around her jaw. I can smell her shampoo from where I'm standing—something sweet like apricots. That scent used to comfort me. Now I just associate it with her showering far too late in the day.

Mom looks up and meets my gaze. "Are those her things?"

She hasn't said Nell's name in a very long time. I nod in response, my voice lost somewhere in my throat.

She nods back. Her eyes linger on the box for a moment, then come back to me. For some reason, I can't seem to catch my breath.

"It doesn't look very heavy."

I shake my head; no, it's not heavy.

"You should get to bed," she says, sounding defeated. "It's late." Whatever strength propped her into a sitting position is beginning to fail. I don't tell her that she couldn't possibly know what time it is. She hasn't bothered to reset the blinking alarm clock since our power was shut off two months ago. It took a rushed payment to the electric company and some sweet talking from Aunt Becca to get it turned back on.

I hang in the doorway, then start to leave without a word. I wouldn't be able to find one anyway, at least not one that would come out sounding nice, and I can't stand to see her cry anymore.

"I'm trying, honey. I swear to God I am."

And then that mean word almost surfaces from the pit of my gut, and I almost can't suppress it this time. I walk away before I say something I know I'll regret. I walk right past my room and straight into Nell's, closing the door behind me.

I stare at Nell's mirrored closet doors. I haven't opened them since she left for Oakside. I always used to borrow her clothes without asking. After she died, the thought of wearing her clothes made my hands tremble.

Because Nell's door stays shut most of the time, her room's cleaner than the rest of the house and definitely more organized. Her knickknacks remain on her dresser: a seashell she pocketed on our trip to San Diego when I was ten and she was twelve; a ratty drawstring purse she used all the time even though it was out of style; a makeup tray glittery with the sprinklings of eye shadow and blush; a tube of soft-pink lip gloss too light for her olive skin, but which she wore nearly every day.

I lift the lid and upturn the box on her bed: the jeans and T-shirt she'd been wearing the night she was admitted (the blood gone, probably laundered by Oakside); a few pairs of underwear and bras; Oakside-issued scrubs in light blue (though not the ones with the frayed hem that she was wearing when I saw her); and Babs, the cloth doll Aunt Becca gave her before I was even born. As I figured, no sign of Nell's silver ring. I'm still disappointed, though.

I scoop the contents back into the box and put it on her dresser, then lie on the bed and reach underneath the mattress. My fingertips find what they're looking for, and I slowly ease my treasure from its hiding place.

Like a ritual, I hold the journal in my lap for a second. I don't know if I'm sending up a prayer, and if so, to whom, but it just feels like the respectful thing to do. I doubt she ever shared this with anyone.

Well, almost anyone.

The marbled cardboard cover stares up at me, and like I always do, I think about the first day I laid eyes on it almost six months ago. I still can't understand Nell's reasons for fleeing to Jerome, with its dust and thin air. When I went to see where they'd found her, the notebook had been left for me on the driver's seat in my unlocked car. I nearly collapsed when I first saw her handwriting. I actually expected her to be there, alive, waiting for me under the nearby tree. Waiting there under the tree where the police found her hanging in a way no one should ever hang from anything. Like a mistake of nature.

I ease the journal open as carefully as I can. The cheap binding is already beginning to release its grip on the thin pages. The book automatically opens to the middle, where someone pried a page from it. I trace my finger along the soft tear marks, willing the page back into place. Then I flip back to the place where I left off. I know all her entries practically by heart, but each time I read them, the pain feels fresh and alive.

Nell David

November 1

Anger is the worst thing to feel in this place. And even though no one tells you it's dangerous, you'd have to be . . . well . . . crazy not to know the trouble that anger can get you into here. They put angry people in restraints and dope them up with brightly colored pills. And there are tons of pills—Dixie cups overflowing with them, it seems. And they're huge, those pills. I can't believe you're actually supposed to swallow them.

There's a guy. I call him LM. He seems really tall to me, but I saw his chart once—the orderlies leave them around like gum wrappers—and he's only five foot ten. I guess he seems taller because he's built like a cube. His stomach hangs over his pants, and his shirt is tight around his shoulders, too. He's older than me. Maybe even in his thirties or forties.

It's hard to say. Everyone looks old around here. For some reason, the orderlies shave LM's head every three days or so like clockwork. They won't let even a half inch grow before they take a razor to it. I'd bet it's because he pulls it out. He has deep grooves along the sides of his head. They look like trenches made by nails. But it's his eyes that I notice the most about him. They're bright and blue, and they're always darting from one end of the room to the other. He never looks content. Maybe that's why I decided he and I were going to be friends.

I get the sense he wants to talk to me, too. When other people stare at him, he hurls a wad of spit at them. But when he catches me watching him, he just nods slightly, or blinks really slowly, like a cat. But he never says a single word. Not to me.

Whenever he has a major freak-out, Dr. Keller or one of the other people in white take him down the same hall they took me down last week. The one with the room of mirrors.

I close the journal with a trembling breath. Because I know that even though I'm not the reason she ended up in Oakside, I could have done something to stop it. I could have said something. To my mom. To Aunt Becca. Instead I did the worst thing possible: nothing.

I ease the journal back between the mattress and the mattress pad.

"G'night," I say to no one in particular, but for some reason, it feels good to say it aloud.

5

I'M NOT JUST LATE FOR school today. I'm so late that I've actually missed first period, and I'm close to missing second. I considered ditching school altogether, but it's Friday— Aunt Becca's day off—and sometimes she does a drive-by to check on my mom. I learned that one the hard way. At least in a few hours I can go home and forget how totally screwed I am in the grades department. Of course, whenever I'm home, I remember how totally screwed I am in the family-and-everything-else department.

I slept like crap last night. I had a dream about Nell, as usual. The one where I see her in the middle of a clearing, a single, impossibly tall pine tree beside her. She looks over one shoulder, then the other, like she's being hunted. I woke up sweating and scrunched in a ball under my bedspread, wondering, as I do every time I have this nightmare, if that same terror is the last emotion Nell felt before she died.

Then I had a dream about Evan. That was new. In the dream he kissed me, which was so incredible it makes my skin hot just thinking about it. But then he pulled away and looked at me with so much disgust. He said something after that, or at least he tried to say something, but I couldn't hear him. He was moving his mouth, but instead of words coming out, it was that horrible murmuring.

"Sophie D.," says a voice that brings sweat rushing through my pores.

Evan's at the end of the nearly empty hall, leaning against a locker by a window. The sun casts a harsh glare over him so I have to squint to make out even the outline of his face.

"Oh, hey," I chirp back, trying for a casual tone, as if last night wasn't the most awkward evening ever. Let's see. Uncomfortable phone conversation: check. Abandonment in a parked car while I disappear into a loony bin for what must have felt like years: check. Retreat back to his car as fast as he possibly can once we're within sight of my house: check.

"What's up?" I finish. *One profound response after the next. God, could I be any lamer?*

Evan looks at an imaginary watch on his wrist, then shakes his head slowly, or at least I think he does. Staring into that glare is starting to give me a headache.

"Forty-five minutes late is what's up," he says, a mocking tone of disapproval coating his words. I put my head down to hide the smile I can't keep from my lips. Does that mean he was waiting for me to get here?

"Yeah, kinda got a slow start this morning."

"Well, you're going to need to know what you missed in chemistry," he says, still pretending to scold me.

"Aren't you in physics first period?" I ask, genuinely confused.

"Is that your way of telling me you don't want to hang out with me tomorrow?" He's still leaning against the lockers like he doesn't have a care in the world, but something's shifted in his tone.

"Er, no. I mean, yes. I mean, sure," I stumble through every possible answer.

"So, does that mean we're hanging out, or . . . ?"

My heart starts racing so fast that I'm afraid to say anything for fear it'll jump out my throat and fall onto the floor. *Is he seriously asking me out?* And then reality strikes: What if he wants to come over again, and this time actually come inside?

I picture my mom all boozed up in her bathrobe, swirling

ice in her glass, rattling a bottle of Ambien in her pocket like a hidden maraca.

"We can't go to my house," I blurt.

"Good!" he says a little too quickly (not that I blame him), then follows with, "I mean, I already had something else in mind. Meet me in front of my house tomorrow? Around eleven?"

"All right."

The creak of a metal door opening at the end of the hall breaks the echo between our voices.

"Gold!"

Evan's hand slips from the locker, and I can see his silhouette stiffen like a soldier coming to attention. The door momentarily blocks the sun's glare, and I can make out Evan's adorable profile, even with Coach Tarza's stubby neck competing for space.

"You planning on joining us for class today, Rookie, or spending the whole period flirting in the hall?"

"Just on my way in, Coach," he says, breezing past Coach Tarza with only a glance back at me. And it was probably my imagination, but I swear I saw him flash me a wink.

"How 'bout you, Ms. David? Trying to set a record for most Sweeps in one semester?"

"Nope!"

I spin toward Mrs. Dodd's classroom, practically tripping over my own ankle. When I get there, I swing open the door, slamming it into its doorstop and shocking the entire class—including Mrs. Dodd—into rapt attention. All eyes are on me sweating with God-knows-what expression all over my face.

"Sophie, just in time," Mrs. Dodd practically sings.

I slide into the closest chair and crack open my copy of *As I Lay Dying*, wanting desperately to lose myself in the strange poetics of William Faulkner.

"Now, we were just about to get into the mother's role in the lives of her sons," Mrs. Dodd recaps for the class, but really I know it's for my benefit since I'm late. "Who can tell me why the kids continue on this journey to bury their mother?"

"Because it's their mom," someone speaks up.

"But what about that relationship keeps them going?" Mrs. Dodd presses.

"Because love isn't always about sparks and tears and all that," I find myself saying.

"Go on, Sophie," Mrs. Dodd encourages me in her quiet, motherly voice, a voice that I shouldn't be hearing in the classroom, but at home.

"Because sometimes things happen in your family that are out of your control. They happen to you or around you, and sometimes you just do things your family needs you to do, like keeping your mouth shut instead of saying something that'll only start a fight, because if you actually stopped to think about it, you'd realize how pointless life is."

Mrs. Dodd says something about what I just said, something that I'm sure would be encouraging if I were in any frame of mind to listen. But I don't want to think about family and obligation and keeping my shit together right now. I want to think about whatever Evan Gold is planning for tomorrow, and why the hell he'd want to plan it for me.

Nell David

November 12

I met someone today. It's not often that I can say that. This place isn't exactly known for its social scene. Dr. Keller says making sarcastic remarks is a defense mechanism. I imagine he'll read this at some point. It's not like I have any expectation of privacy in here. I hope he reads this and understands it's not a defense mechanism, it's me giving him the finger. I can't really see how journaling is much different from talking to myself, and isn't that exactly the kind of behavior that lands a person in a place like this? Whatever. The orderlies say a lot of things that are supposed to explain away questions like that, but mostly, they provide

gelcap answers in little white Dixie cups. And no, Dr. Keller,
if you're reading this, I haven't been hiding the teal ones.
And if I was, good luck finding them. I totally feel like I'm
channeling Sophie's rebelliousness right now.

But this guy. This guy is different. He doesn't act like
the other orderlies or smoke like some do. Especially the man-
child. That one sweats and smokes more than any of them.
This new guy, he said he's been working here forever, but
today's the first time I saw him. He brought my lunch (dry
turkey on white with a banana—delish). He has to be the
tallest person I've ever met in my life. So of course that's the
first question I asked him: How tall are you? What is it with
me? I can't seem to filter anything when I get embarrassed or
nervous. It's like whatever is in my head just falls out of my
mouth. Only Sophie would understand. But the guy barely
flinched. Six foot nine. Then he told me his name is Adam.
A good name. So nice it doesn't need a nickname.

Most orderlies set the tray down and leave without a
word. Occasionally, the old one tells me to "eat up, dear"
("dear" . . . seriously). But this guy sat with me for practi-
cally ten minutes. He asked me what my name was, and
how long I'd been here. It was weird having a normal
conversation with someone. We talked about poetry, about
T. S. Eliot and Ezra Pound and Sylvia Plath. He caught

me with my journal open and saw a poem. And he asked me if I write those a lot. I have no idea why, but I started crying. Just sat there bawling like a two-year-old.

And that was that. He might have left quicker if I'd lit him on fire. It's hard to say who was more embarrassed.

I can't imagine he'll be back after the way I fell apart. But if he does come back, I'd talk with him again.

into the recycling bin at the curb and wiping his hands on his jeans.

"You kinda have a thing for Gatorade," I observe, trying not to sound like I'm making fun of him. I'm not good at that, though, and everything comes out sounding snide. At least that's what Mom says. Mom has charm, or at least she used to. So did Nell. I have sarcasm.

"I have a thing for whatever keeps me hydrated so I don't heave up my lunch during practice," Evan says, wiping the sweat from his upper lip with his forearm. Then he licks his lips absently to rewet them. I look down at my shoes to keep myself from wishing he'd do that a hundred more times.

"So where are we going?" I ask, trying to sound like it doesn't really matter to me.

"It's a surprise." As I reach for the door handle, he's at my side in an instant, pushing away my hand gently, then letting his fingers linger on my skin. A cool rush surges through me.

"Here, lemme get that," he says, drawing his shirt up from the bottom to cover his fingers and open the passenger door. "It gets kinda hot."

I catch a glimpse of his stomach and the seam of his gray boxer shorts poking above the waist of his pants. Once again, I find my shoes to be the most interesting thing in the universe.

6

EVAN'S LEANING INTO HIS CAR when I pull up to the front of his house, which was as easy to find as he promised. He lives a couple of neighborhoods over in one of the "newer" developments, which means his house was built in the eighties not the seventies. His front yard is sparse but manicured. That's more than I can say for ours.

He doesn't hear me as I pull up—remarkable considering I'm driving my mom's rumbling old Buick. He's holding an armful of what look to be empty Gatorade bottles and take-out bags from every fast-food restaurant within a five-mile radius. I'm out of the car before he looks up, startled, embarrassment overtaking his face.

"Just cleaning up a little," he says, depositing the trash

I get in and gingerly pull the seat belt across me, sucking in my stomach as the hot metal clasp finds its other end. I can't even count how many times I've burned myself on those damn metal buckles. Evan slides into the driver's seat and leans across me to point the air vent in my direction.

"Better?" he asks, just inches from my face.

"Perfect," I breathe more than say. How does he still smell so good even in this heat?

"It'll cool down in just a second," he says apologetically. "My car may not look like much, but this baby's AC still works like a champ."

"So, how soon do you have to be home?" he asks, and I want to say never. Aunt Becca said she'd drag Mom out this evening, to a meeting or a class or something. Some sort of effort to get her out of the house on a Saturday night. I have to go home at some point, but not as early as I might have to otherwise.

"I don't know. I can stay out a while," I say, hoping that was the right answer.

"Okay," he says. "Good. Then my plan's not shot."

I breathe a nervous sigh that does nothing to settle the fluttering in my stomach.

In minutes, we're climbing the ramp to Interstate 17 heading north. Evan's fiddling with the radio, and an old U2 song rattles the speakers between us. His hand rests on the gearshift, mine in my lap, cooling under the icy air (he was right, the AC works just fine). We don't talk at all, and I let myself close my eyes and think what it would be like if this was all normal, if this was like any other day.

"Hey, you okay?" Evan's voice drifts into my thoughts, and I open my eyes. We're not driving anymore, and the music has lowered to a faint, tinny babble. We're pulled over at a rest stop that looks only vaguely familiar, somewhere off the Interstate amid honest-to-God tumbleweeds.

"Oh!" is all I can say, embarrassed beyond belief. I'm not sure I've ever been that lost in a daydream. I must seem like the biggest freak of nature.

He laughs. "I can take a hint. You're bored."

"No!" I say fast, grabbing his hand without even thinking about it, then immediately let go like it burns my skin. This just makes him smile that incredible smile, and my heart melts to a little puddle inside of me.

"You need a restroom break?"

I shake my head. What I really need is a break from my thoughts.

"Well, since we're here, I'll be right back. I just have to grab something really quick," he says, and slides out of the driver's seat before I can ask what he's doing.

Evan disappears around the corner opposite the men's room, his hand fishing for something in the pocket of his jeans. He returns with a handful of yellow packages, but dumps them in the trunk before I can get a better view.

"Sorry, we're good to go now," he says, starting the car up. "You ready?"

"I have no idea," I say.

He smiles again and peels back onto the interstate, continuing north.

I'm in a state of perpetual anticipation: what he'll say, if he might brush his hand against mine. I worry he'll ask me to pick the music, and then I'd be forced to admit I have zero idea of what's considered cool. All Mom and Aunt Becca ever listen to is music from the 1960s, and Nell and I grew up thinking it was totally normal to be more familiar with the Rolling Stones than anyone contemporary. So I busy myself with the view out the window, grateful that Evan's already picked a classic rock station.

I have seen this same stretch of road too many times to count. Soon, this dusty path will turn from cacti and Joshua trees to pines and agave shrubs. Growing up, Mom and Aunt Becca would pile Nell and me into the back of Mom's car, and we'd take a day trip to the strange, exotic forests of Prescott or Flagstaff that would suffice as summer vacation.

It all seemed lush and special. We didn't know we were taking a day trip because Mom could never have afforded to treat all of us to an amusement park or a hotel. We had fun running wild in the woods anyway—smelling pine cones as if we were the first people on earth to discover them; collecting honeysuckle plants and swearing we'd keep them alive long enough to replant them at home and protect them from the scorching Phoenix sun.

I drove this stretch of road less than a year ago in Mom's car. Only that time I was alone. I traveled I-17 for nearly two hours—up the switchbacks to the top of a hill called Cleopatra, and straight to the edge of a town that should have burned down three different times but didn't. I headed for the state park with its museum dedicated to the mining industry, and on to the stamp mill where they used to crush the ore they'd dug from the mountains. That's where the Yavapai County sheriff found Nell hanging from a tree by her big toe. Three weeks later, the old sheriff decided to hang up his gun and retire, leaving her case unsolved.

I stare at the dotted lines separating the traffic lanes until they start to look like chalk outlines of her body. When I look at the clock on the dash, I'm stunned to find that we've been driving for nearly an hour.

"So . . . where did you say you were taking me?"

"I didn't," Evan says, smiling slyly.

"Well, can I at least have a hint? Should I have packed an overnight bag or something?" As soon as the question is out of my mouth, I realize the implication and immediately envision any scenario in which Evan and I would be spending the night together. Now I want to hide in the trunk along with those mystery packets that Evan threw back there at the rest stop. I'm guessing Evan is imagining the same thing because he gets super quiet, then starts messing with the radio, complaining about the static even though there's no static I can hear.

"It's, well, I wanted it to be a surprise. We're still about an hour away—I didn't quite realize how far it was. It's just that you said you're into scary movies, and I thought you might like this as a . . . well, a field trip . . . like a date or something."

My face is so hot, I am sure it's going to catch fire despite the arctic chill of his freakishly cool AC.

"I didn't mean to ruin the surprise," I say, not worried about the surprise at all. Did he just say "date"?

"I thought it would be fun. It's supposed to be, like, the most haunted place in the West."

My stomach falls.

"What?"

"It's this town I read about. They say it's the . . . what's the word they used? The most something place in the West."

My palms are sweating. I can't feel my fingers.

"Wickedest?"

"Yeah! How'd you know that? Oh man, I guess I'm not that original," Evan frowns a little. He looks embarrassed. If I look as horrified as I feel, I can pretty much guarantee that this is the last time Evan Gold will take me anywhere.

"Evan, you've got to pull over," I say, not really knowing why until I say it. All of a sudden, I think I might pass out.

"Damn, that lame, huh?" he tries to kid, but I can't focus on anything except trying not to keel over in his car.

"Seriously, Evan. You need to pull over."

"Okay," he obliges. He sounds really worried. We're conveniently approaching an off-ramp, the first in a series of exits leading to Black Canyon City. Evan's driving faster than he was on the freeway, and my stomach is lurching trying to fight the momentum of the car.

He makes a quick right, then another immediate right into a parking lot with several motorcycles lined up next to a restaurant advertising "Fresh Homemade Pies Daily!"

Sliding into an open space in the dirt lot, Evan throws the car into park and unhinges his seat belt in one fluid motion, reaching for my shoulder with so much concern that all I can do is put my head between my knees.

After a few minutes of staring at the pores on my legs, I bring myself back to an upright position, wondering how long I can avoid Evan's worried gaze. From what I can see out of the corner of my eye, it's pretty intense.

"So, do you want to start or should I?" he asks.

"Start what?" I ask, still avoiding eye contact.

"With the awkward conversation. I mean, somebody has to take the first step and talk about what just happened."

I laugh a little, and he looks slightly more at ease. Well, he doesn't know I'm crazy. I suppose it's just a matter of time.

"Maybe we should get a little food in you first, huh?" he suggests. Just before he pulls his key from the ignition, I see it's already noon. Since I skipped breakfast, lunch sounds fantastic.

"Come on," he says, squeezing my clammy hand. I swing my door open to rewelcome the baking sun, and I follow him to his trunk, where he removes a blue-and-white camping cooler. The yellow packages from the rest stop are peeking out from underneath the lid. Peanut M&M's.

"What's this?" I ask, genuinely surprised.

"Just a little something I put together. Follow me."

We hike past the motorcycles around to the side of the restaurant, through some overgrown desert scrub to a clearing with two moldy-looking wooden picnic tables with attached benches. There's an overflowing garbage can in the corner of the clearing with fat flies circling its contents.

"Not exactly what I had in mind for the ideal setting, but whatever," Evan says.

I force a smile, feeling guilty for ruining his plan now that the initial shock of where we were headed has finally subsided.

Evan brushes some dirt and crumbs from the bench and starts pulling out a seemingly endless quantity of food from the cooler: two sandwiches wrapped in plastic, grapes, six granola bars, a box of crackers, a long orange block of cheddar cheese, and of course, Gatorade.

"Oh my God, is the football team meeting us here too?" I blurt out.

He laughs easily, his jaw flexing.

"I wasn't really sure what you would like, so I kind of brought it all. Peanut butter with strawberry jam," he says, offering me the least dented of two sandwiches, the grapes having squished them both in the cooler.

"Strawberry's the best," I say. "Why does everyone go for the grape stuff?"

"I know, right? Only the best for you," he adds, and my face heats up.

"Glacier Freeze or Riptide Rush?" he asks, holding up both sweating bottles of Gatorade.

I grab for the Glacier Freeze. My mouth is so dry, I feel like downing the entire bottle on the spot. How is it Evan can look so relaxed, even after my epic freak-out just minutes ago? Because he's perfect, that's why.

We eat in silence, and I take a look around at the clearing and the back of the little shed that serves pies. With all those motorcyclists, I guess I would have expected loud music and some brawling over a pool table, like I might have seen in a movie somewhere. But the clearing is so quiet, I can actually hear both of us chewing. I'm sure Nell would have something more poetic to say than that.

"What're you thinking about?"

"Oh, it's uh . . . nothing. Nothing really," I stumble.

"You're a bad liar," he says through a mouthful of peanut butter—which for anyone else might be gross, but on him, it's totally adorable. "Like, the worst liar ever," he keeps going. "You stutter when you try."

"When have I ever . . . ?"

But before I can finish the sentence, I hear myself on the phone with him, trying to come up with some excuse for why he couldn't come over—then for why he couldn't come with me inside Oakside. In fact, it seems like nearly every sentence I've uttered to him has been some sort of half truth.

"It's okay," he says, then ducks his head a little. "It's kinda cute."

I'm suddenly fascinated by my peanut butter sandwich—afraid to look at anything but the strawberry jelly squishing out the sides where I've nibbled the crust.

"What happened back there?" he asks, nodding toward his car in the parking lot.

Here it goes. The fantasy couldn't last forever. What was I thinking, assuming I could have a normal life?

"I'm sorry," I say, putting down my sandwich in defeat. "I know I totally lost it."

"Hey, I'm not blaming you or anything. A bad idea is a bad idea," he says shrugging, but I can feel his foot wiggling really fast under the table. I guess this is what self-conscious is like on him.

"No! It's not that at all."

He smiles a little, just so the corner of his lips crease. "So, what was it then?"

I take a deep breath and go for it.

"I know you're kind of new here, so you're probably the only person in a hundred-mile radius who hasn't heard, but my sister . . . my sister, almost a year ago . . . she . . ."

"I know," he says, rescuing me. "I know about her."

I nod. Of course he knows.

"So then you know where they found her," I say, starting to get a little angry. If he knew, then what was he trying to accomplish by bringing me—?

Oh my God. It's a joke. This is all just a joke to him. One of his football buddies put him up to it. He's messing with me.

But Evan just looks at me, puzzled. "Where they found her?"

"Yeah, you know, the police. Where they found her. Her body."

He shakes his head slowly, never pulling his gaze from mine, and we allow the words to hang in the air for a moment before I come out with it.

"She was in Jerome. You know, the wickedest city in the West? That's where they found her." I say that as evenly as possible. I want to see how he reacts.

Evan casts his sandwich aside and drops his head to the table, groaning.

"Shit, I'm such an idiot," he says, shaking his head slowly. Then he looks up at me, his eyes wide.

"I had no idea. Jesus, Sophie, I swear I had no idea. I just thought it'd be fun to go somewhere with this, you know, eerie reputation. I swear to you, I didn't know."

And I believe him.

"It's okay—"

"No, it's not," he interrupts me. "See, there's more to it than that."

The reassurance I'd felt a second ago quavers under the weight of doubt. I knew he was too good to be true.

"I had another reason for wanting to go there with you."

"Yeah, and what was that?"

He pokes at his sandwich, then sighs. He starts to open his mouth, but reaches for my Gatorade instead of his own and takes a long swig. For the first time, he actually looks nervous around me. But it's not the kind of nervous I feel around him. This is familiar.

And then it hits me. The way he's fidgeting, the way he won't look at me—it's as if I'm two seconds from betraying him or uncovering what a freak he is. He has a secret too. One that he isn't sure he can share with me. With anybody.

So I take a chance.

"Hey, it's okay, you know. You can tell me."

I reach for my Gatorade, and he lets it go like he's ready to forfeit it to me, but I take his hand instead. Its wet chill from the condensation quickly warms in my hand. I have no idea where this boldness is coming from, but I don't fight it. And he doesn't either. In fact, a little smile creeps back to his lips, and his eyes finally meet mine again. I'm liking that more and more—when he looks at me.

"I wanted to find someone," he says. "In Jerome."

I'm not sure what I was expecting, but this definitely wasn't it.

"Who?"

He drops his gaze to the table again.

"This is kind of hard to explain."

I laugh. "That's usually my territory."

He crinkles his brow like he's about to ask me something, then shakes his head and continues. "I had this cousin—*have* this cousin," he starts. "Deb. We were pretty tight growing up. Neither of us has siblings, and our families lived right around the corner from each other, and we might as well have been brother and sister."

Hearing the word "sister" from his mouth distracts me, but I try to stay focused. I can tell that whatever he's trying to say means as much to him as what happened to Nell means to me.

"We grew up going to private school together. We were the only kids in my neighborhood who did, so we relied on each other. She's a couple of years younger than me, but still, she and I were sort of a team, you know?"

"Yeah, I know," Nell and I and my mom and Aunt Becca were the same way. We may have gone to public school, and Nell might have been popular, but when she came home, it was just the two of us. Plus, she and I were the only people I knew our age who actually read books for fun—she with her poetry, me with my fiction.

"So anyway, we used to tell each other things. And she told me some . . . some pretty strange stuff."

I keep quiet. Evan starts squirming around again.

"When we were really little, she used to say that she could see things. Like, things that weren't there."

I want to say something but I can't. This all sounds too familiar, like he's somehow read a transcript of what Nell used to tell me.

"I'd play along when we were little because I thought we were just pretending. But then we got older, and she didn't stop. She wasn't pretending. And when I told her I was, she got scared and told her parents about what she saw.

"So my aunt and uncle started taking her to this doctor. And for a while, we weren't allowed to hang out together. They made her take medicine. I heard my parents talking about it with her parents. And then I didn't see her for almost three months straight. They pulled her out of school. I'd ask my aunt and uncle about her, but they wouldn't tell me anything."

Evan stops and looks at me as though he's forgotten I've been listening the whole time. "Is this too much?"

I want to ask him which part. It's felt like life in general has been "too much" for the past six months.

"No, it's okay. Keep going," I say instead. He looks relieved.

"Almost two years ago, my aunt and uncle moved away. They just up and left their house and moved east, to Florida I think. I asked my parents where Deb was, but they didn't even know, just that my aunt and uncle must have taken her with them. How could they not? My parents never heard from them after that."

He nods toward the candy he bought at the rest-stop vending machine.

"They were Deb's favorite. After she went away, I don't know . . . I guess I just sort of picked up the habit. Almost like a tribute to her or something."

I run my finger over the outside of my silver ring. I know a thing or two about tributes.

We let a few more minutes pass with us just looking at our sandwiches. I hear the flies buzz around the trash can a few feet away, and I wonder how long it's going to take them to make their way over to our untouched picnic lunch, which Evan so conscientiously packed when he thought this might be a somewhat normal date. And it occurs to me—he still hasn't told me why he wanted to go to Jerome.

"Sorry, I still don't really understand."

"Yeah, I know. It's a lot of weird," he says apologetically, but at least now he's looking me in the eye again.

"No, I mean, what about today? About—"

"Jerome. Right," he nods, fishing around in the bag of grapes and plucking a few from their stems. But he doesn't eat them, just juggles them in the palm of his hand like dice.

"When I couldn't get any answers from my family, I started doing my own digging to try to find out what happened to Deb. The problem was, I didn't have enough information. I only knew what she said she was, you know, seeing."

He finally pops one of the grapes into his mouth, but he doesn't seem to register that he's eating. As soon as he swallows, he continues.

"I started searching the Internet. I'd type in her symptoms— seeing things out of the corner of her eye; hearing whispers in her ear. Believe it or not, I found lots of information. And not just what you'd expect about schizophrenia and stuff like that. I mean, that came up too. But there was more."

Up to this point, Evan's story about Deb had been the same as mine. But this was new. I might actually start to get answers about what happened to Nell. And even though I know this should make me happy, part of me feels like I'm in a speeding car headed toward a cliff. I'm not sure I want to hear it.

"What kinds of stuff?" I can't keep myself from asking.

He leans in a little closer. "Stuff that makes you think maybe she wasn't imagining it. Like it wasn't all in her head."

A shudder runs through my body so violently that I nearly tip backward off of the picnic bench.

"You mean, like what she was seeing and hearing was . . . ?"

He nods slowly. "Real."

"Oh God." I wrap my arms around myself. No one has put words to what I've felt ever since they started calling Nell schizophrenic—that there was too much that didn't add up. Schizophrenia seemed too easy an explanation.

"You wouldn't believe how much is out there. Blogs and databases and websites, all of them saying the same thing. That these people aren't crazy—that the voices they're hearing, the things they're seeing, are real. There are doctors, psychologists who are studying these so-called sick people. And not all of those doctors are good."

I'm starting to feel like I might pass out again. All I can hear in my mind is the fake empathy in Dr. Keller's voice, the unidentifiable threat hiding behind his words.

"Anyway, one site gets updated pretty frequently. The guy calls himself 'the Insider.' A lot of the people behind these sites are total nutcases, but this one seems like he's been there. It's just a gut feeling, but I think he knows what's going on. Nobody knows where the Insider is hiding out, except—well, I think I figured it out. I think he's in Jerome. I guess I thought that if I could find him and talk to him, maybe—"

I stand up so fast that I bang my knees on the underside of the attached table. I start pacing in the clearing.

Evan's voice floats to me as if from someplace far away. "What a lame date, right? Here I am, trying to make it sound like I'm taking you someplace original, but I really had this selfish motive. And then it turns out it's the place where your sister—oh man, I suck."

"Evan, stop. Okay? Just—just stop for a second." My voice sounds low and froglike.

My head is spinning so fast it blurs my vision. Evan thinks the Insider is in Jerome. The same place Nell died after she ran off with—

"This guy—the one from the website—doesn't he have a name?"

Evan shakes his head slowly, his lips pinched into an upside-down crescent. "The Insider."

"Right," I say. "Well, I think I've got a name for you."

Evan lifts his chin a little higher.

"Adam Newfeld." Now I place my hands squarely on the table and lean toward him, making sure I have his full attention. "Otherwise known as the orderly my sister ran away with."

Evan's mouth drops open as he connects the dots. "Holy shit."

"Yeah, holy shit." I rub my temples against an oncoming headache. "And believe me when I tell you, he might be this 'Insider' guy, but there's no way he's in Jerome anymore. Not with all those unanswered questions about my sister."

Evan and I consider the flood of information that's just passed between us. I try to slow my thoughts by focusing on the landscape. The spindly paloverde tree in the corner. The cluster of stones at the base of its neon-green trunk. The faded green and yellow awning shading the back window of the tiny restaurant. Evan looks like he's processing something too, though what that might be I couldn't even begin to guess.

"So," he says, standing slowly and looking wearily at his cooler full of untouched food. "Want some pie?"

Exhausted in the way that only a mind full of fresh questions and a stomach full of banana cream pie can make you, Evan and I drive home from Black Canyon City in near silence, careful to say only things that have to do with the music selection and the temperature of his car. This has quite possibly been the worst date in history, and yet, for some reason, I don't want it to end.

After Evan pulls up in front of my house, we sit in his idling car for a moment. Pretty soon, it occurs to me he might be waiting for me to leave, so I reach for my bag at my feet.

"Hey," he says, going for my hand, hesitating, then closing his long fingers around mine. "Your hands are cold," he says, pressing my palm between both of his.

"Must be that awesome AC of yours." I smile a little, then find his eyes, which are already on mine.

"Look, I know this was . . . well, I don't know what it was."

I shrug a little, doing my best it's-cool-this-kind-of-stuff-happens-to-me-all-the-time impression, which in a way is honest.

"So, since we know this much about each other already, what would you say to maybe finding out a little bit more?"

My heart pounds behind my sternum.

"I mean, not like that—not that I wouldn't want to, but what I meant was—" He starts stammering. "What I'm trying to say is, would you want to come over sometime so I can show you what I've been reading about all this stuff?"

On the one hand, I would do just about anything to spend more time with Evan. I'd search sewers for rats if he called it a date. But this is something else altogether. If Evan had any idea that he was dating a girl who sees things from the corner of her eye, just like his cousin did . . . well, he'd probably have me committed to Oakside. Unless he was crazy too. Which he isn't.

"I don't get it," I say. "Why me?"

I hope he doesn't think I'm saying no. I'm glad he picked me to be his companion in all this. But nobody ever picks me. Not for anything. He's the only guy to show me more than a minute's worth of attention, well, pretty much *ever*.

Evan looks at the dashboard as if the answer might be there, then answers with startling purposefulness. "I figured you'd understand. There's something quiet about you, like you've lived an entire lifetime already."

I let his words settle into my mind like seeds in soil. I don't quite know what to make of it.

"Plus you've got a rockin' body," he says with an enormous smile. I try to jerk my hand away, but he only holds it tighter.

Serious again, he says, "Please, Sophie." Suddenly I can't remember any of my reasons for saying no. So I say, "Yeah, okay. Maybe."

I ease out of the car, already missing the way his hands felt around mine, and watch his white Probe disappear around the corner, leaving me to wonder what it was I'd just agreed to.

Inside the house, there's no sign of Mom, but her remnants are everywhere—the smell of Jergens body lotion, a TV flickering with its sound turned off in the living room, a sweating liquor glass in the breakfast nook. I guess she's not going out with Aunt Becca after all. I know I'll find her passed out in her bed, but I don't want to go back there yet. I just want to linger in the feeling of being wanted by Evan a little bit longer.

I sit in front of the TV for a while and watch the characters of some syndicated sitcom silently play out their conflicts. I empty Mom's glass of its melted ice cubes and swipe away the ring of condensation from the tabletop with a clean dish towel. I pace the floor of the kitchen, retracing my steps over the bubble in the linoleum that's been beside the refrigerator for as long as I can remember. Nell used to try to scare me by telling me there was a tiny troll who lived under the house, and that was where he'd built his little underground chimney.

With nothing else to do, I'm about to head to my room when I decide I should check the voice mail. I'm sure Aunt Becca's left a message for Mom scolding her for staying home to drink instead of getting out of the house, and it'll end with a request to have me please call her so she can quiz me about what Mom's doing.

I lift the receiver and find the skipping dial tone, telling me there's a message waiting. I punch the code and wait for Aunt Becca's voice. Instead, I find a different voice, one I wasn't expecting but that's becoming almost as familiar.

Good afternoon, Ms. David. This is Dr. Jeremy Keller from the Oakside Behavioral Institute. I'm calling—again—to discuss a matter of great importance with you. It's regarding your daughter, Sophie, whom I had the pleasure of meeting the other day here at our facility. It's very important that I speak with you about some observations I made while she was here. I apologize for being so cryptic, but I'm sure you understand the, er, sensitivity with which this must be approached, especially given the, well, the family history. Ms. David, please give me a call at my personal extension as soon as you receive this message. The number is—

I hang up so fast I nearly knock the phone off the wall. What does Dr. Keller mean "observations"? What the hell is he doing calling my mom about me? I pick up the receiver and select the option for deleting the message. I stare at the phone for another few minutes as though it's betrayed me. Whatever he wants to tell Mom can't be good. And where does he get off calling like that anyway? Like he knows our family?

Yet, the fact is, he does. Dr. Keller knows all about us, all about Nell. And if he knows all of Nell's secrets, what if he somehow knows mine, too? Snippets of my conversation with Evan stream through my brain. I think about institutions and experiments, doctors with malicious intentions. I busy myself

with chores—dusting, straightening, sweeping. I check on
my mom, who is buried under her comforter with her back
to the bedroom doorway. I lock all the windows and doors,
partly out of habit, though now I feel compelled to double-
check them once I'm done. I try to erase the voice of Dr.
Keller from my mind like I erased his message. I do this for
the rest of the day and into the night—tossing and turning
instead of sleeping.

7

I'VE SPENT ALL DAY ON edge, and not just because of every-thing that happened yesterday with Evan, or even the message Dr. Keller left for my mom. Aunt Becca's coming over for dinner tonight. This could mean one of two things: either Mom will be in great spirits because she's forced to get out of bed and interact with family, or Mom will completely fall apart because she's forced to get out of bed and interact with family. Falling apart will set her back a good month (and set me back God knows how much longer).

"Hand me the pepper grinder," Mom says more to the steaming pot on the stove than to me. I have absolutely no idea what she's making, but so far I've seen noodles, butter, onions, peppers, and about ten different spices disappear into the scratched-up blue saucepot that hardly has any more Teflon on its bottom.

I hand the pepper to her over her shoulder, and our fingers brush as she takes it.

"Thanks, hon," she says offhandedly.

She's trying. At least, I think she is. So far, so good. Of course, Aunt Becca hasn't shown up yet.

"Should we have a salad?" she asks, still talking to the pot.

The steam is starting to make her sweat, and the heavy brown waves around her face are curling with the humidity. Still, all I smell is whatever she's putting into her concoction and the faintest whiff of her conditioner. No booze. She's standing at the stove—two steps from the liquor cabinet— but she hasn't had a drop of alcohol since she's been in the kitchen.

"Definitely salad," she answers herself almost too decisively, peering into the fridge and rummaging through the crisper.

She puts me to work chopping random vegetables and throwing them into a wooden bowl. I've almost forgotten my anxiety over this evening when I hear a knock at the door.

"I've got it," I say, dropping the knife and hustling to the front door.

Aunt Becca plants a rushed kiss on my temple before

handing me one of the two paper grocery bags she's balancing on her hips.

"How's she doing?"

I bite my tongue before blurting that I have no idea, that I shouldn't have to keep tabs on my mother, that I'm not exactly fine myself. My face hurts from forcing a smile for everyone else's sake. All so Mom can recover from *her* loss.

"Who knows?" I say instead, mustering my best *I'm coping* tone.

"Guess we'll know soon enough," she says before whisking past me into the kitchen.

We eat in the breakfast nook, the three of us quietly marveling at the creation Mom's managed to slap together. I have to admit, I had my doubts. And I still can't exactly name whatever it is that she's made. But it's warm and savory, and I'm so happy to be eating it. Aunt Becca brought a crusty sourdough baguette and some cheese, and I'm wolfing it down so fast I'm about to slip into a bread-and-cheese coma.

"What kind of cheese is this anyway?" Mom asks before slathering a slice of baguette with the soft white stuff.

It makes me irrationally giddy to see her eating.

"Camembert, I think," Aunt Becca replies. "Who knows? I grabbed the first thing I found next to the bread."

"I can't remember the last time I've had really good

cheese," Mom says with nostalgia, and I wonder if she's working up to more important things to remember fondly. "I don't think I've had really good cheese since Mom died. Do you remember how she used to be such a food snob?"

"Yes!" Aunt Becca climbs onboard. "She was always bringing the girls those fancy French cheeses made from goats' this or that. The girls loved it, didn't you?" She turns to me.

I shrug. Nell had taken to Nana's eccentricities more than I had. I suppose I didn't have the right sophistication—the same quality that made Nell so good at poetry. She and Nana had always had more in common.

"Do you remember that trip we all took to Oregon?" Aunt Becca continues the happy memory game. I'm still just glad to be eating a home-cooked meal.

"Oh God, the cheese factory! I'd almost forgotten all about that!" Mom starts to laugh, and it sounds out of practice in her throat. Still, shaking off the cobwebs is a good start. The Oregon trip was one of the only out-of-state vacations I remember. Mom and Aunt Becca got some sort of discount for going to a hair show.

I watch Mom's face closely from the corner of my eye, and though she looks a little nervous, her smile doesn't disappear as she forks the next bite into her mouth.

"Do you remember that, Sophie?" Aunt Becca tries to draw me in, no doubt hopeful that a shared memory will start the healing process right here in the breakfast nook over a plate of mystery noodles.

"Sort of." I'm hoping if I don't join in, this conversation will pass. This sort of reminiscing can't end well.

"She might have been too young," Mom says.

"I guess she was pretty young. But don't you remember, Sophie? You have to remember. You were the one who almost got us kicked out for stealing crackers from the gift shop!" Aunt Becca hoots, looking at me with a rapt attention that only comes with remembering something that was fun once upon a time.

But her face is tight, desperate, like she's trying to re-create that feeling all over again.

She's talking so fast, I can't stop her before she says, "And then you told the security guard that you weren't stealing it. You needed it for your low blood sugar. Ha! How could a girl your age even know what that was? And then to pull that out of thin air, I just couldn't believe—"

"That was Nell," I correct her quietly.

For a second, we all sit in silence, forks resting on our plates.

"That's right. I'd forgotten that. She was always coming

up with . . ." Aunt Becca trails off as I shift my gaze between the two of them.

Mom's face stiffens. She hasn't looked up since I invoked the unmentionable name of Nell.

"Yep, I remember," Mom finally says, reaching slowly for another hunk of cheese and spreading it on some bread with a zombielike movement.

"Only she didn't make up *everything*, did she?" I aim the question at my mother, but I'm hoping Aunt Becca catches some of my tone too. I'm suddenly overwhelmingly suspicious, like they've conspired to keep me in the dark all these years. I have absolutely no idea where it's coming from— maybe it's everything Evan told me yesterday, all the stuff his aunt and uncle kept from him about his cousin—but the feeling pours over me like oil on a blazing fire.

"It's not that simple," Mom's answer is infuriatingly quick, and she reaches for another chunk of cheese and slathers a second piece of bread before she's touched the one that's already on her plate.

"Yeah, but it kind of is. I mean, either she made everything up, or she believed what was happening to her was real," I push on.

"Sophie," Aunt Becca cautions. I've been warned away from this topic too many times. I'm through walking on egg-

shells. I'm through being responsible for the sake of everyone else while I suffocate under my own questions. Questions like why nobody at Oakside ever told Nell that she was crazy. And why Mom and Aunt Becca went along with whatever treatment Dr. Keller proposed, like the drugs she talked about in her journal. And what happened in the mirrored room.

"No, seriously. Which was it? Because either way, I can't see why Nell would have run away unless there was something else. Something, I don't know, that they were doing to her at Oakside. Or *making* her do."

I can see my mom's and Aunt Becca's shoulders rise in unison, like a barricade against my questions. Still, not a word leaves either of their lips. We all chew on silence like it's a sourdough baguette smeared with Camembert.

"Is somebody going to answer me?" I demand, slapping my hands on my thighs like a two-year-old.

"Goddamnit, Sophie, drop it!" Mom says, setting her water glass down hard and gripping the edge of the table. "You have no idea what you're even asking about."

"You're right. I don't, which is exactly why I'm asking—"

"I *said* drop it," she repeats through gritted teeth, her jawbones jutting out below her earlobes.

Mom's eyes spark in my direction as if I've betrayed her, as if somehow she knew I would all along. I want to scream at

her, to stand up from the table, to slam the door and never come back.

"I think I've had enough for tonight," Mom says, finally unlocking me from her gaze and starting to clear the table.

"Miri, let's go for a walk or something," Aunt Becca tries, pretending I'm no longer at the table.

"It's too hot."

When Mom reaches for a glass in the cupboard near the stove, that seals the deal. She's done with both of us for the night.

Aunt Becca finally ventures a glance at me with anger or pity, I can't tell. Anyway, I think she's aiming it at the wrong person, and I shoot her a look that I hope tells her so.

"Miri, we need to talk," she tries again, attempting her firmest older-sister tone, which never worked on Mom, even when she wasn't like this.

"I'm done talking," Mom mumbles.

"Well, I'm not," Aunt Becca persists.

I have to say I'm impressed. Well, I *think* I'm impressed. Nobody's listening to what I say anymore tonight.

"I've got a number for you," she continues, and I know she's dangerously close to pushing Mom past her breaking point.

"Of a guy? Not in the mood," Mom makes a bad attempt

at a joke. These days, her jokes are like mine: full of acid.

Aunt Becca fixes a stern gaze at the bottle in Mom's hand. "Of an AA chapter. It's three blocks away on Pima. They meet Tuesdays and Thurs—"

"God, Becca. Seriously, not this again." Mom sounds more like a teenager than I do.

I'm instantly pissed at Mom, and I want to throw my plate of food right at her head. Not that I'm any huge fan of Aunt Becca at the moment for stonewalling me about Nell, but at least she's trying to get us all to move on. Anything's better than staying in this limbo. But it's like Mom's completely given up. And right now, that's all I feel like doing too. My head is pounding like a snare drum, and if it weren't still more than a hundred degrees outside, I'd probably run until I hit Mexico.

Instead, I slide from my chair without saying good night to Mom or good-bye to Aunt Becca and drag myself down the hall toward my bedroom. In my wake, I can hear them arguing, their sisterly voices sounding nearly identical the more walls I put between them and me. My bedroom looks somehow foreign in the orange dusk that slips in through the window. Being in there isn't any more comforting than being in the kitchen with Mom and Aunt Becca.

I push open Nell's door and lie down on her bed, the box

of her Oakside belongings right where I left it on top of her dresser. I close my eyes to block the sight of it, to block anything that isn't the picture of Nell curled up on this very bed, knees under her chin, and a journal splayed across the bedspread, left hand flying across the page as the poetry spilled from her mind. I want to remember the way she used to pull my hair into tight braids after a nighttime bath and instruct me not to toss and turn in my sleep. In the morning, she would unravel the coils to reveal wavy hair just like hers, just like I'd always wanted. I want to remember how she used to tell me, her voice strained and urgent, that if I ever thought I saw things that no one else saw in the dark, if I ever heard things when no one else heard them, to know those things could never hurt me.

I let my head sink into Nell's pillow, trying as best I can not to crease the sheets I'll only let myself lie on top of. My mind wanders to the times after Mom had gone to bed, exhausted from ten hours of making people's hair gorgeous, and Nell would tell me about what she heard when she was alone. She said she thought she might be going crazy, only there was something about the way she would push on the words, as if pressing a cut to make it bleed more, that made me think she *wanted* to believe she was going crazy. Because then whatever was scaring her wasn't real. I replay those late-night scenes in my head, imagining myself saying something that might have helped her, that might have made things different. I picture myself telling her what she used to tell me: Whatever it is, it can't hurt you. I imagine my words releasing Nell's shoulders from their vise around her ears, her eyes softening and her pupils returning to their normal size inside her deep-green irises.

But then the image is shattered. In my mind, Nell's face twists at the approach of something only she can see.

What is it, Nell? Tell me what it is.

She shakes her head as if I can't understand. As if I won't *try* to understand. She looks like a child, small and afraid, her bottom lip trembling.

Nell, tell me what to do. What can I do?

But she can't hear me, and then, I can't hear anything but the faintest whisper. It's more tonal than a whisper. Like mumbling. Words indistinguishable from one another slur together like overlapping shadows. The wispy sounds fill my ear and command my attention. Nell's face has gone completely still, and soon she's rising from the ground, and flipping over like an upturned hourglass. An invisible hand grasps her toe, drags her up the wall, and suspends her from the ceiling so that she's ready to listen to the words I can't quite hear from the thing I can't see.

As Nell listens, her face goes slack, her eyes widen, and her body drains of life. One leg falls to a bend behind her straightened knee, a ballerina poised in upside-down relevé. And as her eyes find me one more time, they plead and apologize and accuse in one stare before losing the light behind them.

"No!"

I gasp awake, blinking spastically in the gray that surrounds me. At first, I only register the horizontal stripes of silver in front of me. The miniblinds, partially closed, let in cracks of moonlight, illuminating the front wall of Nell's room.

The digital clock by her bed reads 2:36 a.m. The air is alive with the sounds of the desert night: chirping crickets, a croaking toad, and, from a distance, someone's dog barking at all of it.

I stare foggily at the box with its big black letters: DAVID, NELL.

My gaze drifts over the rest of Nell's room to the things that feel less and less like hers the longer she's gone and more as though they belonged to someone who was never real.

I find my own reflection in the mirrored closet doors. My body, once curvy, is now sinewy-looking, and there are purplish rings sagging below my eyes, which I haven't even bothered to brush with mascara in more than six months. I look at my stringy hair, which is too dark for my complexion and needs brushing but instead just gets the abuse of an elastic band or clip, if it gets anything at all.

"God, what am I doing?" I'm not even sure what I mean. But at this hour, I suppose I can't expect too much of myself.

I begin to slide off of Nell's bed, already counting the time I have left to sleep before school, when out of the corner of my eye, I see a flicker of movement.

Movement that isn't mine.

I stare at the far corner of the room where I saw the movement. But the only thing I see is the silvery light jutting through the half-open miniblinds.

I tell myself it was a bird or a bat flying past the window and give Nell's room one last look before closing the door quietly behind me. I reassure myself that the little black smudge I saw on the mirrored closet door has been there forever.

I'm in my own bed and drifting back to sleep when I remember my dream. The murmuring filled my ear so insistently that I can practically feel the dampness of the breath curl the hair behind my ear.

I tell myself it was just the dream that left my ear and neck moist with sweat. Just a horrible dream that I'll forget by morning if I keep repeating those words to myself.

It was just a dream.

Nell David

November 19

MM has been here for too long. We've all been here for too long, LM the longest, but MM's the one who makes me the saddest. She doesn't feel sorry for herself—that doesn't seem to be her way. But she has a melancholy that's slowly killing her, like the tide wears away at rocks over time. It's smoothing her, sort of dulling her out. I try to make her laugh to get some of that life back, and sometimes I think it even works.

The other day, MM and I laughed so hard that the orderlies separated us. It's like they have to snuff out any trace of humanity that we try to regain. I even got LM laughing. What a feat. I don't even remember what I said.

But MM laughed, straight from her belly, and it was beautiful.

8

SCHOOL WAS A TOTAL BUST today. I could have saved myself a headache and a boatload of guilt over not doing a single second of homework by staying home and sleeping the day away. Mom might not have even noticed. I could have kept my bedroom door closed, pulled the sheet over my head, and created a little cocoon for myself the way she does pretty much all the time. But the need for some semblance of normalcy won out. I spent the entire day like a zombie instead.

Worst of all, I didn't have a single Evan sighting. I even took a while getting to most of my classes (not much new there), but this time it was in hopes of being Swept by my favorite monitor. No luck.

After Saturday, I wasn't sure I would want to see him again

and be reminded of his cousin, or of the blog he's been read-ing, or of Adam, who took my sister and never brought her back—the same Adam who is the only one who could tell the police what the hell actually happened to Nell that day.

So by the time I get home, I tell myself it's probably a good thing I didn't see Evan. I mean, who needs a reminder of all that?

I've almost convinced myself of this when I feel my phone vibrating in the side pouch of my messenger bag as I unlock the front door.

As soon as I see the screen, my former resolve falls away.

"Hey, Sophie D."

It's taking everything I have not to ask him where he was all day.

"Anybody there?" He asks after a second. Then silence.

I wonder if Evan's holding his breath on the other end. It takes me a second to realize that *I* am, which explains why no words are coming out.

"Yeah, I'm here," I say, shrugging even though I know he can't see me.

"I feel bad about the other day," he says, the awkwardness from our first phone call returning. He sounds shy; I can almost see him digging his toe into the ground while he talks to me. "I kind of avoided you today because I didn't know what to say."

"Why? You didn't do anything," I tell him.

"Well, that's just it. I didn't do anything. I basically unloaded all this baggage on Saturday without warning you and then left you to think about it for the rest of the weekend. I forget that not everyone is living in my world, you know?"

"Yeah, I get that," I say, knowing he can't possibly know how much I get that.

"Anyway, I was serious about you coming over to look at those websites."

My hands grow cold.

"I don't know, Evan."

"Okay," he says slowly. "You don't know because you're not sure you want to read about what may have been happening to your sister, or you don't know because you're not sure you want to hang out with me anymore?"

"The first one." What am I going to say? Yes, please invite me to your house so I can have any excuse to be in a room alone with you?

If it's possible, I hear him smile over the phone. And just like that, his confidence returns.

"What're you going to do now?"

I smile. He's not ready to hang up yet. Neither am I.

"Uh, I don't know. Maybe watch a little TV or something."

"What, no homework?" he teases.

"Yeah, that might be on the agenda at some point," I say a little sheepishly.

Why do I even care if he knows I'm slacking? Because he's perfect—that's why. Evan Gold doesn't ditch class. He doesn't skip his homework. He might saunter in late sometimes, might be a little tardy with the work, but he's so damned nice. I don't think any of the teachers reprimand him too seriously.

"So, meet me in the parking lot after school tomorrow?"

"Okay, but you owe me a Glacier Freeze Gatorade," I scold.

He chuckles.

"What? You practically drank my whole bottle on Saturday! I was really looking forward to it," I say, starting to laugh a little myself, something I wasn't sure I'd ever do on this porch again.

"Three thirty at my car," he says, then, "Catch'ya later, Sophie D."

I hang up, but instead of going inside, I sit on the front step and pull out the reading assignment for Mrs. Dodd's class that I should have done over the weekend. I try to concentrate, knowing the fresh air will be better than the stale air inside my house. But it's impossible to focus. Right now, all I want to do is enjoy the echo of Evan's deep laugh.

Nell David

November 26

Puncture it until it pops,

Bleeds like a wound filling to the very top,

Filling like a water glass, too tall, too high,

Optimism brimming over.

I am not optimistic.

I can see for miles,

Through that puncture wound.

I can crawl out, if only for a second,

Breathe the air of something easy.

To breathe would be something easy.

Adam and I talked about trees today. It's always about trees, or poetry, or food. He's so funny and formal. He's more serious than any other guy I've met. It's like he was born into the wrong decade or something. He talked about roots, about how they keep trees stable and upright, how they allow a plant to feed off of the most crucial elements from the earth to survive. But roots also make trees vulnerable to harm from toxins. They're the source, he said, of all the good and all the bad, and that's what makes roots so beautiful.

After Adam left, Dr. Keller took me to the room with the mirrors, and all of my beautiful thoughts about trees and roots disappeared. I tried to write about pretty things when I got back to my room, but I couldn't.

I told Adam. I told him everything. He told me about how he grew up. About the things he's seen, too.

9

EVAN'S ROOM SMELLS LIKE DRYER sheets. It's way cleaner than I was expecting, given how he keeps his car. His deep-blue walls should make the room feel dark, but a giant window by his double bed (with sheets pulled so tight they threaten to bend the mattress in half) lets in the strong glare of late afternoon sun. The only thing that keeps the sunlight from blinding us both is an olive tree with pale bark and waxy leaves weaving a screen of protection. There are only two things hanging on the walls of Evan's bedroom: a framed Arizona Diamondbacks pennant and an old Arizona State University jersey signed by Jake Plummer. His desk is clean save for a closed laptop and a mechanical pencil. His dresser drawers are closed without a single stray piece of fabric peeking out.

The carpet under my feet is a pleasant light gray, the same as the rest of the house, and vacuum marks still stripe the floor. I'm in the world's cleanest room.

"I like to keep organized," he says when he catches me noticing.

"I wish I was that organized," I say. "One time, I swear to God I lost my cat in my room for three days. I could hear him, but I couldn't see him. He's dead now, though."

My laugh comes out like a bark, so I turn away and gaze out the window like the tree outside is the most interesting thing I've ever seen. I know I'm a freak, but why do I have to be even more freakish whenever I'm around Evan? Someone finally pays attention to me, and my mouth mutinies.

Then, out of nowhere, I can smell him. And it's warm behind me. I turn my head slightly, and his broad shoulders are inches from my own. He's so close to me, I can hear his nose whistling faintly as he breathes.

"My parents planted that tree two days before I was born," he says, his voice deep and rich. I open my mouth to ask him what tree he's talking about, but then I remember I've been pretending to stare at the one outside of his bedroom.

"Deb and I used to pick the olives from it and stomp them on the sidewalk, then try to make up stories about whatever we saw in the splatters. Kind of like those inkblots shrinks use. What're they called? Rorschach tests." His voice is quieter now.

I can't think of a single thing to say in response, because I know what he's thinking about. He's thinking about Deb and the tests she might have been subjected to wherever it was her parents sent her. I know, because I've wondered a million times what Nell went through at Oakside. I could probably fill an album with all the horrible images I've conjured—images that weren't quite verified by her journal but I've imagined enough to get me thinking.

Evan's quiet for a long time, and I actually get a little lightheaded from holding my breath. I'm afraid to make a noise or even move. I am a wreck, feeling him this close to me, but I don't want to break the moment.

"Sometimes I forget what she looked like, you know? It's hard to believe I could, but I do. I have pictures, but whenever I think of Deb, it's not her face I think about. It's that tree. Stupid, huh?"

This time, I respond. "No. Not stupid at all."

When he doesn't say anything in return, I finally work up the courage to face him. But when I turn, I'm surprised to find Evan at his desk hunched over his open laptop, his back to me. He's typing in a password, and before I can get self-conscious about why he wanted to get away from me, he turns to me again, his lips parted in a smile that makes my arm hairs stand on end.

"I've never told anyone that before." Instead of looking vulnerable the way a guy might on some stupid TV show after he's just poured out his heart to the girl he suspects he's falling in love with, he looks almost giddy. He's finally found someone he can talk to who will understand—a freak like himself. A freak buddy. I smile and try to disguise my disappointment. I'm suddenly desperate for an excuse to leave.

"Yeah, I have that effect on people," I say, playing the role of the self-deprecating pal.

God, what was I thinking? Of course a guy like Evan Gold isn't going to be into me. He's a football player. Sure, he made that comment about my "rockin' body" or whatever, but maybe he was just trying to lighten the mood. What's he going to do? Explain to all his football team buddies that he's with me because we have this deep, profound connection that only two people who have lost a family member can share? That he finds my loner behavior and the fact that I'm quite possibly on the road to a straitjacket fitting totally hot? I guess it makes perfect sense that I'd assume he liked me. Delusions are quickly becoming my specialty.

Evan has his back to me again, pulling up a search engine and clicking on a link.

"I haven't ever shown this to anyone else. I've never really felt like I could—like anyone would—" he stammers, then stops himself, sounding like he did that first day he called me on the phone.

I can't think of what to say to that, so for the second time today, I choose to say nothing. I walk to his side and shift my focus to the screen.

What I see there is less than comforting.

A page titled Truth Seekers is loading blue link after blue link, all with excerpts starting with words like "criminal," "negligent," "horrifying." The familiar panic creeps in.

"So what are we looking at?" I try to sound casual but fail miserably.

"It's a database," Evan says, his eyes shining from the light of the monitor. "I found it about a year ago, and I've been following it ever since. Some of it is total crap, but some . . ." He trails away.

Bold black letters at the top of the page read:

These facilities are NOT what they seem. They purport to heal the sick and counsel the mentally disturbed, but their REAL intentions are far from pure. <u>This is by no means a definitive list.</u>

It seems that every month, a new institution is featured, each given a snazzy nickname like "Haven Hill—House of Horrors" or "Juniper Springs—A Bouquet of Lies." A list to the right is archived in chronological order. Somewhere toward the middle is "Oakside—Phoenix's Mad Science Lab," a website owned and operated by the Insider.

"Adam," I whisper.

Evan nods. "Guess so."

He moves the mouse over the link.

"Wait, Evan," I say, but it's too late.

He's clicked the link, which opens an entirely new page— a blog just as Evan described. Even though I haven't really begun to read, there's urgency to the text. There are lots of exclamation points, phrases in all capital letters, and italicized, bolded, and underlined words.

Evan looks up at me from his desk chair. "Maybe you should start at the beginning."

I take a deep breath, my eyes reading even though I'm not sure I want them to. I release the air from my lungs in one push. "Yeah, okay."

He stands up and gestures toward the chair. "I'll go grab us something to eat."

But I don't answer him. I'm already too engrossed. I scroll to the first blog post and stop.

April 20th.

Exactly one week after Nell's body was found in Jerome.

The Insider *has* to be Adam.

Well, nothing left to do but . . .

Read.

April 20th

I never asked for <u>any</u> of this. I never wanted it. I know a lot of you out there are going to dismiss what I say. You're going to shake your head at your computer screen in doubt. Imagine it's my eyes you're looking into while you refuse to believe. You might pity me for what you call my delusions, or *laugh* at me when I share the horrors that I've witnessed firsthand. The horrors that I might have had a part in, unwilling or otherwise. Or you might believe me. And to be honest, if even one person believes me, what I've done could have all been worth it.

No, not <u>all</u> of it.

Because once you've lost someone, nothing can convince you that their sacrifice was for a greater good.

NOTHING was greater than her.

Warm tears well in my eyes, and I wipe them absently and keep reading.

April 29th

I'll start at my beginning, but that's not <u>the</u> beginning. This thing—this horror, this pain—has been around longer than me or anyone reading this. It's been around for as long as people have been living and dying. But I can only share my story with you. I will tell you the place where real evil is being cultivated. Years of therapy tells me it's worth the risk I'm taking to post this online—that it will be therapeutic. Maybe afterward . . . **long** afterward, I won't be so fucked up. Or maybe I don't even know what's normal anymore, so trying to be that way is pointless.

I started exhibiting "symptoms" when I was six or seven. I was hearing things, seeing things that my parents didn't think could be real. I would swear they were real, and my parents would whisper between themselves that I needed help—that I wasn't normal. The doctor they brought me to see really *listened* to me. He believed everything I said was happening to me. I know it sounds stupid, but that meant a lot. Pretty soon, I was going to see him so often that he suggested my parents let me stay at a residential facility so he could treat me full-time. They were probably thrilled to have me off their hands. I never saw them again.

At the hospital, the visions started to get worse. A shadow just out of reach, a distorted reflection, like a motion from behind the mirror. I asked the doctor why this was happening to me. Why ME? He told me it was because I was special.

I'm not certain why this doctor believed what I was experiencing was more than just my imagination. I think maybe he *wanted* to believe me. It wasn't until I told him what I heard — THAT'S when he knew I was telling the truth.

Up until I was seventeen or so, I only ever heard mumbling. It was as though something was trying to get me to hear, but I could never quite understand. And then one day, I **DID** hear — it was the only time the mumbling actually became clear. The day had been a bad one. I was thinking about my parents. I'll never forget what the voice said: "You promised me you would come back. Is that bracelet for me?"

That's all you get for tonight. If this is entertaining, then you're more messed up than I am. If you believe me, you'll know why I can't say any more just now.

May 27th

It took me a month to find a new place. I started hearing things again. I used to think I could get away from the murmurings. Now I realize I'll be running for the rest of my life. If not from *THEM*, then from the police. I've been lucky so far. I don't know how long that luck will last.

I told you I'd continue my story, but I also need to tell you someone else's. Otherwise, mine won't make any sense. This assumes, of course, there's anyone even reading this. I DON'T want comments. I've disabled that feature. You can't help me, and I don't want to read anyone else's bullshit. I know the truth. My only motive is to share that with other people.

I've told you about the doctor I was sent to live with. If you met him, you might even think he's a pretty decent guy. I did for a long time. But you have to know that he's different now. **AND HE'S DANGEROUS.** Several years ago, he took over as head of psychiatry at Oakside Behavioral Institute in Phoenix, Arizona. That's where he runs his operation. And with his title, he holds nearly infinite and unquestioned power over the patients who reside there.

This place doesn't treat anyone. It's a place that *fosters* things—not people, <u>things</u>. Brothers and aunts and ailing mothers are sent there because nobody wants to deal with them, let alone the voices in their heads. This place is storage for people who really need psychiatric help, and prison for those they're actually interested in "treating."

Again, the name is Oakside Behavioral Institute. Phoenix, Arizona. **And the doctor's name—Dr. Jeremy Keller. STAY AWAY FROM THIS PLACE!!!**

Stopping for tonight, but now I can sleep knowing that I got that message out to you . . . whoever might be reading.

I wipe my hands on my legs. I'm not sure I can read any more of this. If even a fraction of this is true, it's too much. And it almost doesn't matter because I know at least one part is true—we left Nell there. She was experiencing something my mom couldn't fathom—or acknowledge—and I was in too much denial to believe her. I pretended Nell didn't need me. I made myself think she was still stronger than me.

"Hungry?"

I jump at the sound of Evan's voice.

"Sorry, I didn't know you were so engrossed." He sets half the contents of his fridge on the desk.

"Your Gatorade, madam," he hands me a bottle with a little bow, but his face falls. "You doing okay?"

I push myself away from the laptop and cover my eyes, speaking through the split between my hands.

"Evan, I can't do this. I can't read anymore."

"Hey, hey," he says, putting his hand on my shoulder.

"I'm sorry, I just can't. I know you want to find out what happened to your cousin—and trust me, I want to understand what happened to Nell—but this is all just too . . . close." I shake my head in an effort to block the information that screams through my brain at warp speed, bumping over question after question on the way.

"Just take your time. I know it's a lot right now, but it gets easier, I swear."

I can't tell where he is anymore. I feel dizzy in the dark I've created for myself.

"No, Evan, you don't know!" I blurt, and before I can stop

them, hot tears are streaking my cheeks, followed by words I can't catch before they shoot from my mouth.

"These people he's talking about in these posts, they're just like Nell. She was basically sacrificed to all of this. I know that's just one Oakside statistic to you, but . . ."

And then a memory blinks into view like a slide show clicking to its next image.

"That night we went to Oakside together. You knew I'd missed that turn. You'd been there before, hadn't you? After you found out what Dr. Keller was doing, you went there yourself, didn't you?"

My tone is accusatory, but I can't quite figure out why.

"I should have told you that before," Evan says, flustered, then ashamed. "I wanted to see if Dr. Keller would see me, if he would be straight with me. I wanted to know if he might be able to tell me something that might, I don't know, lead me to Deb. But when I tried to talk to him, he wouldn't see me."

And then I realize why I'm accusing him.

"So I was your ticket into Oakside—to Dr. Keller. That's why you didn't tell me you knew about that place."

Evan's face crumples. "What? No! Of course not!"

"Really, so that was all just coincidence?" I say, folding my arms across my chest.

"Yes, it was. You don't really think—God, Sophie. I've

never been able to talk to anyone about this before. I didn't know how to tell you, and I'm sorry. I shouldn't have—"

But he stops there. Now we're both staring at each other with fire and defeat and hurt.

"Hey," Evan says again, and this time his face relaxes into actual concern. The fire seems to have died out. Then he moves a little closer to me. Then very close. And soon, I can feel his hands on the sides of my face, and without thinking about it, I stand up from the desk into his reach. His palms are warm and calloused, but they feel so good against my skin.

"I'm so sorry," he says. His eyes are the color of honey. I feel like I could stare at them forever and never find the center of him. "I should have told you everything. I should have known I could trust you, that you wouldn't think I was crazy."

"I know what it's like," I say. "To finally find out that someone else has been where you've been."

"We're going to figure this out. Whatever happened to your sister, none of it was your fault."

My heart continues to thrum in my chest, my cheeks heating in response to Evan's touch.

"I should have listened to her. I should have—"

"Shhh," he says, moving closer, so now all I can see are

his lips, full and puckered into a loose O. And then they're touching mine, lightly at first, but then my body relaxes into his, and his hands fall from my face and lightly press the small of my back, pulling me closer to him. He moves his lips against my mouth, and it feels like we're talking to each other in a whole new language. I'm positive he can feel my heart slamming against my chest, but I don't care. For just this second, I don't care about anything.

By the time Evan pulls into my driveway, the house is dark except for the porch light, and that's only because I forgot to switch if off last night.

"Okay," he says.

"Okay," I say back. We stare at each other in the dark of his car, the radio no longer keeping me from having to fill the silence.

"Guess I'd better go in," I say. *Seriously? That's the best I can come up with?*

"Yeah, guess you'd better," he says, but now I know he isn't just hanging out to see what a freak's sister is like up close— or using me to get closer to his own freak past.

And besides, after everything that happened tonight, I can't muster the strength to be self-conscious anymore, which is why I get out of the car before he can try to kiss me again. The first one was incredible. I don't want to doubt the second one. I hear him drive away and know too late that I really did want him to kiss me again, but the minute I step through the front door, the usual exhaustion consumes me. All I can remember is what I read on Evan's computer screen, the frantic, italicized, underlined, and bolded words of the Insider—Adam.

I pull the refrigerator door open with robotic movement, knowing that I should be hungry but unable to locate even the slightest craving. I stare at the clock on the microwave and watch as two minutes click by before I register that it's 9:23. I was over there for practically six hours, and Mom never once wondered where I might be.

I pick up the phone—another automatic habit—and I'm greeted by an interrupted dial tone telling me we have a message. I punch the code.

The saccharine tone of a familiar voice fills my ear, practically dripping through the receiver.

Yes, hello, this is Dr. Jeremy Keller from the Oakside Behavioral Institute. I'm leaving this message for Sophie. I would very much like to continue our conversation from the other day. I believe you know what it's regarding. I'm confident that I can be of assistance to you and trust you feel the same way. Don't worry about making an appointment. Stop by any time you want to talk. I'll make myself available. I hope you'll agree that this should be soon. Your situation is . . . well, I'm afraid you know your situation all too well, having seen it play out before. Come see me any time.

I hold the phone to my ear for so long it's as though I've forgotten how to hang up. Finally, I key in the command to delete the message.

How can such a kind voice from such a handsome mouth be so . . . wrong? It's as though he's threatening me. He knows something about me that I've never told anyone, not even Evan, which after tonight feels strangely like a betrayal of trust. And yet Dr. Keller knows.

What if he really is the only one who can actually help me? If he knows Nell was hearing the murmurings, and that she was seeing what was lurking just out of her sight, won't he be able to help me make it stop? Would it be worth the risk to find out what he wants from me?

I'm so trapped in my thoughts, it takes me a moment to notice the breathing on the other end of the line.

It starts quietly enough, inhaling and exhaling in synch with my own breathing. Then the breathing turns raspy. It struggles for air, loses its pace, gasping on the other end of the line.

Then the murmurings begin. Words tumble together as if a tongue is wrestling to form syllables. The mumbling doesn't get louder, but it feels closer, as though it's bypassed the receiver entirely and found a new means of transport. Like it's hovering inches from my ear, which is sweating into the cup of the phone. Clipped, wordless phrases swirl faster and closer.

Closer.

I slam the receiver back onto the hook.

I hold down the phone with an unsteady hand. I squeeze my eyes shut and force my breathing to slow.

When I open my eyes, the clock on the microwave reads 9:40. It took me fifteen minutes to regain my sanity. I can't help but wonder if eventually I'll lose it forever.

It's that same concern for my sanity that makes me log back onto Adam's blog. I need to hear from someone—*anyone*—who knows what I'm going through. I reread the entries I read at Evan's, poring over every word.

Then I read more.

June 29th

You may think that I'm a less than reliable source. After all, I have told you nothing of myself. Not really. You know some of the more intimate details of my life, but you know **nothing** of the basics—my name, my location, my reason for creating this blog, for exposing Oakside. And what you do know about me—that I see and hear unusual things—may make you think that I was more in need of Oakside's services than I'm willing to admit. You'd be right, but these studies are indeed being conducted at Oakside, and if you don't believe me, <u>submit a formal inquiry to the Mental Hygiene Administration of Arizona</u>. In fact, **I'm begging you to.** There are people at Oakside who need the intervention, and NO ONE IS LISTENING TO ME.

It's time I tell you why Dr. Keller knew that the voice I heard that day wasn't a figment of my imagination.

What I was hearing were words—no, <u>shadows</u> of words— once spoken by someone in Dr. Keller's life, someone who meant a great deal to him. This person was killed violently and suddenly, right before his eyes, and Dr. Keller was helpless to stop it. He knew nothing of what that sort of death can produce, not at the time. It was only when he heard me utter the last words spoken by his loved one that he understood what I was hearing. He believed it was her spirit reaching out to him, but that cannot explain what we discovered later.

He <u>provoked</u> the voice. Dr. Keller learned how to *make* it whisper in my ear. After our most intense sessions—the sessions in which he would delve into the memories of my parents that brought me the most anguish—I would hear the murmurings. Not everyone hears the same thing, if they're "lucky" enough to hear what it says at all. It tells you what you <u>want</u> to hear. That's

how it tries to find its other half. I desperately wanted to please Dr. Keller, so I let him lure the whispering again and again.

Dr. Keller grew impatient. It was rarely clear what the voice said, and when it did speak to me, it was only those same two sentences: "You promised me you would come back. Is that bracelet for me?" He wanted more.

And soon, he got more.

He performed experiments on me. He wanted to know what it was I was seeing from the corner of my eye. He hooked me up to machines and showed me images. But none of the tests showed anything new, and as his frustration increased, his treatment of me became less fatherly. I became little more than a lab rat. I'm bitter about it, but I'm not making any of this up. My life was already fucked up enough. One more person letting me down wasn't going to break me.

The shadow on the edge of my vision didn't reveal itself until it was ready. A half-living thing I can't describe here with any accuracy. I won't try. The memory of it alone is enough to make me fear I might conjure it again, and I won't risk that.

The *thing* only appears in reflective surfaces. **Can you think of a better way to see weakness?** But the **WHAT** is more important.

Dr. Keller didn't care how hideous it was (yes, he could see it too. He couldn't hear what I heard, but once the *thing* appeared,

there was no denying it was real). Dr. Keller *believed* it was the person he'd lost.

Here's what I believe:

There are Takers in this world, and there are people who see them.

I can feel acid creeping up the back of my throat, but I keep reading. Because I know that even though the Insider hasn't named her, he must have believed that Nell could see these Takers. And if he believed Nell could see, does that mean I can too? Does this make me more insane or less?

July 14th

I'm still looking for a more permanent place to lay low, and so for now, I'm staying where I can. There's a reason Cleopatra built this hill so high. Up here, the air is thinner, and that makes it harder to think. I don't expect you to know what that means, and I don't really want you to.

I told you there are Takers in this world. **Taker** is the term I've given them, but just because there hasn't been a name for them before doesn't mean they haven't been around for longer than I care to imagine. As I said, I think Dr. Keller was half right. What I see and hear is the remnant of someone who has passed. But there's something else. I believe when a soul is taken violently,

it splits in two. I don't know where one half goes, and I won't speculate. I'm more concerned about the part that *stays*. Because that is the part that I see.

For as little as I know about this creature I call a Taker, I believe _it_ knows even less. I think that it only has one intent—to find its other half. Whenever it senses pain in someone, I believe it sees its other half because that's the last thing it remembers feeling before it died. This is the only way I can understand Dr. Keller's success in provoking it. Who better to know how to make you suffer than the person who knows the source of all your misery?

Why do I call this being a Taker? Because that is what it does. **It TAKES**, or at least it tries.

I believe a Taker tries to possess the body of whoever it thinks is holding its other half. And when it tries to usurp this body, it fails, killing the body it wants to inhabit.

I know this because I've seen it.

It takes something else, too. Some sort of object. Almost like an artifact—a possession in place of a body.

And so the people who can see this happen—the people who hear the murmurings, who catch the flicker of movement in the corner of their eye and dismiss it as imagination—I call them Seers. That name sounds more hopeful than their fate, but I can't think of what else to call them other than the word that defines their burden. Because as far as I know, there's **no** way to rid oneself of this awful gift. It's a curse you're born with.

And Dr. Keller will stop at nothing to understand this strange phenomenon.

I made the mistake of thinking I could escape the Takers, and I was wrong. I wish to God I'd been the one to suffer the consequence of that error. But it was someone else who suffered instead.

There are no more entries to read, so I reread each post three more times. I read until my eyes sting from the harsh computer-screen light. I read until my stomach tumbles with guilt and fear and confusion. I read until Adam's experience has superimposed itself over my own life and I know just what Adam went through for all those years. I feel as if I'm the one who was raised by Dr. Keller and his false fatherly concern. I feel like I know Adam and his rage at learning about his new reality. I imagine how that anger looked to Nell, if she ever saw it. I pretend that I'm not afraid of him, of Dr. Keller, of Oakside.

I crawl into bed at 3:00 a.m. and drift into another restless sleep. I've already made the decision to skip school tomorrow and to go see Dr. Keller.

10

A DIFFERENT ORDERLY OPENS THE sliding glass door when I arrive at Oakside. She wears a different expression from the typical apathy. She is suspicious. And she looks hungry, much like a dog looks right before you take a scoop of its food and rattle it in front of its bowl.

"Check in at the counter," she says unnecessarily through the intercom before admitting me past the second set of sliding doors.

I've seen her before. She has a long, shriveled neck and a tiny head topped with a bun, which conjures the image of a shrunken head a boy in elementary school once showed me in a textbook. As soon as the second doors slide open, the woman's out from behind her Plexiglas enclosure and next to me like we're old pals.

"Just sign your name right here, Ms. David, and I'll let Dr. Keller know you're here." Apparently, I'm familiar to her, too. She's smiling in a way that tells me her face isn't used to doing that. I want to laugh at her, but I'm still too unsettled by this place to do much of anything other than look at her.

She taps her bony finger on the line where she wants me to sign.

"I know the drill," I say, not masking my dislike of her even a little.

Her back goes erect so fast, she looks like she might get whiplash. The fibers of her neck strain against her yellowy skin. A quick swipe of her tongue wets her parched lips, which, when pursed, look remarkably like a short beak. She looks like a scrawny pigeon in a white, boxy uniform.

"Well, then, I'll just run and get Dr. Keller for you," she says, her voice syrupy sweet. The smile hasn't come back, and that's fine by me. This place is creepy enough.

I scan the room behind me for unseen danger. I could feel it lurking somewhere behind these walls before. But now that I've read Adam's blog, I feel even more vulnerable. I reread his last post again this morning, the one dated July 14. I can't keep his words from passing through my brain like a toy train on a track, circling round and round in a self-abusive mantra.

I made the mistake of thinking I could escape, but I was wrong.

Escape from what, exactly? And there's something else that's been gnawing at my mind—just one more feeling of dread to add to my ever-growing list: Why hasn't he written since July 14? Have the police finally caught up with him? But if that's the case, why haven't we heard anything? And why am I suddenly hoping he *hasn't* gotten caught?

Then, like some sort of omen confirming my unease, I catch the glare of a bald head out of the corner of my eye.

It has to be LM, Nell's—I suppose "friend" is the only word I can use—from her journal.

His head is a shiny dome at the far edge of the room. He carries an armful of Legos—towering blocks of primary colors. His face is set in a rigid, singular thought, one I couldn't even begin to guess. The woman with the tight topknot catches me staring and follows my gaze.

"Wait here," she commands.

This was a bad idea.

I'm already taking a backward step toward the sliding doors when a girl's scream, like something straight out of a horror film, makes us both jump. From behind the bird-like nurse, sneakers squeak on the linoleum floor, announcing someone's approach—and judging by the speed of the squeaking, that person is approaching the corner at a run. Another movie-worthy scream follows, this one closer. It grows to a shriek so loud it makes my eardrums pulse. A small-framed girl with stringy blond hair and enormous eyes swings around the corner, a blur in light-blue cotton heading straight for us. Another blur, this one in white, chases closely behind, but he looks like he's having trouble keeping up. The orderly is clutching his side like he has a cramp. The girl with the stringy blond hair doesn't look like she's having any trouble outrunning him.

The pigeon lady turns calmly, having recovered from shock much faster than I am able to. She faces the girl and subdues her with frightening efficiency. Before I can blink, the Pigeon has her scrawny arm across the narrow expanse of the girl's shoulders and is holding her from behind while her counterpart is busy rubbing the cramp out of his side.

The girl with the blond hair is still screaming, but it's more noise than words. She kicks her legs and tries to free her arms from the Pigeon's hold, but she's not fast enough to escape the poke and plunge of the syringe that's somehow materialized in the Pigeon's fingers.

Just before the needle pricks the girl's skin, I watch her eyes find LM in the recreation room, and something in her gaze shifts. Her once fanatical, darting gaze is clear of its mania for a fraction of a second. Almost imperceptibly, her head nods on her straining neck. I turn to LM just in time to see his head rise in response.

"Come on, Ms. Lasky. Let's get you back to your room," the Pigeon says like a tired babysitter, yet I hear satisfaction in her voice. She knows she's won, and as much as I didn't want to be bowled over by the crazed blond girl, I really didn't want the Pigeon to win either.

Still, as soon as the three round the corner, I can't help but notice that I'm all at once unobserved.

I turn to my right and find LM stacking his Legos with renewed concentration. His meaty hands hover over a pile of loose pieces, and then, with the care of a surgeon, he lifts a yellow block from the pile and affixes it to his growing tower, nodding with approval and repeating the same task twice more.

I walk over slowly, deciding it's probably best to approach him as if he were an animal with a reputation for biting. Only now, if he *does* bite, there's no one here to help me.

"You came back," he says without looking at me. His voice is soft, almost pouting. He sounds surprised, maybe hurt, that it took me so long. I find myself wondering again how old he is. He looks about forty, but his tone is so young-sounding, I can't tell.

I nod at first, then remember that he's fixated on his blocks.

"Yeah, I did." I say, hoping this is enough. I reach for the chair nearest him and, as quietly as possible, pull it out from the table where he's set up his operation. "Okay if I sit here with you a second?" I ask, trying to make my voice low like his. But I'm way too shaken up for that. It comes out like cooing.

"I don't have enough greens," he says, and this makes his brow crease. He looks at the tower he's built; it's probably three feet high.

"I—I'm . . ." I have no idea what to say to this. I want to apologize for some reason.

"They take them on purpose. They only give them to me if I show them," he says, looking more disturbed by this notion than by the absence of the green pieces.

"Do you mean the orderlies?" I ask, looking over my shoulder for the Pigeon or the guy with the side cramp. Either one could be back at any second. Something tells me it isn't going to take long for them to strap the poor blond girl to a mattress and pump her full of bedtime meds.

"They think it's funny," LM says, and smiles. He has the creepiest smile I've ever seen in my life. His eyes get huge and his bottom row of teeth jut out to create an under-bite like a bulldog's. If he didn't look psychotic before, he sure paints the picture now.

I'm desperate for him to stop smiling, but I'm not sure it's worth pissing him off. I opt to look down at my hands instead.

"They don't treat you so great in here, do they?" I ask, this time achieving the sympathy I actually mean. My heart throbs as thoughts of Nell wash over me. Adam's words haunt me once again.

This place is storage for people who really need psychiatric help, and prison for those they're actually interested in "treating."

"It's dangerous stuff. Nobody really knows." He might as well be talking to his blocks for all the sense he's making.

"The Legos?" I ask, my voice barely above a whisper. I don't know how a person like LM reacts when a person like me gets the answer wrong.

"No!" he scolds, and I lean back so hard that I almost tip over in my chair.

"Not the Legos! Christ, how far gone do you think I am?" He looks at me with betrayal, and confusion at my confusion.

He doesn't know the half of it.

My throat goes dry, and I quickly realize it's because my mouth is hanging open. I snap it shut and accidentally bite my tongue. Trying to recover, I stare with salty eyes at the suddenly lucid-seeming man Nell had affectionately referred to as LM.

"What's your name?" My words sound mushy with my swollen tongue.

"Kenny. And I'm not . . . you think I'm crazy, don't you?"
There's desperation behind his tone.

"No! No, no, no!" I reassure him, but I'm not fooling any-one. If I even had half a hope that LM—Kenny—could give me some answers about Nell, that hope is gone. I've offended him, and there's no way I'll be able to make up for that insult before the orderlies come back.

"You do. Everybody thinks so. Everybody except for them," Kenny says, nodding his shining globe head toward the hall-way. "*They* know I'm not crazy, but it's almost worse that way. Because they make me show them . . ."

Kenny has crossed his arms over his chest and tucked his chin, creating the appearance of a snowman, all round sur-faces with no limbs.

"I won't make you do anything, Kenny. I swear. I don't want to upset you. I'm so sorry if I did."

I start to reach for his arm to comfort him, but his wild blue eyes shoot me a look that is somehow inviting and warn-ing all at once. Like he's dying for an excuse to lash out at me, but the part of him that keeps control is telling me to back off before it's too late.

I retract my shaking hand and sit on it. But I'm not ready to give up. Kenny and MM, whoever that is, are the only two people (aside from Adam) Nell ever mentioned trusting, and even then, she only dared to confide this to her journal. She never told me a thing. This could be my only chance to understand what she was too afraid to tell me.

I peek over my shoulder and assure myself the Pigeon isn't coming. Then I turn back to Kenny—who is now holding a coveted green Lego and staring at me with that hungry/wary look.

"Kenny, I need to ask you something, okay?" I start carefully. Maybe if he feels like he's in control, he'll be more forthcoming. Though he *is* in complete control. If I'm being honest with myself, I'm terrified of him.

"Can you tell me what the doctors made Nell show them? What they make *you* show them?"

Kenny looks so shocked that for a second I think I might have sprouted a second head. It might not be the strangest thing that's happened in this place.

"She never told you?" His upper lip starts to perspire, and he breathes heavily. It takes me a second to understand why: Shoes squeak down the hallway behind the reception counter. The Pigeon is coming back. If she sees me talking to Kenny, she's going to know something's up.

I struggle to answer his question. "I never . . ." The guilt in my stomach is suffocating, and I can't unbury the words I need. Finally, they manage to come out: "I never asked her."

I try to remember all of the italicized and bolded parts of the Insider's blog posts.

"But I think I know now," I hurry, words spilling from my lips faster than I can edit them. "Tell me why. Why are they making you show them the thing? The unfinished soul. Damn it, what's it called? The Taker? Why are they making you show them that, Kenny?"

"You have to go!" He says through clenched teeth, his entire face turning red. I look down at his hands—one fist squeezes the green Lego so hard I'm afraid he's going to draw blood.

"I can't. Not yet. I need you to tell me. Kenny, what are they trying to do? Is it Dr. Keller?"

I know Kenny's perilously close to losing it, but I've come this far, and I'm not going to get another shot at talking to him without arousing too much suspicion.

"Leave! She's coming back. She's not just an orderly. She can't know that you know anything or they'll take you, too!" he cries, his face crumpled like a raisin.

His hands are shaking, his upper lip covered in beads of sweat that drip down his face. His trembling knees are making the table with its Lego tower rumble.

"Kenny, I won't be able to come back. They'll catch on. Tell me. Please, tell me!"

The squeaking is getting louder, and I can hear the echo of a voice. It's the Pigeon, and she's close to the end of the hall. She'll be rounding the corner any second, and once she does, she'll look for me.

"Kenny, just tell me—"

The voice creeps around the corner, oozing like toxic smoke. "She'll be out for at least eight more hours . . . ," it says. The white of her smock is visible now.

I see a flash of primary colors in my periphery before the side of my head feels like it's caving in. I'm on the ground, staring at the ceiling, the chair underneath me jutting into the small of my back. A vent is blowing puffs of humid air. Then everything goes blurry, and the pain in my head makes my stomach roll so violently that I'm sure I'm going to throw up. I can feel something brush my side, near my waist, and then I can't see or feel anything. A beautiful darkness takes over.

"Ms. David, can you hear me?"

My pool of darkness is being disturbed. Someone is swimming in my nice calm pond. My mind is frayed, fuzzy.

"Ms. David, if you can hear me, I'd like you to open your eyes."

I can hear too well. I want the voice to stop. Oh God, my head feels like it's ready to split open.

"Easy now, that's right. Take your time."

I know this voice. There's a reason I hate it. Not just because it's rippling my nice calm pond. It's the same voice that has haunted my answering machine for months.

"There, there. Everything's okay."

But everything is not okay.

A light pierces my eyes like a sharp blade, and I squint to keep it out. But the squinting only hurts more, so I open my eyes again. I roll to my side, sure I'm going to puke all over the place. But the nausea fades, and in its place a warm, pulsating pain radiates in the back of my head. I shift slowly to a sitting position, wincing at an unidentifiable crinkling sound as I make myself as upright as possible.

"Slowly now, Sophie. We don't want you to move too fast. You took quite a blow to your head."

The voice is warm and thick. I want to scream at it, and I just might if I wasn't absolutely certain that my head would explode if I even tried to whisper.

"Eyes up at me now. Let me just check those pupils."

My vision returns slowly, and I stare at a handsome face that is just as smooth as the voice that comes from it. Dr. Keller holds my chin with one delicate finger. His hand smells like a nice, mild soap. I resist the urge to flick away his touch as he shines a light into my eyes again.

"Looks fine. But you definitely shouldn't drive yourself home. Maybe you should stay with us for a little while longer."

"I have to go," I say, and my words sound strange, like someone else has taken over my body and is moving me like some awkward marionette.

"I'm afraid that's not possible," Dr. Keller soothes, but I couldn't be less comforted.

He has his tiny flashlight in one hand, but his other is pressing down on mine, keeping me bolted to the gurney I'm sitting on. It's on wheels, meant to transport a person who's not able to walk. An unconscious person. The room that I'm in has those same bland walls that are indistinguishable from the floor. There's a tiny window close to the ceiling, but the light from the outside is dimmed by the mesh covering it.

I was *brought* to this room.

Why isn't there a nurse in here with us?

"My mom's expecting me at home," I say, suddenly aware that the door is closed.

Dr. Keller's response is wordless. His smile shifts from placating to something else. This smile knows something I don't want it to know.

It knows that my mom isn't waiting for me, at home or

anywhere else. I told him everything he needed to know about my mom when I was the one, not her, to retrieve Nell's box of belongings.

"I'm sure she can wait a little longer while I ask you some questions." His hand presses harder on mine, pushing the blood to my fingertips. "Just so we're certain you're not hurt."

He's mocking. He can see what I've tried to keep him and everyone else from seeing.

"What kinds of questions?" I ask, hating my voice for betraying a quaver.

He moves his little flashlight to my other eye, and I'm temporarily blinded by the brightness. He's so close to me that I can feel his breath on my face.

"Oh, just some standard questions."

I know he's lying. There's nothing standard about any of this. And what's worse is that I think he knows he's not fooling me. I don't think he cares.

"I really do have to go—"

"I'm surprised your sister never shared any of our little talks with you," he continues. It's like he wants to see how much he can rattle me. I'm beginning to lose feeling in my fingertips under the weight of his hand.

"I . . . we didn't really talk after she . . ."

"Yes, so sad. Unfortunate indeed."

I've never wanted to leave a place more in my life than I do at this second.

"I always got the impression Nell was . . . saddened by your distance," he continues, and I hate him for talking about my sister like he knew her. I want to punch him in the nose, but I'm still seeing spots from the light, and my free arm feels like Jell-O.

"She told me a great deal about you, Sophie," Dr. Keller says, and switches off the little flashlight. He stares into my eyes with such intensity I can only stare back.

"She told me everything."

I hear the echo of a bolt slip in a lock, and the door to the little gray room swings open, revealing a shocked-looking Pigeon.

"Oh, Dr. Keller! I didn't realize you were in here."

Her eyes are embarrassed, darting from Dr. Keller's handsome face to the floor, then back to his face. Eventually they find their way to me, and in that instant, the pressure of Dr. Keller's hand releases from mine.

"That's all right, Gladys. I was just making sure our patient here was okay after that knock to her noggin. Ms. David, you've met Gladys? She's my second-in-command here at Oakside."

His confident smile has returned, though he isn't looking

at me. He is saving his charm for Gladys. Somehow, he has managed to move to the far end of the room, putting a healthy distance between us. I'm so shaken, I can't remember him moving away.

"Forty-five's too old to be playing with toys if you ask me," the Pigeon says. "You should know better than to get too close to that man's Legos. Surprised your sister never mentioned that."

"I should have known better," I say in response, knowing I'm not just talking about Kenny and his Legos. Her words chase one another through my mind, inverting and rearranging—"that man's Legos." Man Lego. Lego Man. LM, Nell's nickname for Kenny.

I slide from the gurney and try to walk calmly toward the Pigeon, but my legs shake under my weight. My head still feels unsteady on my neck, and a fresh jab of pain rocks the back of my skull. But I'm not about to spend another second in here with Dr. Keller.

"Sorry for disturbing L—I mean, Kenny," I say to them both, anxious to ensure a smooth departure from Oakside. I only want to go home and piece out what just happened.

"Ms. David, everyone here is disturbed," Dr. Keller says, his voice as slick as oil.

The Pigeon chuckles a deep, throaty laugh and bats her

eyelashes flirtatiously at Dr. Keller. I force a smile to my mouth.

"Wait, didn't you come to see Dr. Keller? Now's your chance to talk." Gladys the Pigeon turns to me, the charm draining from her voice.

"Oh, right, I uh . . ." My head is killing me, and I can't think of a lie fast enough. The words feel lost in the back of my brain.

"Yes, Sophie. I was hoping you'd come because of my calls, but it seems you're in a hurry to leave before we've even had a chance to chat." Dr. Keller's face creases in concern, but his meaning is unmistakable. He's onto me.

"I . . . well, I just . . ." I fumble for words, but still nothing comes.

"You've had a traumatic day. I'm sure it can wait," Dr. Keller finishes for me, and the crooked smile returns to his face.

"Yeah, okay," I croak in response, my heart racing so fast I'm sure it will burst from my chest. "I guess it'll come back to me."

"Well, we'll be right here when you're ready," he says, his voice barely concealing the threat. "Do come back and see me soon. I'm very eager to speak with you."

I move my mouth up and down a few more times before

I give up. I'm halfway down the corridor before I remember to breathe again.

At the Plexiglas door, I pause for only a second to peer at the place where Kenny usually stations himself building his towers. The chair where I was sitting is still on the floor, its legs jutting out like roadkill. Scattered Legos litter the carpet. Kenny's broken tower lies amid the wreckage on the floor—cracked into pieces, probably because it was used to hit me in the side of the head. I try to make my brain focus on what happened right before he snapped, but everything hurts. I just want to get out of here as soon as possible.

When I look up to the little room for someone to activate the inner Plexiglas door, Gladys the Pigeon is poised with her finger over the button. She hesitates for a moment, staring at me like she's trying to decide whether or not to let me go. I stare back, hoping the fear doesn't show on my face.

They couldn't really keep me here, could they?

Before I can answer my own question, the inner door swishes open. I'm in the vestibule once again, staring at the foggy reflection of myself, which is thankfully me this time—not the horrible thing with the wordless mouth and stretched lips.

The second set of doors slides apart and ushers in the smell of the desert. I can hear the last hums of the cicadas before they quit for the night, and their shift is slowly being picked up by the chirping crickets and groaning toads of a nearby pond.

I slide into the driver's seat of Mom's old Buick and immediately lock the door behind me—a silly precaution, I'm sure, but an urge I don't fight. The thought of Gladys the Pigeon or Dr. Keller climbing into my car and dragging me back to that little gray room is enough to make my breath catch. I keep my gaze locked on the sliding glass doors just in case they try to approach.

I fumble through my cluttered messenger bag and quickly find what I'm looking for. Evan's number was the last one I dialed. I hit the call button and pray he picks up.

"Hey, I was just thinking about you." His voice sounds so good, I have to smile, even though my head still feels pulverized. "I didn't see you at school today."

"Hi," I say, not even bothering to mask my relief. "Can you come and get me? I'm . . . I'm at Oakside."

"You're what? You went there alone? What were you trying to do?" He sounds genuinely worried, and I'm just fine with that.

"I have no idea," I lie, but the silence that follows makes me try a little harder. "I'm okay, I just can't drive. I'll figure out how to get my car later."

"I'm not thinking about your car," he says sternly, but then his voice softens. "I'll be right there."

"Don't worry, okay? I'm all right," I say, not really believing that's true, but hoping it'll be enough to keep him from worrying, at least until he gets here.

He doesn't sound satisfied, but he says, "I'm on my way."

I lean over to toss my phone back into my bag when I hear a crinkling from someplace inside my jacket. When I press my side, I hear it again.

Reaching into my inside pocket, I pull out a wrinkled white piece of paper, folded into quarters. My finger brushes the margin's frayed edge where it looks like it's been torn from a book or binding of some sort. Faded pink lines cross the page, and I can just barely make out the impressions of writing on the inside. Before I can even read what the words say, I know who wrote them.

It's Nell's handwriting. And I know exactly where the page came from: the middle of the composition book I found on my car seat in Jerome a week after Nell was found dead.

Nell David

December 6

There's a reason Cleopatra built her hill so high.

Up there, the air is thinner, and it makes it hard to think.

There, the cottonwoods breathe in shallow gulps.

And the ladies rock

Cribs for babes whose cries make men flock.

And the ground is hollow.

The cacophony will hush beneath so much pain.

Jeweled wrists will wink, but we don't know why.

Time is captured like a ship in a bottle,

Its waves long dried up, turquoise stains all that
remain.

Holes that hold more than the mistaken treasure

Tunneled away, smuggled strife.

11

I'M DRIVING US TO JEROME, mostly because I'm the only one of us who has ever been there, but also because I don't want to risk getting carsick. I'm normally fine, but the switchbacks leading up Cleopatra Hill are enough to make even an iron-clad stomach feel unsettled.

But if I'm being totally honest, that's not the only thing that has my stomach in knots.

"So you haven't been back here since that time . . ." Evan starts to say, and I shake off the idea that he's somehow managed to see straight into my brain.

"Right," I say, doing my best to sound like I'm completely okay with visiting Jerome. It might have been my idea, but the thought of going back has left me with a hollow feeling deep in my gut all week. I can feel flutters in the space where my organs should be. It's like I've been dreading it and restless to get there all at once.

"Well, I pulled up directions just in case," he says, jiggling his phone, a little smile sneaking to his lips. "Not that I don't trust you."

I just sigh and roll my eyes. I have no real reason to be irritated with Evan, but I've been resisting the urge to pick a fight with him all morning. As the days of the week crept by, the thought of our trip consumed me like some sort of disease. If it'd been up to me, I would have come here the day after my ordeal with Kenny and Dr. Keller and the Pigeon at Oakside. But Evan had a game on Friday, and he couldn't risk ineligibility by skipping class. Coach Tarza has this policy about ditching. I, on the other hand, couldn't give a shit about school right now. I guess I should be thanking Evan for making sure I don't get kicked out of high school, but I seem well on my way to trying to make that a reality.

"Did you bring that sheet of paper Kenny gave you?" Evan asks while he fiddles with the GPS feature on his phone.

"Yes, of course I did," I say testily, jabbing a finger toward my messenger bag on the console between us.

"Yikes, sorry," he says, but he starts digging through my bag for it anyway.

"Careful, don't spill all my stuff," I scold.

"Just watch the road. What? Are you afraid I'll find your girly things and know how hard you try to look pretty for me?" he teases, but he doesn't sound confident.

I keep my eyes on the road, my fingers gripping the wheel with forced concentration. "No," I say, indignant as a five-year-old. "Just . . . just be careful with everything in there, okay?" I say, hoping he understands I need him to be careful with one thing in particular.

As I finish my plea, his hand emerges from my bag with the page from Nell's journal, still folded in quarters, just as it had been when Kenny slipped it into my pocket. Among the hundreds of questions I've asked myself since my last trip to Oakside, the question of how Kenny had Nell's journal page is at the top.

"I promise you I'll be careful," he says, and in an instant, all my frustration with him evaporates.

Evan unfolds the page gingerly, and his head bows to look at Nell's faint writing.

"Can you read it to me?"

Evan starts to read, clears his throat, and starts again.

I regret it almost immediately. Hearing Nell's words on someone else's lips—even lips I'm dying to kiss again—feels wrong. I can't shake the feeling that I'm somehow betraying her by letting someone else read her poetry.

But if I can trust anyone, it's Evan. After all, he's sort of in the same boat as me. If this were Deb's journal that someone had secretly smuggled to him, I know he'd want to share it with me. I guess I'm just not used to feeling . . . not alone.

"What do you think she meant by that part about cribs? 'Cribs for babes whose cries make men flock.' I mean, I don't claim to get, well, *anything* about poetry. But that part has me really confused."

I shrug, a casual response to a question I feel anything but casual about. I've retraced that same line over and over since Monday, scouring the words for any hint of a clue. But I've come up short every time.

"I have absolutely no idea. I don't get any of it," I tell him.

"Oh," Evan grunts, but I detect a hint of disappointment.

"Hey, just because I'm good in English doesn't mean I get poetry. It's like a whole different language." I know I shouldn't be so defensive. It's hard to explain what I'm feeling. It's like I'm ashamed that I couldn't figure it out. Like Nell's left me this clue, and I've got one last chance to try to help her, but I can't crack the code.

Once again, I'm letting her down.

"Sorry." Evan rests a big, calloused palm on my thigh. My leg tenses so hard in reflex that I almost shove my foot straight into the pedal and send us careening off the road.

"No, *I'm* sorry. I'm just a little on edge."

"I don't know how you wouldn't be."

We're silent for a while. Evan finds a playlist on his phone and plugs it into the adapter I can't believe I actually remembered to bring along. We listen to his mix of Portishead and Mazzy Star and Jeff Buckley. It's strange how the simplest things can stay constant when everything else seems to be in chaos. A life can come to a stuttering halt, but the music, the lyrics, the melodies—they'll never change. It's like they stay the same just so you have one thing you can hold on to.

"Have a thing for the '90s, huh?"

"That and Gatorade," he replies. I sneak a look at him just in time to catch his wink.

"Hey, can you pull over for a sec?" he asks, and I obligingly pull off the road at the next rest stop.

We're directly in front of the small stucco building before I recognize where we are. Evan unfastens his seat belt and slides out of the car. He disappears around the side of the building, his hand fishing in his pocket, and I brush off an expected tingle of déjà vu. When Evan reappears, he's rattling two yellow packets in his hands like maracas. He climbs back into the car with such ease, I get fluttery in my stomach just like the first time he did this.

"A little nostalgia for the road," he says, his brilliant smile lighting up his entire face.

"M&M's!" I gush like I've just won a million-dollar prize. "Sir, you're too kind!"

I reach for my packet, but he snatches it back.

In one quick movement, his lips are on mine, both soft and commanding. They move from my upper to my lower lip, fast at first, then slower as we find a rhythm. Jeff Buckley's version of "Hallelujah" pipes through the speakers with the same kind of urgency as my thrumming heart. Evan's hands move from my hair to my neck, from my neck to my shoulders, my shoulders to my back.

He pulls away just long enough to find my ear, his lips brushing my earlobe as he breathes into it: "You have no idea what you do to me."

I feel the faintest tickle of his tongue as it lightly skims my neck before his lips find their way back to mine.

It takes every ounce of strength I never knew I had to pull away.

"We, uh . . . we should probably get back on the road."

Evan's cheeks are splotchy, and his eyes search my face as though looking for the proper response before he nods his agreement.

"You're right. You're right. I guess I just—I didn't mean to—"

"No! No, no," I try to reassure him, but I sound frantic. Who could be reassured by that? "I wanted to, it's—let's just get going," I stutter, but he smiles that amazing smile that tells me he understands, and I pull back onto the highway a little too fast to be fooling either of us.

"So how much farther is it?" I ask, desperate to find a safe topic of conversation.

Evan checks his phone's GPS. "Looks like about sixty-five miles."

"Guess you'd better find us another playlist."

I'm only going about fifteen miles per hour, but it doesn't matter. After almost half of a mile uphill, the switchbacks make both of us feel like we are going to pitch off the side of Cleopatra Hill at each sharp turn of the steering wheel.

"Jesus, how much longer?" Evan asks, his hand shielding his eyes. I know the feeling. Nell and I used to hang on to each other in the backseat on trips up here, our stomachs unaccustomed to experiencing this feeling outside of a roller coaster.

"We're about halfway there," I say, getting only a groan in response.

"Don't you get hit in the stomach, like, every day?" I tease, but I keep my eyes fixed to the road in front of me, glad to focus on something other than the sheer drop to my left.

"Okay, first of all, getting hit in the stomach when you're on level ground is nothing like being dropped off a mountainside in a car," he pipes up while gripping the passenger door handle. "Second, I have pads, and I only get hit when I'm not the one hitting first. And third, did I mention that I don't play football on a mountainside?"

"Don't worry," I say. "It's a lot better on the way down."

"I bet it is," he says. "Less distance to fall when we go hurtling to our deaths."

"Exactly."

Half an hour later, Evan and I climb out of my car and do our best to breathe the thin, mile-high air of Jerome, Arizona—the "Wickedest City in the West." For the millionth time, I scold myself for forgetting to slip a travel deodorant into my bag. The tense drive up the hill has left wet rings under my arms. I've parked us in the nearest lot I could find. Outside the visitor center, which is inconveniently closed today, the asphalt square of the parking lot is nearly empty.

"Closed on Saturdays? When do they expect people to visit, during the week?" Evan complains. He's still grumpy from the trip uphill.

"I'm not really sure they could have helped us anyway," I try to reassure him, but he just gives me a look.

"What were you expecting?" I ask. "'Excuse me sir or ma'am? Can you please help us translate my sister's modernist-style poetry to determine where her former boyfriend-slash-conspiracy-theorist might be hiding out blogging in your fine town?'"

Finally, I unearth a smile from the usually affable Evan.

"Okay," he says, hands raised in surrender. "You're right. I was hoping I'd have some sort of a plan by the time we got here, but now I don't have shit for ideas. I don't have a clue where to start."

"I know what you mean," I say, pulling the poem out of my messenger bag for what feels like the eightieth time. "I thought instinct would guide us."

I sigh and refold the poem a little more harshly than I'd intended, nearly tearing the frail creases with my impatient fingers.

"Shit." I examine it for damage, relieved not to find any. I glance at Evan. If I look half as defeated as he does, we're doomed.

"Are you hungry?" I ask.

"Always," is his reply.

"I know a place."

We walk in silence, taking in the scenery. I've been here a handful of times, but I'm acutely aware that this is Evan's first visit. He greedily takes it all in—the pines and cottonwoods, so different from Phoenix's paloverdes, olive trees, and cacti. The wind at this altitude is free and unencumbered, unlike the swirling gusts that flow through the valley. The historic buildings from the late 1800s and early 1900s have clapboard exteriors and balconies laced with intricate woodwork, and are worlds away from the siding and shingled roofs of a modern sprawling city.

"Have they changed anything here since the city was built?"

"Sort of," I answer, happy to be the one to relay some information to Evan for a change. "They've preserved what they could. There were fires—several of them, actually. They built the city around copper mines, which have been caving in at places, so some of the buildings kind of slid."

"Slid?" he asks, looking at me like I've made a mistake.

I laugh. "Yeah. The old jail used to be across the street from where it is now."

"Damn," Evan says in awe. "So, who lives here now?"

As he asks, a couple walks by us on the sidewalk pushing a stroller, a kicking toddler squealing in delight underneath a protective sun bonnet.

"Families. A lot of them relatives of those who stayed around the mid-1900s. I think the population dropped to about fifty or something like that before tourism picked up. Then the artists moved in, so I think the town's got about four hundred fifty residents or so."

Evan cocks his head to the side.

"What?"

"Nothing. You just sound a little like you should be working in the visitor center."

"Hey, you asked," I say defensively. "It's all online."

"You could probably convince me to hang out here for a while. Hell, I might just set up camp to avoid going back down the hill."

We're quiet for a while longer, and I allow my mind to drift. That's normally a dangerous endeavor, but something about the light, clear air and the fatigue from the drive makes me relax into it.

I think about the first time I saw the thing in the mirror— the night Nell cut herself in the bathroom. Was that really the first time? Surely I'd been hearing the murmurings before then. I had dismissed the sounds more times than I probably even realized. I couldn't have been as young as Nell when she first started hearing them. I know that for certain. I would have given anything to be like her. If I'd had any opportunity to mimic her in some genuine way, to share a "grown-up experience," I would have jumped at it. So what made the voices start murmuring to me? I'd always assumed it coincided with Nell's breakdown, but why would that be? Adam's blog didn't really explain that, from what I could recall.

"Hey, when did you say Deb started hearing things?"

Evan looks a little bewildered, and I realize I probably just interrupted his own train of thought.

"I don't know. When we were pretty little. What about your sister?"

I nod slowly. "Same."

Then I remember something the Pigeon said the last time I was at Oakside.

Forty-five's too old to be playing with toys if you ask me.

Kenny is forty-five. Forty-five and he's still hearing things. Seeing them, presumably. I can only guess that he's lasted that long because he's complied with whatever it is the doctors want him to do in Oakside. They offer him some meager form of protection, if you can call it that. But what if he started experiencing things later in life? Even later than I did? It might not be significant, but I can't seem to convince my brain of that.

Inevitably, my thoughts return to Adam and what answers he might have for us if we can track him down. Questions compound and multiply, racing incessantly through my brain. Who is Adam really? What was it that made him run away from Oakside with Nell and seek some sort of refuge in Jerome of all places? Why did he stay here?

Before long, Evan and I are standing in front of a

dingy-looking white cement building, bold black letters painted across the top: The Wicked Kitchen.

"I think I read online that it's the oldest operating restaurant in the West," I say more to the building than to Evan. "Anyway, we used to come here when I was a kid. They have great burgers."

"Now burgers I can get behind," he says, leading the way through the dirty glass doors.

The restaurant itself can't be more than a thousand square feet, including the kitchen. I get the distinct feeling it used to be a tiny house in the early days. It has an enclosed porch for extra seating—seating they need, judging by the crowd. I don't remember it being quite this bustling when I was little. Our waitress has brittle red hair, loads of makeup, and the fastest hands I've ever seen in my life.

"What'll it be, kids?" she asks, a pad and pen materializing before we've even gotten menus.

"Um . . . burgers?" I ask Evan, who nods eagerly.

"Burgers and fries, and two Cokes, please," I request, frankly a little intimidated by our waitress's frantic pace. I can see at least three heads leaning from their tables in search of her. It looks like she might be the only one working today. Her nametag says BONNIE in big blue letters. I would not want to be Bonnie today.

"Coming right up," she reassures, but I'm not holding my breath. I arch my eyebrows at Evan, and he smiles in agreement. If we were looking for a peaceful place to regroup, we sure didn't find it. I was expecting the sleepy little town of my childhood—of several months ago, even—but I'm glad for the buzz of the surrounding crowd. It feels good to not be so alone.

"All right," Evan says. "Let's see that poem again."

I sigh and pull it from my messenger bag. I know he's right, but each time I look at Nell's cryptic writing, I get more and more frustrated.

Evan's amber eyes scan the page again, and I watch him concentrate. I'd like some of his determination to rub off on me. I don't want to give up, but I'm just so tired from trying.

"I keep coming back to this line," he points to Nell's line, the same one he repeated in the car. "'Cribs for babes whose cries make men flock.' I don't know why, but there's something about that line that feels like it might mean something."

"It *all* means something. That's the point. That's also the problem." I put my head down on the sticky table, not liking the way my forehead adheres to the surface, but not caring enough to pick it back up.

"All right, all right," Evan says. "Don't get like that. We'll figure it out. So tell me about how Nell liked to write," he prods.

"Maybe that'll help us figure out what she was getting at."

"You mean what type of poetry she wrote?" I ask the table.

"Yeah. You said something in the parking lot about modern . . . modern-something-or-other."

I lift my head up slightly. "Modernist. It's a style of writing. Kind of like T. S. Eliot. He was her favorite."

Evan gives me a look like I should know better. "Do I look like the kind of guy who sits around reading poetry? You're going to need to help me along a little more than that."

"Sorry." I smile. "He wrote a poem called *The Waste Land.* It's one of his most famous works. It's super hard to understand, but Nell got it."

"Okay, so what was it about?" Evan keeps trying to jog the conversation.

"It wasn't so much what it was about," I continue, understanding what he's getting at now, "but Nell was really into the style. What that type of poem was trying to do."

Evan looks relieved that I'm finally catching on.

"It was more what the poem wasn't saying than what it was saying, you know?" Now I'm starting to get a little excited.

"No, I don't." Evan jabs a thumb at his chest. "Clueless about poetry, remember?"

"Think of it like metaphor. Like everything that the poet says stands for something else. It's like trying to draw a giant picture by using totally unrelated images to make up the larger picture."

"Sounds a little indirect, but okay."

Now Evan looks tired, but I think he is on the right track. Rather than trying to decipher individual aspects of Nell's poem, maybe we need to understand what she was trying to say about the big picture.

"We're pretty sure she was writing about the same stuff Adam's blogging about now. About Takers and Seers and whatever Dr. Keller's trying to do at Oakside," I say. I'm shredding a flimsy paper napkin in my lap. I can't seem to keep my hands still. For the first time, it actually feels like we might be getting close to understanding what Nell was trying to tell us.

Evan nods, wanting to follow my lead. "Yeah, that's probably a safe bet."

"Then we've got the big picture! And we know that something made her and Adam decide that they were going to be safe in Jerome, right?"

I turn the paper so we can both read it and point to the second line so Evan can see.

"'Up there, the air is thinner, and it makes it harder to think.' So we know what it's about, and we know something about the *where*."

Bonnie slides our burgers, fries, and Cokes in front of us so fast, I actually jump. She leaves the check under Evan's plate in the same motion, the tail of the ticket flapping in her wake.

We eat in silence, our eyes glued to the poem in the middle of the table. We're chewing lunch, but it feels like we're chewing Nell's words, slowly trying to digest them. Once we've finished eating our lunch, I feel satisfied physically, but my brain hurts with the effort.

Evan and I pool some cash and leave it on top of the ticket.

"So we're right back where we started," Evan says. "With Oakside and Jerome and cribs with wailing babes."

"Oh yeah, cribs. Can you imagine what it was like back then?"

It's Bonnie, not Evan. She's reappeared out of nowhere to count out our change from a wad of bills in her apron pocket.

"Wait, you know what that means?" I ask.

"What, cribs?" Her frizzy red hair shakes under the air vent above us.

"Yes!" Evan beats me to it.

"Uh . . ." Bonnie looks like she regrets engaging us in any sort of conversation. She eyes the full tables around us.

"What? What does it mean?" I plead.

"The Cribs district. Across the street in the back alley. It's where all the prostitutes used to hang out. You know, hawking their wares and whatnot."

"Oh my God," I stare wide-eyed at an equally wide-eyed Evan. "Babes. She meant prostitutes, not babies. I think that's where she and Adam must have been hiding out!"

Bonnie frowns. "Not likely. It's just a bunch of shacks now. And you two shouldn't be messing around over there. Place is haunted or some crap like that." She nods to a table across the restaurant. "Be right there, sweetie."

"Bonnie!" I exclaim, reaching for her hand. "You're a lifesaver. Thank you! Thank you so much!"

She yanks her hand from my grip with the same efficiency of motion she'd used to bring our food. "Whatever." She hustles away from our table.

We leave Bonnie an extra big tip and exit the Wicked Kitchen in two seconds flat. The row of shacks across the street is easy to spot.

"Come on!" I prod, but it's not necessary. Evan is already two steps in front of me.

"Shack" really isn't the right word to describe the buildings in the alley. They're more like gutted and abandoned brick rooms. Aside from one larger building, they're not even big enough to be called houses. A placard at the edge of the road explains the alley's history, and it's much like

Bonnie described. The prostitutes started out on the main road, but after pressure from politicians, many of the lower-charging ladies were forced out of sight of Jerome's commercial square.

"Well, this is one part of the town my mom and Aunt Becca never showed Nell and me," I say, taking in what's left of the old red-light district, weeds and desert shrubs crowding the ruins.

"I can understand why," Evan says after reading the placard. "Well, let's start looking."

"You don't think we're going to pop our heads into one of these abandoned buildings and find Adam waiting for us, do you?" I ask, losing some of my excitement.

"No," Evan says, dragging out the word. "I was kind of hoping we'd find a clue that they'd squatted here for a while. Something to tell us we're on the right track."

I look around at the weedy, crumbling brick-and-mortar structures lining the secret street. There's hardly any protection here from the elements, let alone any privacy. I can't imagine my sister trying to hide here from anyone.

"Come on," Evan nudges my arm and ducks into the first doorway. I follow him into the dark one-room structure.

Light cuts through the cracks in the facade, forming tiny spotlights on the dirt floor. There are four walls (or what's left of them) and a deteriorated roof that's partially open to the sky.

"Well, guess that's all there is to see here," Evan says, and I nod, doing my best not to sigh and tell him it's pointless. I already feel defeated.

We move on to the next building in the alley and find it looks pretty much the same. I hear giggling and poke my head out to the alley. A couple a little older than us steals looks over their shoulders as they grab each other's belt loops. He moves his hands to her back, then down. They disappear into one of the smaller buildings at the end of the street. I feel my face grow hot as I picture Evan and me doing the same thing, if we wanted to. But now that we have a clue, I can't bear the thought of stopping, even if our make-out session at the rest stop is still fresh in my mind.

The next building we explore is larger. It's practically a mansion compared to the other two. I can imagine women calling to men from these doorways more than a hundred years ago. These would have been the less "classy" of the prostitution houses, the younger, prettier women occupying rooms at the bordellos closer to the main street. But the larger building has maintained some of its original architecture. It looks like it's in the wrong place, as if it slid, like the old jail, from its original address and landed here.

"Fancy," Evan says, but his sarcasm is halfhearted. I can tell he's thinking the same thing I am. This ramshackle house with its shuttered windows and carved wooden banisters along the porch—and the fact that it even has a porch at all—make this place different. And what's more, the walls and the roof are completely intact.

We pass over the threshold, and I hold my breath for just a moment. I'm sure I was imagining it, but my ear felt like it was about to pop, like when the pressure leaves the room and a silent vacuum sucks all the noise out with it. I've come to hate this feeling more than anything. The murmurs always follow.

"Sophie? Hey, you okay?"

Evan's beside me now, the light from the narrow doorway the only thing illuminating him in the otherwise dark room. The wood plank floors are buckling in several places and echo, like it's hollow underneath. It feels as though we could fall through them at any second.

"Yeah, I . . . I just thought I heard something is all," I half lie.

"Easy to think that in this place," he says, his voice quieter than when we were outside. Neither of us seems to want to disturb the silence.

"Let's just take a quick look around and—"

"Over here!" Evan hisses with restrained excitement. He squats over a shadowy pile in the corner of the room.

"Evan, if you're looking at something gross like a dead rat, I think I'll pass."

"No, come here," he motions to me over his shoulder, but doesn't look up. Then he reaches into his pocket and pulls out his phone, pressing a button to illuminate its face.

All at once, I see what he's staring at: a fleece blanket. The stiff, clinical kind. And it's embroidered with the words OAKSIDE BEHAVIORAL INSTITUTE.

"Oh my God, they were here," I breathe. The pressure in my ear constricts again. I swallow to try to relieve it, but to no avail.

"Yeah." Evan gingerly picks up the blanket, shaking it out onto the ground, releasing some gravel and a few blades of desert scrub.

"I'm going to search the other room," I say, and hurry through the other doorway.

"Hey, wait. Be careful of the floor. Maybe you should slow down a little!" Evan calls to me.

But I'm already in the next room. My heart races. "Nell, if you're here, if any part of you is in here, give me a sign," I whisper.

The pressure in my ear releases. A damp, rattling croak

creeps down the back of my neck. A gasp sounds like it's struggling, like it's climbing out of some dark hole.

I hold my breath while it inhales and exhales into my ear. I'm waiting for the murmuring to start, waiting for the word-less command. My eyes go wide in the dark.

"Sophie, are you—"

The floor creaks, then splinters. My stomach drops from under me as the floor parts.

"Sophie!"

When I open my eyes, Evan is above me, and I'm a foot lower than I was a second ago, now standing on the dirt ground beneath the floorboards. My leg is burning.

"The floor. It just . . . it just cracked open!" I stutter.

The wood underneath where he's standing starts to bow.

"Evan, I think it's going to—"

Transferring weight to another, sturdier floorboard, Evan puts his hands under my arms and lifts me out of the hole, but not before the splintered wood drags a second path down my shin bone.

"Ow! Damnit," I grumble, and before I can say another word, he picks me up and hustles me out into the sunlight.

Easing me back to the ground, he squats to examine the damage. "Ouch," he says.

I don't want to look. With the breeze hitting it, the cut

goes cold, then burns like fire. I know it's bad, and I can feel something damp puddling around my sock.

"It's deep, but I don't think you'll need stitches or anything," Evan says, his face surprisingly close to my shin. I'll say this for him—he has an iron stomach, despite how he looked on the switchbacks. I can't look at my own blood, let alone anyone else's.

"Those floors are rotted to hell in there. I tried to warn you." He looks apologetic and protective as he squints up at me from near my feet.

"I had to see if there was anything else," I say. He nods and gestures at my shin. "We should probably get this cleaned up. You got a first-aid kit in the car?"

I do, but I'm not ready to leave yet. There are still a few more shacks we haven't checked. Of course, one is probably still occupied by those kids from earlier.

As though reading my mind, Evan coaxes me back toward the main road. "That was the sturdiest of all the shacks. If your sister and Adam were going to hang out anywhere for a while, that's the one they would have stayed in. Clearly no one's been in there for a while. You saw how nasty that blanket was. After Nell—after everything—I'm sure Adam figured he had to find somewhere else to stay."

Evan helps me limp over the curb to the main road, then

across the street and onto the sidewalk that leads to the car. I thought answers would make me feel better. That blanket is the only bread crumb we've found on this trail. And we have no idea if it was left there before or after Nell died. In other words, we barely know more than we did before we came up here. I am beyond discouraged. I feel like I've been punched in the stomach. And the shin.

At the car, Evan does his best to bandage me up, and I do my best not to let him see tears pool in my eyes—from pain and loss and hopelessness and frustration. As he eases gauze over my freshly disinfected wound and affixes it with first-aid tape, I reread the poem for the thousandth time. Now I understand that Nell and Adam had planned to run away to that particular location all along—though why, I still have no idea. I'm back at the beginning.

"We should probably . . . ," Evan starts, and it's obvious he doesn't want to finish. He doesn't want to admit defeat either, but the sun is starting to drop. At this rate, we could bumble around Jerome for a hundred more days without getting any closer to finding the clues Nell buried in her poetry.

"I know," I say. "Look, can you drive? My shin is still pretty sore."

"Not that I'm glad you hurt yourself or anything, but I'm happy to avoid sitting shotgun for those switchbacks. Even if it is easier going downhill."

We fall into our seats, neither of us masking our sighs, and slowly pull onto the road. I turn Nell's folded poem over in my hands. Just holding it somehow comforts me.

"You want to give that a rest?" Evan asks. From anyone else it might sound impatient, but from him, it only sounds worried.

"I will. I just don't want to stare out the window."

I know he knows I'm lying, but he leaves me alone and focuses on the hairpin turns.

"'Holes that hold more than the mistaken treasure. Tunneled away, smuggled strife,'" I recite.

"What's that now?"

I repeat the line from Nell's poem.

"She really was good, wasn't she?" he says, and the tenderness in his voice makes me uncomfortable. It's as though I'm the only one who's allowed to respect Nell's writing on such a deep level.

"Holes," I repeat, then look out the driver's side window at the side of Cleopatra Hill. "I never noticed that before."

"Noticed what?"

"How many abandoned mines there are. They're at practically every turn. Did you see that on the way up?"

"No," he smirks. "I was focusing on not losing my breakfast. But yeah, you're right."

"Evan, stop the car. Stop the car!"

Evan pulls to the left so fast that a cloud of smoke and

dirt kicks up around us. He throws the car in park, yanks the emergency break, and turns to look at me. He's wild-eyed and sweating.

"What the hell? Are you okay?"

But I'm not looking at him. I'm still looking past him out his window.

"Sophie, what . . . ?" He follows my gaze.

There, about fifty feet from the side of the road, lies a fenced-off area enclosing what looks like a small oil rig—a mining lift. I remember seeing something like it online. They were used for lowering men into the mine towers. Spray painted on a splintering piece of wood in big block letters is STRIFE MINE. KEEP OUT.

I fling open my door and spill out of the car, but I'm still not quick enough to beat Evan to the mine's entrance.

A forbidding steel door, sealed shut with rust, covers the mine pit. The surrounding fence warns us to stay back in three different languages and threatens us with fines, arrest, and certain physical danger should we try to climb the crane without express permission—permission from whom, I have no idea.

"Well, Adam's not hiding out in the mine, that's for sure," I say.

Evan chuckles, but it doesn't sound like his usual breeziness. "Kinda hard to get a WiFi signal down there, I bet."

I look at him and crinkle my brow.

"For blogging," he explains, and now it's my turn to laugh uncomfortably.

But the momentary excitement of seeing the sign with the same words from Nell's poem has quickly faded upon seeing the mine itself.

"I was sort of expecting something else," I confess.

"I know what you mean," Evan says as he drags his hand along the diamond cutouts in the chain link. "If only it was a cave or something. And when we went inside, there he'd be with his little fold-up table, typing away on a laptop."

I stare for another minute at the antiquated machinery, the door covering the hole to the depleted treasures below the ground, and I say what we're both thinking.

"Maybe she wasn't talking about a place where they were going to hide out. Maybe she was talking about actual strife— a feeling, not a place. Just words in a poem."

Evan envelopes me in his arms, and we stand that way, looking at the mine lift for another moment before succumbing to the same defeat we felt leaving the Cribs district.

As we turn to go, I see something I hadn't noticed upon our approach. Tucked behind the rusted lift, set back several yards from the enclosure, sits a squat portable building with brown siding that can't measure more than a hundred square feet.

And in its single window, I swear I see the flutter of a dirty white shade.

"Did you see that?" I ask Evan, pulling him to my side so he's looking in the same direction as me.

"See what?"

"In the window of that building. I think I saw something move."

"Not a chance. I'm sure that thing's been locked up tight since the fifties," Evan says, but he's walking toward it in step with me.

"I'm sure you're right. Probably abandoned like the rest of this stuff," I say as we approach the building with a little more speed.

"I'll bet folks have forgotten all about these old buildings. Half of them are boarded up anyway." He squeezes my hand tighter. Pretty soon, I understand why.

The door looks boarded up, but not well. Almost as though it was rigged to *look* like it's boarded up.

I point to the door with my chin, and Evan lifts an eyebrow.

Shrugging, I reach for the board. It's so easy to pull away, I almost fall backward, expecting more resistance.

Propping the board against the flimsy siding, I raise my hand to knock.

"Hello? Anyone home?"

Our only answer is a faint creaking from inside.

Evan tenses beside me. I grab his arm.

"Well," I say louder than I need to, "guess nobody's here. You were right."

Evan shakes his head and starts to say something, but then he catches on, and responds, "Yup, guess so. Got a long trip back to Phoenix."

Another creak from inside, and the faintest shuffling.

"Told you it's all crap. There's no such thing as the Insider. Just some psycho looking for his fifteen minutes of fame," I shout.

Silence is all that follows. Desperate, I turn to my last resort.

"I guess Nell was just making it up."

The door flies open and I scream. In the same instant, Evan has my hand and is edging between me and the doorway, but not enough to block my view of the person standing in it.

His closely shaven black hair nearly skims the ceiling of the room behind him, and he has to duck under the doorway. He is perhaps the tallest person I've ever seen. Maybe seven feet tall, like a basketball player, and just as lanky. His hands are huge. His knobby knuckles bulge at the joints. In fact, his entire body looks that way—spindles connected by huge bolts. It's so unlike Evan's muscular proportions. This guy's face is also long, and his ears push outward, as though trying to fill him out and give him width. Black eyes, set deeply into his head, are fixed on me in the most unsettling way.

"Everything she said was the truth," he says quietly. "You know it and I know it. The question is, What are you going to do about it?"

12

EVAN AND I SIT SQUEEZED together on a bench that folds out from a half wall. A narrow table folds out from a perpendicular wall, locked in place by a bar below. Adam sits across from us on another fold-out bench, but he sits in a sideways sort of way, his legs too long to fit underneath the table with ours. Everything about this ramshackle building is too small for him. Even his clothes look wrong for him, faded red cotton shorts and a tan T-shirt that looks about three times too wide. It's as if he plucked his clothes from a clothesline when no one was looking. His whole appearance would be funny if it weren't for his eyes. Never in my life have I seen eyes so dark they look black.

"Ask me what you want now," Adam says. "I won't be here if you come back."

"Because you think we'll turn you in?" I ask. I've been so eager for answers, it never occurred to me I might notify the police of Adam's whereabouts.

"Won't you?" Something in the way he asks makes me think he *expects* me to turn him in—to blame him. Maybe I do.

"We've read your blog," I say, not yet ready to answer his previous question. I'm in more of an asking mood.

"But you didn't need to read it, did you?" Adam tilts his head at me in what feels like an accusation.

"Not all of it, no." I meet his challenge, even though my stomach is starting to twist into a knot.

"And why not? Why didn't you need to read all of it?" he asks.

Evan tenses next to me, but I put my hand on his knee and squeeze it under the table. This is a conversation that needs to happen.

"I already knew some of it," I say, hoping I sound brave.

"Because her sister—"

Adam cuts off Evan with a twitch of his hunched shoulders. "I'm not talking about Nell."

Evan opens his mouth, but I interject before he can ask more. I'm not ready for him to know I hear the murmurings. Not yet. Besides, I have a bigger demon to face.

"You're right," I allow, though I can't seem to unclench my

jaw when I say it. "I wasn't . . . I should have been there for her."

This is the first time I've said it aloud. I've been trying for so long not to, and now that I've unleashed the words, I feel empty. Adam looks down and squeezes his eyes shut behind thick black lashes. The angry veneer he's been holding over his face dissipates, and what's left looks exposed and pale.

"We both should have been there for her more," he says so quietly I almost don't hear him. "I knew more than you did. I should have been the one to protect her. I tried to. I . . . I tried."

Adam's voice breaks under the weight of what he's saying, and I don't even think before I reach across the flimsy fold-out table and put my hand on his wrist. He flinches at my touch, but then his black eyes meet my gaze. It's strange to be sharing my grief about Nell with someone I've never met. But whatever suspicion or anger I was feeling toward Adam a second ago has given way to relief.

"So you *are* the Insider, right?" Evan asks, stunned by our exchange, and clearly uncomfortable with my touching Adam. But I can't let him go. Not yet. However sympathetic Evan might be, he can't know what it felt like to lose Nell.

Adam nods, his face crinkling against more unseen pain. "I am. Or I was. I haven't written for a while. There's just not much more to say."

He looks toward a laptop plugged into an outlet in a tiny kitchenette. The outlet shares space with an ancient coffee maker, which looks like it's filled with coffee. Come to think of it, the whole place smells like charred coffee.

From where we're sitting, I can see the whole room: a squat fridge and a narrow, antique-looking stove, a small unmade bed, and a door, which is ajar revealing a closet-size bathroom with toilet, sink, and shower stall. A space on the plaster above the sink—roughly two feet high and oval-shaped—boasts a slightly cleaner surface, as though something used to hang there.

A mirror.

"Are you living here?" I ask, hoping the question isn't offensive. It's just so hard to imagine.

He nods again and looks surprisingly unashamed. "I think it used to be the foreman's lodging or something. I don't know. But it's pretty much got everything I need." Then he chuckles a humorless laugh. "Everything but running water, that is. There are places I can go in town for that, though."

"How is there even electricity here still?" Evan wonders.

"Dunno," Adam shrugs, and I guess I wouldn't question it either if I had it when I needed it.

"You've been hiding out here ever since?" I ask, knowing Adam knows what I mean.

"Almost." The shadow returns to his face. He stands from the table with some effort—the cramped quarters beginning to show their wear on him—and begins pacing slowly. This person in this tiny, self-made prison cell is nothing like the one described in Nell's journal, or even the angry bolding and italicizing *Insider* from his blog. Adam looks utterly vulnerable.

"It was her idea to come here," Adam starts, then looks at me shyly. He's being careful with me. He wants to be sure whatever he says doesn't hurt. I give him a small smile that I hope tells him that's impossible, so he might as well say it all.

"She said she used to come here when she was a kid," Adam continues. "We thought with all of the tragedy that'd happened here, there would be a ton of that emotion still floating around, almost like a cloud of sadness. Maybe it'd be harder to detect *our* pain, *our* tragedy underneath all of that. We'd hoped it would run interference or something. Besides, who would think to look for us in Jerome? Not long after we arrived, I heard that the sheriff was counting the days until his retirement. I guessed it was as good a place as any to get lost and stay that way. All I knew was that the longer we stayed at Oakside, the more danger Nell was in—because of him."

"Dr. Keller," I confirm, and Adam nods.

"He had a special interest in Nell. Said she was uniquely

talented. He's out of his mind." Adam smiles a sad smile. "You know, he used to actually help people. He was almost like a father to me."

"We're talking about the same Dr. Keller?" I ask.

"You didn't know him before," Adam says, his voice soaked in melancholy. "Haven't you ever wished, just once, you could tell someone everything you see, everything you hear, and have him understand exactly what you're talking about? Have him truly believe you, not treat you like some sort of maniac?"

I bite my bottom lip in response.

"You must know what that's like," Adam says, holding my gaze.

"I know what my sister knew," I say, sneaking a glance at Evan as he scans my face for clues.

"I know you're a Seer," Adam says, and my body goes cold.

"What's he talking about?" Evan asks quietly, as though he is trying to block Adam from the conversation.

"He doesn't know?" Adam asks. I look from one accusing face to the other. I feel trapped between two faltering realities.

"I don't know. I mean, I don't really understand what it is myself," I plead.

"You've been hearing things? Seeing things?" Evan accuses me.

"It started less than a year ago, and I'm not even sure I'm actually—"

"She's sure," Adam finishes for me, directing his assertion at Evan, who looks like he wants to punch Adam in the face.

"Excuse me, I don't need your help with this," I fire at Adam, who shakes his head like I've betrayed him in a way I couldn't possibly betray someone I barely know.

"Well you certainly need help from someone," Evan spits at me.

"What are you saying?" I can't believe he could be so mad at me about this. And after everything with Deb! Who does he think he is? "Hey, you're the one who wanted to know more about this shit in the first place. Well, here you go. Take a look," I fire back.

Evan balls his fist and fits it into the palm of his other hand and squeezes. He clenches his jaw so his cheeks hollow out.

Adam casts one more cautionary glance toward Evan, but it's pointless. It looks as though Evan has decided to stop listening, so Adam turns to me instead.

"You want to know more about Dr. Keller."

I lean in, still a little angry at Adam, but at least Evan knows about me now. It's not how I wanted him to hear it, but if this is the only way to find out what happened to Nell, so be it.

"Dr. Keller was the first person who understood me," Adam continues.

I nod, then remember what made Dr. Keller believe Adam.

"'You promised me you would come back. Is that bracelet for me?'" I repeat the two sentences that were whispered in Adam's ear.

He responds with a shudder that travels the entire length of his tall body. Then he wipes his mouth with his enormous hand and begins.

"All he said when I told him that was 'Susan.' Dr. Keller stayed away from me days after that. I thought I'd done something wrong telling him what I'd heard. But he came to see me a week later and explained why he was so disturbed. What I'd heard were the very last words his girlfriend, his first love, said to him before she died. They'd met in high school and were going to go away to college together."

Adam pauses, his lips drawing into a frown. "She was murdered. Stabbed right in front of Dr. Keller by a mugger. He couldn't protect her. It happened just as he was about to give her a present to mark the next step in their relationship."

"A bracelet," I finish.

"A charm bracelet, with a few charms to start her collection. But he only got as far as showing her the box. Dr. Keller's carried the guilt of Susan's death with him ever since. It's why he went to medical school. To maybe, I don't know, save other people since he couldn't save Susan. And the more his grief and his guilt deepened, the more he began to wonder if maybe his girlfriend might assuage his guilt by sending him a sign from the afterlife."

Adam keeps talking, his speech halting, and it occurs to me that it's probably been a while since he's spoken to anyone. I swallow hard as I wonder if the last person he spoke to was Nell.

As Adam tells it, Dr. Keller knew it was dangerous to want a sign from the beyond. After all, before Adam came along, Dr. Keller used to treat people for those types of thoughts. But he began seeing signs from Susan everywhere. His loss was that deep. Somewhere along the way, he began to wonder if what some people—people like Adam—were experiencing weren't delusions at all, but actually communications from the afterlife, someone trying to make contact from the beyond.

"Isn't that the definition of a delusion?" I ask, not certain how I'd rather be defined, as delusional or as a Seer.

"Except for one minor difference," Adam says, some enthusiasm reaching his voice. "If someone's experiencing a delusion, there won't be anything to show for it but someone's description. But with a Seer, there's always a tiny piece of evidence left behind from the encounter. It's easy to overlook unless you know what to look for: something out of place, shifted, or marked."

I automatically reach for my neck, to the spot just behind my ear.

"Like maybe the dampness from a whispering in your ear," Adam says, his eyes following my movement. Then his gaze drifts to my bandaged shin. "Or a mishap right after you think you might have heard something. Seen something."

I turn to Evan, but he's staring straight ahead past Adam, nostrils flaring.

My stomach twists with anger and guilt, but an earlier thought distracts me. I look to Adam again. "You were young when it started for you, right? Hearing things?"

Adam nods, his eyes drooping like the thought exhausts him.

"I don't know why some people experience the whispering earlier than others. I was young, as was Nell. But I've met others whose onset is later. I think the younger ones are less likely to dismiss what they're seeing and hearing. When you're a kid, anything's possible."

"I think it started for me when I was with Nell. The night she went to Oakside."

Adam shakes his head. "It's not like a virus. You can't catch the voices from being around people who experience them. Otherwise, Dr. Keller would have no need for any of us."

We're all quiet for a moment, the only sound the faint whistling of Evan's nose.

"Maybe it's not so much a matter of when it starts as when we start to believe it," I venture. Adam simply looks at me, the deep pools of his eyes unreadable.

Another silence follows. I can't take it anymore.

"How do you know all this?" I ask. I sound suspicious, but who am I kidding? I *am* suspicious of him. How could anybody believe something so unbelievable?

"I told you. Dr. Keller worked with me for over half my life. He shared things with me."

"You and Dr. Keller sound like you're pretty tight." My throat tightens. Did I just see Adam's eyes shift?

"We were," he says. His hunched shoulders take on a new tenseness. "When he became head psychiatrist at Oakside, he made me his orderly, his right-hand man, in a way. By then he knew I could detect a Seer as well as he could. He had me convinced we were going to help people. That we were going to protect them from the Takers."

It's so strange to hear Adam throwing around terms for what I've been experiencing as if it's the most natural thing in the world.

"The split soul." The words feel ridiculous on my tongue.

"Just the one half," he corrects me.

I'm at a loss for what to say next, but to my surprise, it's Evan who chimes in.

"So what, you just left? You'd had enough?"

Adam looks him squarely in the eye. "I fell in love."

"Oh," Evan backs down a little.

"I had to help her. I could see the way Jeremy—Dr. Keller," Adam says, and blushes a little, "was losing it. He wasn't sleeping much, and I hardly ever saw him eat. He was getting more, I don't know, obsessive. He'd been letting his other patients slip—the ones with actual delusions, the ones he keeps on the other side of the ward, away from those he's identified as Seers."

I think back to the day I went to Oakside to pick up Nell's box of belongings. I had tried to turn down one hallway, but Dr. Keller had cut me off at the pass and hurried me in a different direction. I can still hear the sound of his coat as it snapped in his wake.

"They're still there, and the orderlies are the only ones taking any sort of care of them—though I'd hardly call it that. Those patients aren't being given the therapy they need. They're just pumped with drugs to keep them quiet."

"What about the other Seers?" I ask.

"You mean all two of them?"

"There are only two left?" Evan asks. His brow creases, but every other part of his face falls. It's as though he was hoping to hear other news.

"And I can't say how much longer even they'll be around," Adam says, a hardness slipping into his tone. "Dr. Keller's not worried about the safety of the Seers. He used to believe they needed help and protection. Now he just views them as a conduit. A means to getting what he wants."

"And let me guess," Evan continues, apparently one step ahead of me. "What he wants is to find Susan."

Adam frowns so deeply his chin threatens to disappear underneath his bottom lip. "He's convinced that if he can coax out the Taker, he can somehow communicate with her again. He won't accept that she's gone. What's left isn't her at all. It's just some mindless *creature*. The Taker won't ever be his Susan again."

"So you're telling us there aren't a bunch of Takers floating around Oakside, trying to get to the other Seers? It's just this one that was created after his girlfriend died?" I ask.

"That's the one he's attracted, yes. But there are other Takers out there, trust me."

And here Adam stops, like he's lost his train of thought. Nell used to get that same look. I find myself wondering just how many Takers tried to burrow themselves into my sister's body before she didn't have the strength to fight one off any longer.

"But this is the one he's been trying to coax out of hiding through the Seers he's accepted into the facility," Adam finishes once his eyes clear of their shadow. "Susan's Taker probably found Dr. Keller, then after realizing he wasn't a Seer, latched on to the nearest one."

My throat caves in on itself. I cough to clear a passage, but it only makes my eyes well with tears. "That's the Taker that killed Nell?"

Adam crosses the room and kneels beside me, his head level with mine. I should feel swallowed by his stare, but somehow I feel comforted.

"I thought coming here and getting away from him would help." Adam shakes his head slowly, his eyes never letting go of mine. "We were wrong."

Tears spill from my eyes like water overflowing a glass.

"You've got to stay away from Oakside," Adam says. "Nell knew you saw the Taker that night in your bathroom mirror. When she broke it, she wasn't trying to hurt herself, Sophie. She was trying to make it stop. She was trying to hurt *it*, trying to protect you."

I lean toward Evan for support, setting my anger aside,

and his hands squeeze my shoulders, drawing me to him.

"She knew? She knew that I . . . ?"

"You can't go near Oakside. Dr. Keller knows too much. He can open the window to let the Taker in. He can get to you. He can send *it* for you. Do you understand?"

But I'm not listening to Adam anymore. My mind is swimming through the events of the past year. "It was you watching me that day I came to Jerome. The week after they found her, you left the journal in my car."

But I don't need him to answer. I already know.

"I thought after reading her journal, you'd be satisfied. Nell wanted nothing more than to keep you safe. She talked about it all the time. You have to promise that you'll never step foot in Oakside, that you won't let Dr. Keller near you."

I don't promise him a thing. Instead, I say, "You wanted me to find you. The journal, the blog. You even stayed in Jerome. Why would you do all that just to tell me to stay away?"

Adam's jaw stiffens, but he doesn't answer.

"Here's what I think," I continue, finally putting some of the pieces together. "It's impossible to escape a Taker once it's found you. No place is safe if you're a Seer. You've proven that." I lean in. "What you don't want to admit is that with Nell gone, Susan's Taker is after me. Nell told Dr. Keller that I saw what she saw that night in the bathroom. Which means

Dr. Keller knows I'm the next closest conduit to the Taker."

Evan tenses beside me. I put my hand on his knee and continue.

"And that means I can stop Dr. Keller."

Adam says nothing, but he has no reason to. I've said it all for him.

Evan and I leave in silence. We head back to the car feeling no more satisfied than we did when we arrived at the mine so full of strife that they named it accordingly.

13

THE DRIVE TO JEROME FELT like it took days, but the ride back feels like it takes minutes. That's especially surprising considering it's been almost completely silent. Neither Evan nor I even thought to put on music, and now that we're nearly home, there's no point.

"Thanks for letting me drive," Evan finally says, and I'm startled to hear his voice.

"No biggie." Frankly, I couldn't care less who's driving my mom's beat-up Buick.

"It helped me sort some things out," he says.

I'm back to being pissed at him for how he reacted at Adam's place.

"Yeah? How's that going?"

"Not so great," he scowls.

After I've grown used to the quiet again, he pipes up. "How could you not tell me?"

"Are you kidding me?" I ask in full defense mode. "Exactly what would you have wanted me to say? 'Hey Evan, I know we only just started hanging out and don't even know each other's birthdays or favorite movies or what we want to be when we get older, but here's a fun little fact: I hear people whispering when no one's there, which probably means I'm going crazy. Still want to hang out?' Jesus, Evan. I was afraid you'd—"

"What, think you're a freak?" He grips the steering wheel so hard his knuckles begin to pale. "You're forgetting one important detail. *I* shared something with you, something I've never told anyone. I told you about Deb. About what happened to her."

"Yeah, and you also told me that you thought she was crazy just like your aunt and uncle did," I spit back.

"I was a kid!" Evan yells. "What did you expect me to think? By the time they sent her away, I was finally old enough to understand how badly they'd treated her, but I still couldn't do shit about it. I've been trying to figure out what happened to Deb ever since, which by the way is looking totally hopeless now that I know how crazy Dr. Keller is and how there are basically no Seers left at Oakside. Do you honestly think I would have shown you those websites if I didn't think that you would understand?"

For the life of me, I can't think of a thing to say in response.

"After our picnic, I thought we had an understanding. I thought you *got* me."

He pauses before delivering his final blow on my already throbbing heart: "I guess I was wrong."

We pull up to my house.

"You weren't wrong."

Evan doesn't answer me. He stares at the steering wheel, the engine still rumbling.

"I should have told you that I was like Nell. Like Deb. Because I felt a connection too, that day by the picnic benches. You have to understand, I saw what happened when people found out about Nell. They treated her like she had some sort of contagious disease. I just couldn't stand the thought of you thinking of me like that."

He turns to me. "So now do you trust me?"

I think for a second. "I have for a while. I just never told you."

The sun is beginning to make its way down toward the mountaintops. He reaches out for my hand, rubbing the top of it with his thumb. I would give anything to keep feeling this newness. We've had our first big argument, but mutual forgiveness stretches between us. Which is why it kills me to say what I have to say next.

"I'm going back to Oakside."

"Are you out of your mind?"

"No," I say indignantly, though he may be right.

Evan's so flustered his voice actually cracks. "Why the hell would you risk—after everything Adam just told us—do you have any idea—?"

"You heard what Adam said," I try to explain. "There are still two Seers there, and I already know one of them, this guy Kenny. He wants to help me or he wouldn't have given me that poem from Nell's journal. Nell wanted him to have it, maybe so he'd know there was hope outside of Oakside. Or maybe because she knew that somehow it would find its way back to me. The other Seer has to be MM. And if Kenny wanted to help put an end to Dr. Keller's experiments, I'm sure MM will want to too."

"And what, you're going to waltz in there after what happened last time and politely ask to speak with Nell's other friend? You don't have to play the hero!"

"But what if this is the only way to make the Taker leave me alone?"

"Sophie—"

"Evan, I wasn't asking for your approval!" That shuts him up in a hurry.

He puts his hands to the sides of his head and squeezes, like he's trying to find some restraint between his palms. I cross my arms over my chest.

Finally, we both put our hands in our respective laps.

"Look, all-star camp for football starts tomorrow," he says, frowning.

I completely forgot. Winter break begins Monday. I have officially lost all track of time.

"I'm going to be up at Camp Verde until Thursday, and I'm not going to have my phone. Coach Tarza has this no cell phone policy." Evan rolls his eyes more than he usually does when he talks about his coach's rules.

But then his face turns serious. "Please, promise me you won't do anything until I get back."

"Evan, I—" I start to argue, but he interrupts me, this time taking both of my hands into his giant callused palms.

"*Please*, Sophie. I'm asking you not to. I know it's a lot to ask, but . . ."

"But what?"

"I don't know what I'd do if something happened to you."

This is probably the only thing he could have said to keep me from driving to Oakside the minute he left tonight.

So I just nod in response.

"I want to hear you say it," he pushes.

Sighing, I say, "I won't go to Oakside. Not until you get back."

His brow crinkles. He doesn't believe me.

"I promise, okay? Just hurry home." I say grudgingly.

This conjures a tiny smile. "Trust me, I'm going to want to get back in a hurry. But not to go to Oakside."

And with that, he leans across the console, my hands still in his, and finds my lips with surprising efficiency. He kisses me hard. It's as if he's taking out the rest of his anger on my mouth. And while I know this should make me mad, and it sort of does, I find myself pushing back against him, like we're fighting without saying a word. A low groan comes from his throat, and I return it with a gasp, my breath buried under the weight of his mouth. I can't pull away. Then, he moves his mouth toward my neck, his lips soft and pliable under my earlobe. He whispers, "I don't know how I'm going to concentrate on football."

I pull away for the second time today, but this time it's even more difficult than the first. "Just focus on coming home quick."

He unlatches his seat belt and slides from the door, pausing for a second to rest his head on the window, his eyes closed in what almost looks like pain.

"Be good, Sophie D.," he says, sliding into the driver's seat of his car.

I've just turned around to go inside when he says, "Wait."

Leaning into the backseat, he reemerges from his car and trots over to me, a balled-up football jersey in his hands.

I crinkle my nose.

"It's clean," he chuckles. "I don't need this one. Just keep it. To help you remember your promise."

I roll my eyes and take the jersey from him. My lips are still burning from our kiss as I watch him pull away and round the corner.

The house is empty when I walk in.

There're no liquor bottles on the counter, no melted ring of condensation telling me where there used to be a glass. I make my way to Mom's room and find the bed not only empty, but made.

"Mom?" I ask the house, the walls, the furniture, the stale smell that comes from staying in a home without really living in it. "Mom, I'm home!"

When I don't get an answer, I drag my phone from my bag and search for missed calls, but find none.

I go to the fridge and try to find something to eat. I'm not hungry but know my body actually does need food. I forage through the fridge with zero enthusiasm, my mind engrossed in our conversation with Adam. The way he looked at us with his black eyes. The abandoned shack where he'd tried to keep Nell safe when my mom and I couldn't. Adam's words roll back on me like a wave licking the sand, depositing little shells each time it returns.

There's always a tiny piece of evidence left behind.

He won't accept that she's gone. What's left isn't her at all.

Everything she said was the truth. You know it and I know it. The question is, what are you going to do about it?

My appetite is even more dampened than it was a second ago, but I emerge from the fridge with a block of cheese and an apple. That's when I see the note on the fridge.

Going to AA with AB. Should be food in the fridge for dinner.

Love, M

I blink at the note for a few seconds before returning the cheese and apple to the shelf where I found them.

"Well, what do you know?" I ask the refrigerator with enough sarcasm to quell any excitement. I know the disappointment that's bound to follow. This is no different from all of the other times Mom's promised to quit. Sure, she's never actually gone so far as to attend an Alcoholics Anonymous meeting, but that was probably the only way to get Aunt Becca off her back. And when Mom's spooning a bottle of gin in her bed two days from now and apologizing to the air, she'll be the only one who's surprised.

I go to change my bandage and decide to let it get some air so it'll scab over. Then I change into Evan's practice jersey, which reminds me of the way his bedroom smells, and a pair of old cotton shorts and lie down on my bed. Adam's voice tunnels through my brain.

"Enough," I tell it. "Enough for tonight. I can't think anymore."

Besides, if I keep thinking about everything Adam told us today, I'm more likely to break my promise to Evan and go to Oakside before he gets back.

I leave my room and crack the door to Nell's. I still enter her room with the same hesitation as when she was alive. I peer around the door and wait for an approval that will never come. But it still feels right to make the gesture.

I slide Nell's journal from its home between her mattress and the box spring, and crack open the composition book to where I left off: the entry after the poem Kenny slipped me right before he gave me a concussion.

We went outside today, MM and I. They took LM to the room, so it was just the two of us. We couldn't stand waiting around for him to get back.

So we pretended. It was like we were five years old. Neither of us laughed at the other. It was almost as if we had a pact: She could be a fairy and I could be a 1920s Hollywood starlet, and neither of us would call the other one out and say it was stupid. It was stupid, though, and I think we both knew that. But we played for almost an hour out there in the courtyard, making believe cacti were clouds made of marshmallows and light posts were poles that led down to underworld caverns where we could hide out from orderlies and doctors and mirrors.

I stop for a second and close my eyes to envision the world Nell and MM created in their imaginations. It doesn't take me long to picture it. Nell was like a magician. She was always so good at evoking something from nothing. And even though I know what comes next, and even though I hate reading it, I do it anyway.

Then we went back inside and found LM in the rec room. He had a pile of green Legos around him, and we knew. But he wasn't playing with them. He sat there, staring. The way we all do afterward. Just staring.

I knew whatever it was they made Nell do, made MM and Kenny see, it was bad. I'd wanted to believe that Nell was at Oakside to get better. That these treatments were somehow okay. Now I know better. Adam knew how much danger Nell was in with those people at Oakside.

> *I took MM by the hand and we sat next to LM while he stared at the Legos they made him earn. Now that he had them, it was like he didn't know what to do with them.*
>
> *MM tried to make conversation so it wouldn't be so quiet and told me she would give back all the glossy treats in their crinkly bags to be out of this place. She said she'd never eat them again if it meant we could all leave. It's been her home for practically three years, an eternity next to my six months. And I didn't know what to say, so I told her that then I'd have to come up with another name for her. That made her laugh, and that made it a good day.*

I reread the last few sentences. Whenever I'd read this passage before, I'd focused solely on the way Nell had taken this girl as her friend—made it her responsibility, like the big sister she was, to make the girl feel better. In a strange way, it had made me a little jealous to read that Nell took care of other people too. I know it was probably my way to avoid feeling guilty. But something about the passage strikes me differently now.

It's been her home for practically three years.

And what she said about "glossy treats" in "crinkly bags." I think back to Evan returning from the vending machine at the rest stop, little yellow bags crinkling in his grip.

They're my favorite. Actually, they were Deb's favorite. After she went away, I sort of picked up the habit. Almost like a tribute to her or something.

"M&M's," I say aloud to the empty house. "MM. Oh my God," I breathe. "MM. M&M. Nell nicknamed her after her favorite candy. MM is Deb."

I blink at the journal as I let the cover close. I stare at the marbled cardboard for a long time.

Deb is the one Nell befriended in Oakside. And that means that she could be the other Seer that Adam was talking about. Evan's aunt and uncle never brought her to Florida. She's been here the whole time.

And if that's true, she and Kenny are in more danger than even Adam realizes. He wasn't in that little gray room with Dr. Keller like I was. He didn't feel the weight of Dr. Keller's hand pinning him to the gurney.

"I'm sorry, Evan," I whisper.

Because I have to break my promise to him. I have to see if Deb really is the other Seer at Oakside, and it can't wait until he gets back.

I reach for my phone to tell Evan what I've discovered, but

decide against it. If I'm wrong, I'll have gotten Evan's hopes up for nothing. I'll go first, just to verify that MM is Deb. If I'm wrong, Evan will never have to know. But if I'm right, all of this hurt might finally lead to something good.

Nell David—Patient #402

December 21

Things are different now, and I can't help but feel all of this is happening too late. I want to enjoy the feeling. What is it called? Love? How would I know, if I've never felt it before? Dr. Keller, are you reading this? Maybe you can shed a little light on it for me. I'm sure you could, but I won't let you get that close. Bet on that. In fact, consider this the last little window you're going to get into my brain.

For the first time in my life, I feel really heard. When we talk, I get the feeling Adam wants to know more about me. So is that love? Or am I just so desperate to connect with someone who doesn't think I'm a freak that I'm willing to jump at the first guy who doesn't shrink away like I'm infected. Maybe he just cares. To be honest, I almost don't mind if he acts like this with everyone. It doesn't matter if it's love, or sympathy, or how people who work in a dump like this are actually supposed to treat people.

I've told him everything. I mean everything. He knows

all of me now. He knows about the voice, the thing in the mirrors, how I tried to stop it. He knows about my mom and the way she looks at me, about how terrified I am of letting Sophie down, and about when it all started. I feel totally naked around him now, and I don't even care.

I'm still scared. I'm scared all the time. I can't look in a mirror, as much as they get me to try. But now I have someone to tell. And he doesn't pull his hand away. He keeps it on my shoulder, warm and big, as he towers over me like a giant. He's the only one in the world I can see. If he could just stay with me forever, I might be okay.

14

I DIDN'T SLEEP AT ALL last night. Not surprisingly, I had dreams of M&M's. All kinds. Peanut, plain, peanut butter. Red ones. Blue ones. They were falling from the sky like primary-colored snow. At first it was fun. But then they started pouring, and they were whacking me in the head, and I had to find shelter. Evan was there, but he couldn't get me out of the way fast enough, so he took cover somewhere out of sight. Then I saw Nell. She was reaching for me, and I grabbed her hand, but when I looked into her face, it shriveled in on itself like it was decaying. I screamed and let go, but just as I did, I heard the echo of that horrible murmuring in my ear.

When I woke up, my neck right below my ear was damp, and it wasn't from sweat.

Mom went out "booth shopping" with Aunt Becca today. I guess it's too intimidating to say "looking for a job." She's hoping to rent a booth at a salon again. Since Aunt Becca drove, Mom's car was just sitting there, a full tank of gas, waiting for me to take it. The keys dangling from the hook by the door taunting me.

As I pull into the nearly empty parking lot at Oakside, I tell myself over and over that I don't have a choice. If Evan's cousin really is in there—if I can help get her out, if she can tell me what's really going on at Oakside, then maybe I can avoid the same fate. Maybe we can stop Dr. Keller.

I know it's a terrible idea. I thought of Evan all morning, that look he gave me in the car last night, the way he pleaded with me to not do the very thing I'm doing right now. I really did try to talk myself out of it. I tried all day, which is why I'm here at dusk—the exact time of day that I *didn't* want to be here.

There's a reason I never came to Oakside at night. It wasn't just because their posted visiting hours are only during the daytime. If we'd really wanted to, Mom or I could have claimed an emergency and seen Nell whenever we wanted. But as unnerving as this place is during the day, I knew it would be that much worse at night.

Crickets provide the only background noise as my footsteps sound on the parking lot asphalt. I parked under the only functioning lamp; the rest are either burnt out or dying a slow, flickering death. Taking this precaution seems silly now with the gray light surrounding me, but I'll be glad for it when I come back to my car. It'll definitely be dark by then. The problem is, I can't really envision what my return trip will look like. I haven't taken the plan that far yet.

A light is already burning above the "welcome" mat at the first set of sliding glass doors. The hum of its electricity makes me flinch. But the doors slide open on their automatic sensor to let me in, and while I know they're on a sensor, I hate the idea that anyone knows I'm here.

Once they close behind me, I look to the Plexiglas window on my left, prepared to face the grimace of some disgruntled orderly—or maybe even the Pigeon—before they let me through the second door. But for the first time in all my visits, the booth, with its microphone and red admitting button, stands empty.

I step toward the second set of doors, but nothing happens. I tense with the memory of the thing I saw reflected when I came to retrieve Nell's things.

"Hello!" I yell to the window, eager to get in and get out as soon as possible.

My plan is loose, but I've told myself it's enough. I just

need to say that I want to see Kenny, tell him I'm sorry for upsetting him last time. After the way he clocked me, they're probably so afraid of getting sued that I'll get a couple of minutes with him.

I just need to ask him about Deb. I need to know if she's really here. If I can confirm that she's not in any immediate danger, then I'll wait until Evan gets back from all-star camp, and together we can figure out what to do. He'll be pissed I came alone, but when he finds out Deb's here, I know he'll understand why I had to do it. But first I have to get those minutes *alone* with Kenny—asking him about Deb is another story.

"Hey, can someone let me in? Hey!"

Still nothing. The glass contains the volume of my voice, as if I'm a bug trapped in a jar.

"Is anybody th—?"

The doors part.

I glance back at the admitting window. It's as empty as it was before.

I brush a chill from my arm and tell myself that the door must be on a sensor in the evening. Probably some sort of budget cut to keep from having to pay an orderly to sit there during non-visiting hours.

But when I step into the lobby, I'm alone. From the reception desk to the recreation room where I'd had my incomprehensible conversation with Kenny, it is empty and still.

I take a couple of tentative steps toward the reception counter, half expecting some cranky, white-smocked orderly to pop up from behind the desk jack-in-the-box style. But as I stand on my toes to peer over the desk's ledge, I see nothing but boxes of Xerox paper and piles of manila files, each marked with a patient number.

I look behind me again. A single tower of Legos sits in the middle of the rec room table. It is made entirely of green blocks. All I'd wanted was some private time to talk with Kenny. But I hadn't expected there wouldn't be anyone here. It doesn't seem right. Something seems off.

"Hel . . . hello?" I say in a tone hovering just above a whisper. Pathetic. I try again.

"I need to talk to someone," I say in a voice I'm hoping is more assertive than how I feel. But the way it trembles from my lips tells me I came up short.

All of a sudden, getting answers out of Kenny is the last thing I want.

The urge to get out of here is palpable. I've felt afraid before, and I've known when it's my own chicken-shit attitude that's trying to get me to run. But this is different. Almost primal.

I glance once more toward the recreation area before

deciding to leave. I'll have to find out if Deb is MM some other way.

I step toward the doors and wait for them to open the way they did at my entry, but they stay sealed like two tightly pressed lips, refusing to let me out. I duck around the corner. As I go to push the red button, I announce, "I'll just let myself out."

Something sharp pinches the back of my thigh. I stop dead.

"Ow! What the—?"

I turn and scream.

There, not three inches from my face, is a set of wild blue eyes and a shining dome of a head. In his hand, a large plastic syringe drips something clear.

"Kenny, what did you—?"

But I can't finish my sentence. My eyes drop to Kenny's bare feet. I can't think straight. Everything is dark.

"Kenny, help . . ."

"I'm sorry. I had no choice. They gave me all the green ones I wanted." His blue eyes sparkle.

"Now you'll see what she saw."

I can't see. My head is thudding and I can't see.

"Open your eyes. You have to look!"

I can't tell if that's my own voice. No. It's different. High.
Breathy.

I feel like I'm swimming in the dark. Why can't I see?

"Wake up now! You have to look!"

But I can't see. I can't wake up. I can't—

I start to open my eyes, but it's too bright. I shut them
again, squint, put my hands up to shield them. There's
pounding in my head. No, somewhere close by. Pounding
and shouting.

"Now! Look NOW!"

Someone pulls at my hands, tugs them.

I'm in a room with Kenny. His bulging blue eyes are frantic. His chin shakes, and his hands are slick and cold with
sweat. But his grip is firm, unyielding. He lets go of my hands
and turns me to face a mirror.

"No!"

I try to wrench my head away, but his hands hold it in place
like a vise. And soon, I'm staring. There's something there
other than my reflection. Something *behind* my reflection.

The pounding gets louder. Yelling comes in sharp stac-
cato, like crests of high, frothy waves. Only now do I notice
the reflection of a door behind me, the handle jiggling
against the steel bolt of an electric lock. A keypad glows
green. I'm being held captive.

The staff is trying to get in. Trying to get *us* to open the door. They sing a chorus, chanting commands, but all I can focus on is the mirror as it ripples and bends.

"Help us!" I scream, shocked by the power of my voice.

But the Oakside staff can't get in.

The mirror folds in, bulges out, folds in.

"Kenny, we have to go!" I can hear myself shouting, but I can't take my eyes away from the reflection in front of us. I can hear his breath above me, coming in gulps and gasps."Kenny, we have to get out of here! It's coming!"

I tear my eyes from the mirror, wiggling my head out of Kenny's grip, and frantically look for an escape route. It's a smaller room than the one I was in the other day with Dr. Keller. There's a medical gurney, its thin mattress covered only by scratchy-looking disposable sheets with a tiny pillow. Thick nylon straps cross the mattress and hook to metal rods beneath the gurney. This is a procedural room—with a wall of mirrors.

"Kenny, I'm unlocking the door."

"It won't unlock. You need the code," Kenny says, as though in a trance.

I turn back to the mirror. The glass melts into a thick liquid, pulsing like a heartbeat.

"Then tell me! What's the code?" My voice doesn't even

sound like my own. It's desperate. I can barely push the words from my throat.

"I broke it. This way they can't interrupt. They're not allowed in. Just us. It's time for this to end. Look! It's coming!" Kenny is breathless, and it brings a new terror to my gut. Turning back to the mirror, I can see something moving behind Kenny's reflection, like a shadow trying to pull away from its host.

I tug at Kenny's big meaty arm, making his head wobble on his neck, but his eyes, orblike, are fixated on the mirror.

"Kenny! You have to help me with the door! The staff are trying to get in, but they can't!"

I have no way of knowing if Kenny even understands what I'm saying. He doesn't seem to hear any of the noise on the other side of the door.

Before I can plead my case, I see the oily hair. Shaggy remnants fall in pieces around a gaunt, skullish face. Then come the bottomless holes where eyes should be. But it's the mouth, with its cracked lips and protruding teeth, which move in silent, urgent intervals, that I stare at, horrified. I'm fixated by the soundless words it forms, its parched skin pulling tighter and tighter over the bone until it looks like the terrible leathery skin might come undone, revealing something even more hideous underneath.

"We have to get closer," Kenny says, his entranced voice drifting over my shoulder.

I feel his belly against my back. His grip on my wrist has tightened so that I can barely feel my hand. The pounding on the other side of the wall is faster and more feverish than ever, but I still can't make out what the voices are telling me. It wouldn't matter if I could. I can't seem to move from where I'm standing. All I can do is watch that horrible mouth.

"I . . . Kenny, we . . . *please*," I whisper, knowing with terrified certainty it won't make a bit of difference what I say. Kenny's the one who brought me here. And for what? Legos? The promise of something good in a place that's so horrible?

"We have to listen to what it's saying. It's the only way," he says so quietly that I can barely hear him over the pounding on the door.

"Why? Why do we have to listen? I don't understand," I'm pleading with him now. He starts to push me, lean against me to get me to move toward the mirror with him. Closer to *it*.

"We have to know what it wants," he says. Absurdly, his reflection is the most lucid I've ever seen him. But this only frightens me more. He's serious. He's not hysterical. Whatever he's doing, he thinks it's right.

"Kenny, this isn't the way to make it stop! Listen to me. I've talked to Adam, okay? I know what this is, and this isn't the way. Kenny, no!"

He breaks his gaze from the creature and spins me around, his nose inches from mine.

"He's one of them, you stupid girl! And besides, he left. This is the only way."

He turns me and pushes me again, and I can't hold him back. He could throw me into the mirror if he wanted to. He could feed me to that *thing* like I was no more than a raw steak getting tossed into a lion's cage at the zoo.

"But the poem. You gave me Nell's poem. Remember? You gave that to me so I'd know what happened. So I'd find Adam!"

Kenny grits his teeth. "No! So you'd know to stay away. You should have stayed away. Now it's too late! There's no one here for me. Not for us. Just the two of us."

"What do you mean the two of us? Jesus, Kenny, stop!"

Kenny lunges, and I stumble closer to the mirror. Adam's words scream through my head.

It tells you what it knows you want to hear. That's what it murmurs in your ear. That's how it tries to find its other half.

"Sophie, the code!" I hear a voice screaming, but I can't hear what it says after that. Kenny's arm is pressing against my ear.

"Code! You have to . . . we can't from our . . . he cracked the . . . punch . . . Sophie, *listen!*" A voice screams from the other side of the wall, but it might as well be speaking

another language because I can only catch snatches of what it's saying.

"HELP!" I scream.

My feet are squeaking against the dull gray floor. It's only going to be another few seconds before Kenny offers me to that hideous thing in the mirror.

"HELP ME!"

"Kenny, please," I whisper, now completely drenched with his sweat and mine. Our shared moisture slicks the space between us enough for me to wiggle away from his arm. Finally, my other ear is freed.

"Sophie! The code! One-zero-zero-five-eight-five!"

The shadowy shape has begun to bend away from the glass. *Separate* from the glass. It's becoming an entity of its own.

Kenny's arm flexes. I slide from his grip in a single movement, and I'm up against the door, the metal handle pressed into my palm. The digital keypad above the handle glows like something toxic. A single voice still shouts on the other side, but I can barely hear it over the screaming that echoes inside the room.

15

THE THING IN THE MIRROR snatches Kenny. It happens so fast that I'm almost not sure it happened at all. He slides up the mirror, the Taker dragging him by his toe. Then there's blood dripping to the floor, and Kenny hangs from the ceiling above the Taker—suspended by a force I can't see. Suspended by only his big toe.

The shadowy figure spills onto the dull gray floor, leaving something slick like oil in its wake. The stench of rot fills the air. The Taker looks at Kenny, inspecting its work. Its mouth is moving faster than ever.

I grip the door handle behind my back, hiding it like a secret. I don't dare take my eyes from the Taker. Its body is more visible outside of the mirror. It's gaunt, emaciated, like a decomposing shell. The entire room seems to darken and dampen with its presence.

It walks toward Kenny.

The Taker is only inches from his face. He's as still as a fly caught in a spiderweb, and the Taker sizes him up.

Kenny's eyes blink with a steady rhythm. Blood has rushed to his head from hanging upside down, and his blue Oakside-issued shirt has crept up his belly, sticking to his stomach with sweat. *Where is the blood on the floor coming from?*

The shadowy thing lifts what looks like a hand—though its fingers are too long, and too thin, to be any ordinary hand—and reaches for his face.

"Hey!" I yell, the sound leaping from my throat before I can retract it.

The Taker stops cold and slowly turns to face me.

Its mouth moves faster.

"Sophie, you have to unlock the door! The code!" They scream the numbers to me.

But I can't move. I can only stare at the thing. It takes one slow step toward me, then another. Its mouth is in constant motion, its words lost somewhere in the silence of the room. I can't hear Kenny breathing. I can't even hear my own breath.

Kenny moves slightly. The Taker slides back to him faster than I can blink.

"Kenny," I whisper, pleading with him to defend himself. I take a step toward the Taker, my legs threatening to collapse under me.

His eyes shift in their sockets, and for the first time, he looks at me, his face completely calm. It terrifies me. He looks defeated. He's given up.

"Now it's just you two," he whispers, and before I can take another step forward to help him—how, I don't know— the Taker lifts its arm, puts its skinny fingerlike tentacles to Kenny's ear and leans forward to speak.

Kenny's eyes go wider, and just like that, the life in them dies.

My heart throbs so hard in my chest, I think I might pass out.

"The code, Sophie! Are you still there?"

I back up again, groping for the keypad above the door handle. My fingers ache with the strain as I punch the numbers shouted to me from the other side of the door.

Even though I can recite the code from the repetition, my brain can't make sense of it. It's like one of the synapses won't fire. I've forgotten the shapes of the numbers.

I hear a dragging sound behind me, and before I can turn around, I feel the heat of breath on the back of my neck. A putrid smell fills my nostrils and my eyes water. Air catches in the back of my throat, and my trembling fingers stop in midair above the keypad. My muscles feel like they've crystallized.

I can't hear the voice on the other side of the door anymore. All I can hear is the sound of a jaw working, moving up and down, and the clicking of teeth—long, yellowed teeth.

The Taker is right behind me. It wants me to hear. To understand.

"Sophie, unlock the door!"

I'm frozen.

"The keypad, Sophie!"

My shaking finger finds the first number: One. A tiny beeping sound is my reward, and the green button gets momentarily brighter.

As I reach for the next number, the mouth moves into my peripheral vision.

The Taker wants me to turn around and look at it. It wants me to listen to what it's saying. It wants to tell me the same secret that it shared with Kenny. I can see those long fingers reaching slowly for my face. The voice on the other side of the door is silent, and maybe that fear of being given up on searches out my reserve of bravery. I punch the next number.

Another beep, and again as I hit the zero, then the five, then eight.

And just as I reach for the last five, the Taker tries to step in front of me. I squeeze my eyes shut and scream.

"NO!"

My finger hits a button. I have no idea if it's the right one. A beep follows, then a series of three rapid beeps. I can barely hear them over the clicking of the rotting jaw, but I clutch the handle of the door like a lifeline and pull back, desperate to put distance between me and this thing, which seems like it's taking the breath straight from my lungs.

Then I hear another click. This one mechanical. I feel a pinging in the handle. The door has freed itself from the bolt.

I yank the handle so hard it wrenches my shoulder. The door flies open, and when I dare to open my eyes again, I am stunned to find myself staring at a pale, sweating Dr. Keller. He's collapsed against the wall in the hallway, his hands spread against the gray as though they're trying to grip something that isn't there.

"Did you see her?" he asks me, and I can think of nothing to say in return.

His eyes are wide. It's the first time I've ever seen him unsettled. It's as though he's registering a phantom before his eyes. Then his gaze moves over my shoulder, and his terror returns. My stomach sinks like an anvil, and I'm 100 percent sure that the Taker is still behind me. But it's vanished. The only evidence the Taker was here is the residue on the mirror. And what Dr. Keller is staring at: Kenny.

Kenny hangs from the ceiling, one leg bent like a dancer, his foot fixed behind his left knee. His arms are stiff at his sides, not hanging above his head as they should be if gravity were in control. But the most disturbing thing is how Kenny is suspended. His one big toe is hooked into the ceiling panel's seam—his massive weight held aloft in a way Dr. Keller knows, and I know, should be impossible. Yet there he is. The pool of his blood on the floor glistens like some sort of sacrificial offering. The light catches the puddle and the surface shakes. I can now see that the blood is dripping from his ear—the same ear the Taker murmured into.

"Where . . . where is . . ." Dr. Keller breathes his words. He can't take his eyes—or *won't* take his eyes—from Kenny. He seems at once horrified and suspicious, as if Kenny might drop from the ceiling and charge him at any moment.

The Pigeon—Gladys—appears and approaches Kenny with the same caution Dr. Keller and I use to observe him. But she is the only one brave enough to touch him. I watch as her shaking, shriveled fingers reach for his neck, which is about at her eye level. She puts two tightly pressed fingers to his bulging neck, squints, and turns away. She shakes her head at Dr. Keller.

And with that prognosis, Dr. Keller regains his composure. The scared man transforms back into the cunning, handsome doctor I've come to expect in these horrid gray halls.

"Why did you do that?" I find the courage to ask. "Why did you put me in there with—?" A panic seeps into my veins. The Pigeon has finished her inspection and now stands in the doorway, blocking my view of Kenny, which should be comforting, but somehow isn't. Dr. Keller is now at my side, and several orderlies in stiff white smocks round the corner, one of them handing Dr. Keller a stethoscope and a blood-pressure cuff.

"Shhh," he coos. "You've already had quite enough excitement."

Then he presses the stethoscope to my back. The cold slips past the thin denim of my jacket, chilling me to my spine.

"What are you—would you stop?" I flick the stethoscope away and start to raise my other arm, but the Pigeon clasps my wrist with such efficiency, I'm too stunned to move.

"Thank you, Gladys. Sophie, we'll just check your blood pressure here," Dr. Keller continues, his voice even and liquid. Gladys tightens the cuff to my arm as Dr. Keller gently pushes the head of the stethoscope to the bend in my elbow.

"That must have been quite a fright for you," Dr. Keller says. "Poor Kenny, I'm afraid he experienced a psychotic break. He overpowered us, then dragged you into that room."

This is enough to break the spell of Dr. Keller's voice. "You're lying," I spit. "You're all lying. And I'm not the only one who knows it."

I back away, tearing the blood-pressure cuff from my arm, shoving an orderly from my path.

"Oh, I'm afraid you won't be going anywhere tonight, dear," the Pigeon says, her beaklike mouth twisting into her version of a smile.

"Watch me."

I break into a sprint, my mind operating on autopilot. I'm strangely reminded of my fifth-grade teacher, Mrs. Gibbons, telling us about the fight-or-flight instinct and the adrenaline that floods our bloodstream when we're faced with certain danger.

My legs pump, my arms flail, and my heart chugs. I race down the gray hallway, rounding one corner after the other, passing one nondescript door with its tiny rectangular and wire-mesh window after the next. Finally, the lobby stretches before me. Through the sliding glass doors, I can see my mother's beat-up Buick waiting for me under the flickering light of the parking lot.

I can hear squeaking shoes behind me, and orders to stop me, to keep me from leaving.

I lunge for the control room to release the inner door. I punch the button so hard I think my palm might split as the footsteps grow closer. The inner door sighs and eases open. I take my first running step, then another. I'm almost out. My keys jingle in my pocket. I'm almost free.

And then an arm encircles my waist.

The air is shoved from my gut as I'm pulled back inside. Both feet off the ground, I kick, claw, jab. But I can't reach anything. I can't reach.

The door grows smaller as I'm dragged away from it.

"Nooo!" I scream, but a hand eases over my mouth.

"There there, no need to get excited. You're in no shape to go anywhere right now, young lady," a voice oozes into my ear. A Pigeon's voice. "You'll be much safer here with us."

My arms are pinned against my sides by the same strong grip that's pulling me back toward the room where Kenny hangs from the ceiling, where something wants to whisper to me from the mirror.

"It appears you're not just a danger to yourself anymore, now, are you? I mean, look what happened to poor Kenny," the Pigeon says.

Her hand muffles my response.

"Doctor, I think we're ready for you."

Dr. Keller is in front of me now. We've stopped in the

corridor leading to the mirrored room. He unzips a small leather kit, revealing a set of syringes and vials, clear liquid trembling in their bottles. He deftly removes one of each, and piercing the top of a vial with a syringe, draws the liquid into the needle.

"NO!" I scream from behind the Pigeon's hand, but it's no use. I'm too far from the door, not that anyone's there to hear me anyway.

"Now, this might hurt," Dr. Keller warns. "But it's all for the greater good. You're going to finish the job your sister started."

The Pigeon offers Dr. Keller my arm, and soon I'm drifting toward gray.

Gray.

Then darkness.

16

I'M BELOW A TREE, AND it's hard to breathe. Winds swirl around me, almost through me, shaking needles down from the ponderosa pine that towers above me. The needles fall like snow, piling on top of my shoulders, and I shrug them away. Then the needles flatten into little disks and turn color. A train of green Legos forms a trail, leading into a fog that builds all around me.

I look up into the tree. There's Nell, hanging upside down from the lowest branch at least ten feet above me, her arm reaching to me.

"Nell, what are you doing? Come down," I call to her.

But she only shakes her head, her smile downturned and mournful. Still, she reaches for me.

I can hear Mom from somewhere on the other side of the fog.

"But I just don't understand. You think she had something to do with this?"

"It's possible. But it's important you realize, Ms. David, how genetically linked this sort of condition is. Her sister, as you're all too aware, suffered from an acute version of . . ."

The smooth voice that answers my mom fades from my ears, and I'm watching Nell's hand again, her tan arm and slender fingers, with her fingernails filed. I used to love to paint her fingernails. They were the perfect canvas.

"Miri, this might be the best place for her now. We can't let the same thing happen to her as . . ."

Aunt Becca's voice floats by. I watch Nell's fingers as they reach for me. They seem to wave to me as the fog grows.

"I promise you, we'll take very good care of her. We've put in place precautionary measures since Nell was a patient. You have my personal guarantee she'll be safe. I'll just need you to sign some paperwork."

"Nell, stop them. We need to stop them. They can't leave me here," I try to tell my sister, but her fingers have stopped moving. On the tip of her middle finger, a single drop of cherry-red blood has formed. It falls to the ground amid the green Legos and flattened M&M's and pine needles. I look up, and her face has gone slack.

"Nell!"

I wake with a gasp. My lungs feel like they've been deprived of air for hours. I try to sit up, to swipe the hair back from my forehead where it's plastered with sweat. But I can't move my hands. I can't move any part of my body, for that matter. As my eyes regain their focus, I see black rubber and mesh restraints tying my limbs and chest to a gurney. The small room is dark. I can only make out the bed I'm in and a rolling stool with a small folding table, set with instruments—a stethoscope, a blood-pressure cuff, a syringe, a tourniquet.

The scene from the hallway creeps back to mind, and my brain rewinds to the mirrored room. To Kenny. To what Dr. Keller told me right before my vision went to dark.

You're going to finish the job your sister started.

So they *can* keep me here. Mom and Aunt Becca have given them what they need to do that.

The thought of being kept here like this, of Evan trying to warn me, of my mom leaving me here just like she left Nell—I try to hold back tears, but they come in a rush. Soon I'm crying so hard that I'm afraid I might choke.

"MOM!" I scream through the sobs. "Don't leave! Don't listen to him!"

No one answers. I want to sit up, wipe my eyes, bite my nails, throw something, punch someone. But I can't do anything except stare at the ceiling and cry and lie to myself that everything is going to be okay. But it's far from okay. I know that.

I've made a huge mistake. And there's no one who can help me undo it.

I'm sobbing so hard my throat is getting sore. And at first, I barely hear the voice that calls to me.

"Hey. Hey! Nell's sister. Hey!"

Calling isn't quite right. It's more like hissing.

"Stop crying and listen to me. Can you hear me? Say yes if you can."

I try to place the voice, but I can't. Of course, I'm not sure how I could given all the whispering. All I know is it isn't the Taker, and the voice isn't in the room with me.

"You're not crying anymore. Does that mean you can hear me? Yes or no. Tell me now!"

"Yes," I hiccup. "Yes, okay? Yes."

"Good. Listen to me very carefully, Nell's sister. The Doc's going to come in any second. Whatever you do, don't let him get to you. You hear me?"

"Dr. Keller? What's he going to do to me?" I pull against the restraints again. I try to jerk my hands from the wrist cuffs, but I only succeed in chaffing the skin underneath.

"Nothing, you know, physical. But he's going to try to get

into your head. That's what he does. Believe me, he's good at it. Just don't let him in. Got it?"

"Wait, I don't know what you mean."

"Yes, you do. Now quit talking before someone hears. Just remember what I told you, Nell's sister."

"Wait! Who are you? *Where* are you? You've got to get me out of here!"

But my only response is silence. I'm left alone for no more than ten seconds before a tiny tap sounds on the door. Dr. Keller ducks his head inside.

"Hey there, sleepyhead," he chides. "Mind some company?"

He's treating me like a child. As if a lollipop will bribe me to be a good girl.

So I don't give him the pleasure of a response. He doesn't seem to expect one, though. Instead, he rolls the leather-padded stool to the edge of my bed and takes a seat, bending his athletic legs to ease himself down.

"Well then, how are we feeling?"

I stare at him in utter disbelief. Is this guy for real?

"Now, I know the restraints may seem a little unnecessary, but they're for your own protection, Sophie. I don't know if you remember, but you were pretty out of control earlier."

"Oh, I remember," I spit back. I'd hoped to maintain my cool, but he's making it really hard.

"I have no doubt." He frowns. "In fact, I think you have a very good memory. I think you've been carrying a lot of memories around with you. I bet there are some you'd give anything to forget."

His voice is sincere, and for the first time since I've met him, Dr. Keller actually sounds like a decent human being. His face is creased, deep bends around his mouth and crinkles at the corners of his eyes. He looks uncomfortable there on his stool.

Still, I wait for him to talk. I don't trust where he's going with this.

"You were there that night. When your sister cut herself."

My stomach flinches at the memory of Nell, her wrist dripping with red, the flicker of something just out of sight in the shattered bathroom mirror.

"You walked in on her, saw what she'd done. You've had to live with what you saw all this time. No one to talk to about it. Your mother, so unavailable. Your aunt preoccupied with her well-being. Who was left to care for Sophie?"

A knot edges to the top of my throat, threatening to cut off my airway.

"So many nights alone to think about what you saw. So afraid to tell anyone. And the nightmares. I'm certain they've been awful, haven't they?"

I nod before I realize what my head is doing, then scold myself mentally. The whispering voice I just heard. What did it say? *He's going to try to get into your head, and believe me, he's good at it.*

Dr. Keller closes his eyes, and when he opens them, I see a sheen on his irises. Tears. Tears for me.

"Well, that's all going to get better in time. I promise. I'm going to help you, Sophie. I will, I swear it. You just let me help you, and I will make this pain stop for good."

I flinch when he reaches a hand to my wrist, just below the restraint. He squeezes it gently, the kind of gesture that makes me think of Mrs. Dodd's kindness. I want to start weeping all over again. Or screaming. But before I can do either, Dr. Keller lifts himself from the stool, and he's out the door, closing it behind him with a soft click.

Maybe it's the residual effects of the drugs, or the exhaustion, or the trauma, but I fall asleep quickly after that. My dreams stab at my brain, trying to puncture the bubble that's begun to form over my mind. In those dreams, I see Evan's strong hands, his jaw clamped in concern. Then I see the coal-black eyes of someone else who used to feel the gratitude of Dr. Keller's empathy before fear and love drove him to hide in the high desert.

17

THE NEXT MORNING, THE NURSES run a series of tests. Tests on my eyes, my ears, my blood pressure and blood type, my glucose levels, and my level of comprehension. I'm brought from one tiny gray room to the next—each time with a needle in my arm, and an orderly carting a rolling IV behind me as a tube carries medicine to my vein. The needle wiggles at my elbow's bend, and I get a little queasy whenever I become aware of it again. But they keep telling me I need to remain on a sedative so my nerves don't affect the tests, and I have no choice but to believe them because everything they're saying sounds so reasonable. They haven't used restraints on me all morning, so I suppose the drugs are working. There's a thickness spreading across my brain, and for so long, that's all I've wanted. Just something to dull me, to make the distance between what I'm thinking and what I'm feeling grow so I can stop hurting. And while there's something deep inside that tells me I should be feeling something different, I can't seem to figure out what that feeling should be.

All I'm certain of is the needle in my arm.

"Have a seat right there, Ms. David, and we'll be in the next room behind the glass. Just tell us what you see when we turn out the lights and you look up at that big wall with the projection screen. You see that right there?"

It's the Pigeon talking to me now, and she's pointing one of her talonlike fingers at a broad white surface to my left.

"Uh-huh," I mumble. That seems to be the desired response for the orderlies. I haven't seen Dr. Keller all day, and though a loud, muffled voice inside seems to protest, I can't help but feel that it might not be so bad to see him again. Maybe I'd misjudged him. Maybe he was telling the truth. Maybe he really gets what I'm going through. Maybe he can help me get better.

Get better? Or get what he wants?

The muffled voice hurts my brain. Any thinking at all hurts my brain. So I keep uh-huhing and nodding the way I think they want me to.

Only I can't seem to shake the sound of hissing. It's a

vague memory that lingers like a tickle in my throat. It's the sound of a girl's voice, the words *Nell's sister.* The insistent tone made me listen even though I didn't want to. All I want to do now is swim in this numbness, but this persistent tickle keeps me from doing that.

"We're about to begin the evaluation, Ms. David. Please turn your head to the screen and simply watch. That's all you have to do. Just watch. Don't look away. Do you understand?"

The Pigeon's voice pipes through a speaker somewhere above me. I feel a little pull at the skin on my chest and back. I look down. At some point, little suction cup tabs have been stuck to me underneath my blue cotton shirt. My eyes drift down to my ankles. The white of my skin dangles below a slightly frayed hem of blue cotton pant legs. A tingle of memory crops up, and I'm momentarily distracted—agitated. Unhappy, though I can't recall why. My eyes drift to the needle in the bend of my elbow.

"Ms. David, do you understand?"

"Uh-huh."

"Good. Now we'll begin. Just look at the screen."

The room lights dim, and a flickering image pulls into focus on the screen. It's a clearing in a meadow. It's bright and sunny, and there are tall blades of green grass, sun-bleached in places where beams cut through the opening in the trees above. A little girl smiles up at the sun. It's a lovely picture. The next image is a close-up of a rosebud, a drop of dew trickling from its outer petal. The next is a seal pup, white and impossibly fluffy, all black eyes and nose and crystalline whiskers, nuzzled against its mother. The next is a mother holding a wide-eyed baby fresh from a bath, swaddled in a downy towel, pressed tight against her breast.

A flutter in my stomach makes the sensors on my chest and back tingle.

The next image is a photo taken from behind, a silhouette of two girls, their hands clasped together, their little figures stepping in tandem along a tree-lined path with thick piles of orange and yellow autumn leaves piled around them.

Another tingle from the sensors.

"You're doing great, Sophie. Just keep watching."

The next image is of a man smiling down at a child, his hand on her pigtailed head, her upturned nose scrunched in his direction. They seem to be sharing a quiet joke.

The sensors tingle.

The next image clicks to the screen. It's dark, and it takes my eyes a moment to adjust to the picture after such a bright one. This appears to be a room. The only light comes from around the door, like it popped open to a bright hallway on its own. There's nothing to the picture at all, but for some reason, I don't like it.

The sensor tingles on my chest, and as it does, a machine on the wall that is hooked up to the sensors—to me—beeps a single beep.

"Watch the screen, Sophie. Don't worry about anything else."

The next image clicks forward, and it's a girl standing alone in the same meadow as the first picture, but this time it's covered in shadow. The little girl's face is obscured by her hair, and her shoulders are hunched toward her ears.

Another tingle. Another beep.

The next image flicks forward, and it feels like the pictures are playing faster than before. This image is grainy and speckled like an egg, which makes it hard to see. I squint to try to pull it into focus, and when I do, I can just make out a pair of eyes and a wide, oval-shaped mouth. It's not moving, but something tells me it should be, though I don't want it to.

Another tingle, and this time, the monitor behind me beeps three times.

The next image is a tree in a clearing. A tall pine tree disappearing into the clouds.

More beeping from behind me.

"Can I—I need to stop."

The next image is a hand with a ring. A tan hand with flat paddles for fingernails and a silver ring.

More beeping.

My palms are sweating. The tingling from the sensors on my chest and back is starting to make me nauseated. I cover my eyes. The needle in my arm tugs.

"Sophie, we need you to keep watching the screen."

The next image is in shadows—oily hair covering a face, and long yellow teeth inside a black hole of a mouth.

"No! Stop! Let me out! Let me out of here!"

"Sophie, we're not done with the—"

"I said let me the fuck out of here!!"

I tug at the sensors and they peel from my skin, leaving behind sticky residue. I turn from the screen and ball up on the gurney, eyeing the IV cart suspiciously. I want to bend my elbow, to wrap my arms over my body and create an exoskeleton.

I hear a series of hushed voices at the doorway, then a click.

"Doctor, she wouldn't let us finish. She just—"

Then there's silence. After another second, the door sighs on its delay and clicks shut. Someone else is in the room with me. I can feel it.

A hand runs gently over my hair, guiding it behind my ear to expose the side of my face that isn't pressed into the cot. I squeeze my eyes shut. I want the numbness to come back.

"There, there, Sophie. You did really well for your first day."

The voice is smooth like buttered maple syrup.

I open my eyes to Dr. Keller, whose gray eyes stare down at me with concern.

"I'm sorry," I tell him without even thinking. Suddenly I'm sorry for so much. My stomach flops over when I say it, though, and an insistent voice yells at me, scolding me for something. But what?

"I know you are. You did the best you could. I know you want to make us all proud."

I do?

He crouches to meet me at eye level.

"I know you want to make me proud."

I nod and blink. My eyes feel dry. My mouth feels dry. I'm starting to get a headache.

"Don't worry too much, now," he says, squeezing my forearm tenderly. "In time, you'll be able to show us exactly what we need to see. You do want to help us, don't you?"

I want to say yes, to be agreeable. At least I think I want that.

He nods slowly, his mouth pinned in a soft frown. "You

have a very special gift, Sophie. You can hear what it's saying. You know what I'm talking about, don't you?"

I nod. I can hear what it's saying. Well, almost. It wants me to hear.

"Your sister, she had the gift too. But then, I'm sure you knew that."

The tickle in my throat is gone now, and it's been replaced by a lump I can't swallow. My eyes tear up, spill over onto the tissue paper on the gurney beneath my cheek.

"Oh, now, why the tears? Surely you two talked about it. Nell trusted you, I know that. She told me she trusted you. Unless . . . oh dear . . ." Dr. Keller shakes his head slowly, the lines around his mouth deepening, his chin puckering.

I'm soaking the paper under my face, but I can barely feel the tears falling. My whole face feels like it's gone numb.

"I didn't want to believe her," I whisper. My body shakes. I feel like my whole body is crying.

"Of course you didn't." The doctor's voice pours over me. His hand strokes my hair again. "Of course you didn't."

I pinch my eyes shut, my sobs coming in waves, and finally my body stops shaking. Dr. Keller's hand never leaves my head, never stops stroking my hair. It's the only thing that seems to keep me connected to this room. And yet, something inside of me is screaming. Part of me wants to throw his hand off of me or take it in my own hand and break it into a thousand pieces. But why? He's only comforting me. Isn't that what I've been wanting for so long? To feel safe?

Then I hear him stand. His shoes click then squeak on the linoleum as he walks across the room. A drawer opens and closes, and his shoes click then squeak toward me again. The bag on the cart beside me rustles. I feel the gentlest tug on the needle in my arm, and then my arm and shoulder and chest and the rest of my limbs go cold. My heart races with the sensation, and when I try to open my eyes again, I can't.

But I don't care anymore because I'm floating into a gray nothingness.

"Nell's sister. Wake up! Hey, wake up!"

My head is throbbing, and it takes every ounce of strength to open my eyes—not that it does much good once I do. I'm surrounded by dark and shadow. It smells like metal. Or maybe that's the just the taste in my mouth.

"Are you awake?"

I groan in response. I don't quite know how to articulate that I don't know. I can't tell if I'm asleep and having a strange dream or if I'm awake.

"I'll take that as a yes. You've got to stop. You're not doing what I told you to do."

This voice is familiar. Have I dreamt it before?

"You're letting him get to you. That's exactly what I told you *not* to do. Are you listening to me?"

"Go away," I grumble, wishing the voice in my head would stop. When I reach for my temple, I realize there's no tugging. I put my fingers to the inside of my elbow, and I'm rewarded with another dull pain to match the one in my head. It feels like a bruise that reaches to my bone. My ankles and wrists feel the same way. And my shin itches, though I can't remember why.

"Go away? Not a chance. Look, I'm going to help you whether you want me to or not, because frankly, you're probably the last chance we've got."

The voice is a little louder now, like it's forgotten to whisper.

"What am I supposed to do?" I ask. I know it's totally crazy. I'm now talking to some voice I've probably conjured myself. There's no other explanation for it. Unless I'm dreaming again. I don't know what's real anymore. All I know is talking hurts more than anything else at the moment, so I'll do whatever it takes to make it shut up.

"They're going to take us out to the courtyard tomorrow. They want to see what happens when they put the two of us together. They want to see if we can, you know, *make* something happen. Like we're goddamned wizards. We can talk more then. But *not* if you're high as a kite."

"I don't do drugs," I say automatically, like I'm talking to a teacher.

"Well, maybe you don't, but that's not really your choice anymore. Sounds like you're coming down right now. Here's what you're going to do. Listen to me carefully. Are you listening?"

"Yes, yes, I'm listening."

"Tomorrow morning, they're going to give you two pills in a cup with your breakfast. Take the pills. They're sugar pills; they won't do anything. They just want to see if you're done fighting them, which by the sound of it, you pretty much are."

This is the first hint of real anger I've heard in the voice, and it gets my attention. If this voice is just my imagination, does that mean I'm mad at myself? I keep listening.

"Take the pills so they think you're not going to give them any trouble, but *don't* drink the juice. Got it? Take the pills; don't touch the juice. Pour out the juice. Anywhere you can so they don't find it. But make sure you pour it out so they think you drank it. Got it?"

"Okay," I say. Why not? The things the voice is telling me are no crazier than the fact that I'm hearing voices in the first place. I might as well go along with it.

"I hope for both our sakes you're not just bullshitting me," the voice scolds, and then I'm left in silence.

"Hey, you still there?" I ask tentatively. I'm met only by the sound of my own breathing, and I feel strangely alone all of a sudden.

"Best not to get used to that," I tell myself. It's not a good thing to start missing the company of your own delusions.

Not in a place like this.

18

MY HEAD IS POUNDING BEFORE I even open my eyes. The room is bright. I can tell by the way my eyelids feel semi-translucent. I ease them open to a squint, and when I decide my head can handle a little more, I open them to see where I am.

Another gray room. This one looks much the same as the others I remember . . . that I sort of remember . . . assuming I didn't dream them. But in addition to the glaring fluorescent lights, this room has a window high in the wall. It's covered by mesh and out of reach at about nine feet, just below the ceiling.

My wrist and ankle restraints are tied tight. I seem to recall being free of them, even if for a short time. I shift my gaze to the bend in my elbow. It's red and purple with a tiny lump and a little perforation at the top of it where a needle should be, but for once it's not. And though my head is still thumping behind my drooping eyelids, I am glad to be free of the IV. My brain feels whole for the first time in . . . a day . . . a week? I have no idea how much time has passed.

My heart skitters in my chest as I try to fill the empty spaces in my mind.

What do they know about me? What have they been doing to me? How long do they think they can keep me here? *Can* they keep me here at all?

The restraints on my wrists and ankles seem to answer that question for me.

Then a memory—or what I'd like to believe is a memory because I have no real basis for reality at this point—of Mom's voice and Aunt Becca's seeps in. They're talking to Dr. Keller, or rather he's talking to them, and they accept what he says like chicks eating worms from their mother's beak. They swallow every last word. After that, the only voice I remember hearing is Dr. Keller's.

I want to curl into the smallest human ball. I tell myself I'm fine on my own. I don't need Mom or Aunt Becca or anyone else to rescue me. Then my mind scurries to the image of another face, and then I'm thinking about Evan, his calloused hands gripping mine. I want to feel his hands on my wrists instead of these straps. I want him to steady me. My throat closes over fresh sobs, but if I focus on what I want rather than what's in front of me, I really will lose my mind. I may have more questions than answers, and my brain may not be entirely whole, but at least I know that for the first time since they put me in blue scrubs, my brain is *mine.* And I intend to keep it that way for as long as I'm here.

This is what I tell myself to keep the panic that's begun burbling in my chest at bay. Maybe the drugs weren't so bad. Is a Swiss-cheese memory better than this reality?

Shoes squeak outside my door. My stomach reacts with an involuntary grumble. I feel like I haven't eaten in years.

There's a swipe, then a click, and the Pigeon emerges from behind the door in a freshly starched uniform pushing a metal cart with a yellow plastic tray on top. Separate compartments in the tray hold scrambled eggs, a slice of slightly burnt toast, and a cup of fruit cocktail. Not typically my idea of a tasty breakfast, but I'm so hungry, I'd eat just about anything they put in front of me. And at least I know by the meal that it's morning.

"Rise and shine," the Pigeon sings, and I immediately know that she has never been a mother. She's unpracticed in that brand of cheeriness.

I try to sit up, but my restrained wrists only allow me to get up on my elbows.

"Oh, dear. Let me get those for you," she says, that mock soothing tone already grating on my nerves.

She pulls a plastic device from her pocket that looks like a pin and pushes it into a hole on one wrist restraint and then the other. She does the same for my ankles, and once I'm mobile, my limbs feel strangely light.

"Now, eat up," she says, her singsong voice chilling me.

"And don't forget to take your medicine," she says, gesturing to the little paper cup in the corner of the tray with one of her talons. "That'll help with the headache."

I don't like anything about this woman, least of all her ability to divine the pain that I'm in. Suddenly I feel completely naked in front of her.

She leaves me to my breakfast, shutting the door behind her. I look at the food in front of me: The eggs are underdone and runny, the fruit cocktail is heavy on syrup and light on actual fruit, and the toast isn't just kind of burnt but practically charred. The pills in the paper cup are enormous and turquoise, and I've been given a giant glass of orange juice to take them. In fact, the juice is the only thing that looks semi-edible on the tray.

Something flickers at the back of my mind, like a projector trying to play a movie that's gotten stuck in the reel.

"Juice," I mutter to the tray of food.

My head is starting to pound harder, and I suspect it's because I need to eat something. I'm also so thirsty I feel like I'm going to turn into a prune. The juice is looking better and better.

But for some reason, my hand—feeling lightweight and not quite my own in the absence of the restraints—reaches for the blackened piece of toast instead. I eat it fast, almost choking on the charred crumbs. Then I turn to the eggs, which taste excessively salty, and shovel them into my mouth with the spoon they gave me (no sharp objects, I suppose). I move on to the syrupy cocktail before I've even finished chewing the eggs. I drink the syrup, and wouldn't you know it, my headache really does start to subside. The only things left untouched are the cup of pills and the juice.

My mouth has a vaguely metallic taste, and I would give anything to kill that with a little bit of juice. And I'm thirstier than I was before I ate. I feel like my tongue is going to shrivel up and fall out of my mouth.

But I reach for the pills instead. I swallow the first one dry, then the second, producing meager amounts of saliva to slide them to my stomach, a sensation I unfortunately feel due to the ridiculous size of the capsules.

I eye the orange juice again, warily, as if I expect it to do something.

I could leave it untouched, pretend I just didn't want it. But the same feeling that's been propelling me all morning tells me that I need to conceal it. I need to look like I'm playing along.

Let them know you're not going to fight them anymore.

I search the small gray room for convenient hiding places. There are no drains, no potted plants, no holes to pour it down that I can see. It's liquid, and it'll smell if I don't pour it someplace where it'll get absorbed easily. The cot I'm sitting on doesn't have thick enough material. The only other thing in the room is the cart the Pigeon rolled in with breakfast.

A few minutes pass while I hold the giant glass of juice in my hand and contemplate what to do. The longer it takes me to find a hiding place for it, the heavier it seems to get. Before long, I can hear squeaking from what I'm assuming is the far end of the hallway. A swipe and the ping of the releasing lock announce my visitor.

Without much thought, I dump the entire contents of the juice on my chest and lap, the sticky, pulpy liquid soaking my cheap cotton scrubs.

"Oh!" the orderly fails to contain his shock. I guess I can't blame him. I can't even begin to imagine how ridiculous I look right about now.

"I spilled," I say, deciding to go with the obvious.

"Uh," he says, looking around, then behind him, then back at me, then behind him again.

"You got a towel or something?" I ask him, for once feeling like I have the upper hand in this place. It's sad that it took me being on this side of its doors to feel that way. I've never seen this orderly before, and it's a shame that I haven't. I get the sense that I could have gotten a lot more information from this guy than from the likes of the Pigeon.

"I don't . . . you were supposed to drink that," he says.

"Yeah, that's typically the idea with juice," I shoot back, then try smiling. To my surprise, he smiles back, then catches himself.

"Can I get cleaned up somewhere?" I ask, and he looks behind him again.

"You're supposed to be in the courtyard in ten minutes," he says, like I'm supposed to know what that means. He seems to catch himself again, and his face screws in on itself like a button sewn to a shirt too tightly.

They want to see what happens when they put the two of us together.

"Well, I can't go outside like this," I say, then try smiling again. "And honestly, I don't know when I've last showered. I can't really remember how long I've been here, you know?"

He sighs impatiently, then signals for me to follow him.

He looks to his left and his right, his left again, then points a nicotine-stained finger toward the end of a long, gray corridor, and I quickly locate the sign that says WOMEN.

"There are showers in there," he says. "I'll find a female worker to go in there with you."

"I think I can figure it out on my own," I say, a little taken aback.

"Rules," he says.

I start to head down the hallway, then turn back to the orderly. "Can I get a clean set of clothes?"

"I'll find some new ones," he says, looking more agitated now that he's taken a peek at his watch.

"Shit," he mumbles. "Just hurry up."

He scurries down the hall in the opposite direction, and my heart races the moment he leaves my sight.

Because I'm alone.

I know there's no way I'll make it very far unattended. But I creep after the jittery orderly just the same. Sadly, all I find when I round the corner is another gray, nondescript hallway with its own set of unmarked gray doors. I jiggle one handle, then another. None budge.

"Come on," I whisper. "Isn't there anything here that isn't locked?"

But I already know the answer to that.

I'm just about to retreat back to the showers when I hear the familiar swipe of a keycard and ping of a lock undoing itself. It sounds like it's coming from several doors down, but I'm too far away from the corner to duck around it without notice.

"Come on, let's get you out to the courtyard," a woman says impatiently.

An orderly emerges from one of the rooms, and I immediately recognize her as the woman who was operating the admittance doors the day I came to pick up Nell's box of things. She's a pucker-lipped lady roughly my mom's age, and she's pulling a thin arm in her tight grasp. On the other end of that arm is a petite blonde with enormous eyes whom I also recognize; she's the girl who shot down the hallway screaming and had to be restrained by the Pigeon when I came to see Kenny—the day he gave me Nell's poem.

"What are you doing out here?" the pucker-lipped orderly asks. "And where's Robbie?"

"I don't know who Robbie is, but I can't take a shower before I have new clothes to change into," I say, knowing instinctively that my defiance isn't going to go over well with this one.

She has a similar huff to Robbie's. Then she turns to the blond girl whose arm she's still grasping.

"Courtyard," she commands with a look that conveys the consequences for not following directions. "You know the drill. Ring the bell and someone will meet you on the other side of the door.

The blond girl responds by blinking her giant eyes and turns to go.

The orderly ducks into a room to our right and, with one foot propping open the door behind her, leans toward a shelf stacked with blue scrubs, sorted in piles labeled small, medium, large, and extra-large.

While the orderly is busying herself with choosing the right size for me, I hear a hissing whisper at the end of the hallway.

"That's one way to get rid of it," the girl says, then winks one of her giant eyes at me.

The orderly emerges with a folded pair of pants, shirt, and towel.

"Make it quick," she says, giving me a slight push toward the bathroom.

But I barely register the orderly's command. Because my memory has suddenly awoken from its drugged haze. I haven't been imagining that whispering voice. And now I have a face to go with it.

19

THE "COURTYARD" IS ANYTHING BUT. It's essentially a rock garden, and really not even that considering it's composed of maybe two types of gravel—one red and one brown. The yard spans half the length of the building's back wall, probably the length of three houses squished side by side in a typical Phoenix neighborhood. And the courtyard is longer than it is deep. It reaches maybe twenty yards back before it's stopped short by a forbiddingly high cinderblock retaining wall. Concrete sidewalks weave through the garden, and weeds and cacti sprinkle the empty spaces in between. I can't help but wonder how dangerous a place like this might be for someone with actual psychological problems. So many sharp objects.

It's chilly out. Winter has finally arrived. Goose bumps prick my arms, but I'm not about to ask for anything warmer to wear. Something tells me the Pigeon would be more than happy to fit me with a straitjacket to keep my arms warm.

There's a fog of cigarette smoke in the air. A cluster of about five orderlies stand around chuckling and grumbling, some smoking. They're all in matching white uniforms, which are creased at bellies and knees—all except for the Pigeon's. She looks perfectly in order, not a single hair unpinned, not a wrinkle marring her uniform. There's no sign of Dr. Keller.

I scan the rest of the "courtyard" and almost miss the blond girl altogether. She's at the corner farthest from the orderlies, the shadow of Oakside's exterior wall swallowing her in its shade. She sits on a backless concrete bench, her knees making a shelf under her chin. Her wide eyes find me and signal for me to come and sit beside her. After another look at the distracted orderlies, I do—but not without first noticing the Pigeon noticing us. She stays where she is, but her eyes never leave me. I angle myself on the bench so I can talk to the girl while keeping one eye on the cluster of orderlies in the distance.

"You're going to have to find a better way of getting rid of your juice," the blond girl says in a voice so low, I almost can't hear her. Up close, I see her giant eyes are a brown so light, they're almost yellowish. "They're going to catch on if you keep spilling on yourself. Nobody's that clumsy."

"What are you talking about? Exactly how long do you think I'm going to be stuck in this place?!"

"Shhh!" she scolds, shifting her gaze toward the orderlies. The Pigeon's got her laser-tight focus on me.

"You're going to be here as long as they want you to be here, and it's best if you just get used to that right away," she says, her voice even more hushed than before. "Unless of course you have someone on the outside who wants to get you out."

My stomach twists into a tight knot. The girl's implication is unmistakable. What she doesn't say is what I've been trying to deny since my mind has been lucid: No one is coming for me. Mom and Aunt Becca have given me up. What can Evan do for me now? Even if he wanted to get me out, how could he without Mom's permission?

I catch the Pigeon's unforgiving stare. My eyes find the retaining wall behind her. I know it has to be my imagination, but it looks as if the wall is moving. As if it's crawling toward me at a steady pace, pressing the courtyard into a tighter and tighter strip of concrete. My palms are cold, and when I look down at my hands, I realize they're shaking.

"How long have I been here?" I demand of this girl I don't

even know. But for some reason, she seems to have answers.

"Two days," she says.

My hands cease their trembling for just a moment. Two days. My mind has only been clouded and prodded for two days. Maybe two days is not enough time to admit I've been abandoned. Maybe.

"Do you know how they convinced my mom to sign me away?" I ask, the trembling returning, this time all over my body. If Oakside could convince my own mother to give up on me, what hope did I have?

And for the first time since seeing her, the blond girl's eyes lower to the ground.

"What? What is it?" The knot in my stomach cinches tighter.

"Kenny," she whispers, squeezing her eyes closed, her mouth twitching into a frown.

It's as though a locked door has unlatched in my brain. Heavy fog dissipates to a fine mist, and the mist parts to reveal a blur of pictures.

Coal-black eyes and giant hands gripping at stale coffee and stale air.

Shouting in a car.

Evan's pleading, calloused hands.

Nell's finely curled writing across pale blue lines.

Flattened, primary-colored pine needles with MM stamped on their backs.

Kenny's wide red face, hanging upside down.

Now it's just the two of you.

I pull my knees to my chest like the girl next to me, feeling colder than before. I can't stop my body from shaking, and I'm fooling myself to think it's just the weather. My throat is so dry, I wonder if I'll ever be able to swallow again.

By the time I finally glance up at the blond girl, she's opened her enormous orbs to reveal small puddles.

I want to ask her more, but I feel utterly paralyzed.

"Kenny knew what he was doing," she begins. "He'd had enough. When they saw you pull into the parking lot the other night, they knew you were coming to talk to him again. They just didn't know what about. That's what they bribed Kenny to find out. Dr. Keller knew that once he got you to talk, they'd find a way to keep you here."

She pauses, shifting her eyes back to the orderlies. I don't follow her gaze this time. I'm too afraid. When her eyes return, they shift downward again, seeking solace in her knees.

"Kenny told me earlier that he wouldn't let it continue, that if you came back, he'd end it. I didn't know what he meant. Kenny's been . . . he's been gone, you know, mentally, for a long time now. He's been here longer than anyone, since before Dr. Keller even arrived, when Gladys was more than just his sidekick. She was in charge—some sort of administrator. I think Kenny's been in and out of institutions for most of his life. Anyway, when you came back, he just snapped. They promised him all the green Legos he wanted if he got you talking about how you've been hearing things. They said they'd take it from there. But Kenny had other plans."

Now she looks up at me, an urgency filling her face. I have never seen a person so young look so old. From far away, I would have bet money she was my age, maybe a year or two younger. But close up, I wonder.

"He got his hands on a syringe. He knocked you out. And before the orderlies could get to him, he brought you to The Room, then busted the exterior keypad."

"The room with the mirrors," I whisper.

The girl with blond hair blinks in response. "I guess Kenny decided he was going to try to stop what they're doing here. He was going to let it get him. I guess he figured he'd show them what would happen if he unleashed that . . . *thing*. If they were willing to play with fire, he'd give them fire. I don't think he thought about what would happen to you, honestly. I think he just . . . wanted it all to end."

She stops as her voice breaks. I want so badly to comfort her, but she looks too fragile to touch. And while I know it's not my fault that Kenny's dead, a part of me can't help but feel like he might still be alive if I'd just stayed away.

"I never should have come back," are the only words I can manage to eke out. And for more reasons than she knows.

But the girl shakes her head.

"He'd already made up his mind. Kenny is . . . *was* the most stubborn person I know. I think he figured you'd either die with him, or you'd find a way to stop it. Either way, the cycle would end."

We let the ghost of our conversation float between us for another minute, the chill of the morning finally starting to burn off.

"I guess he was wrong about both," I say, the hopelessness of the situation pressing down on me with suffocating force.

The girl with the blond hair searches me with her huge eyes. "Then why did you come back?"

Her question is without malice or accusation. She sounds more defeated than I feel, and that makes me feel even worse. That is, until I remember the answer to her question.

"You're MM, aren't you?"

A watery smile spreads across the girl's face, and tears well in her eyes all over again. "She had a knack for nicknames, didn't she? M&M's were my favorite candy. Until they started using them to bribe me."

My confusion must be pretty obvious because she tries to clarify.

"That's how they used to get me into The Room. They'd promise me all the M&M's I could eat if I'd just stare into the mirror and think about all the sad things Dr. Keller and I talked about in our sessions. They knew that would make the thing appear in the mirror. Then they'd shoo me out of the room, and in Dr. Keller would go, looking all crazy and hopeful and carrying a long, thin velvet box. And every time, I'd have a session with him the next day, and it was more of the same. Except he kept getting sadder and sadder, then crazier and crazier. People like me came and went, sometimes because their parents would pull them out, sometimes because they'd . . . well, you saw what Kenny did."

"And Oakside gets away with it?" I ask, forgetting to check my volume. Her eyes shift to the orderlies, then she nods almost imperceptibly.

"You don't understand," she says. "Most of the time, people like me end up here because nobody else wants to deal with them. That's why . . ." Her voice cracks again, like an enormous weight has dropped on her all at once.

"That's why my parents never came back for me."

I finally find the nerve to put a hand on hers. Her fingers are small and impossibly cold. And it's the only thing that's brought me anything close to comfort since I've been lucid enough to realize exactly how deep I am in this mess.

"Are you Deb?"

Her eyes reach mine, and something shifts in them, like a fire igniting.

"You are, aren't you?"

She nods, her jaw moving up and down like a fish blowing air bubbles underwater.

Just then, a shadow casts a chill over me, and I hear the crunch of gravel underfoot.

"All right, girls. Enough chatting for one day. There'll be plenty more time for that after your individual sessions with Dr. Keller."

The Pigeon is standing so close to me, I can feel the heat radiating from her recently sunned self. She circles one of her talons around my elbow, her thumb pressing on the bruised patch of skin where the IV left its mark. She pulls me from my sitting position with a smart jerk of her arm.

"It was nice meeting you," I say over my shoulder. "I'm Sophie."

She nods once, her face still alight with that spark, and I hope she sees all I'm trying to convey with my eyes. Maybe Kenny was right. Maybe what I told Adam in Jerome was right. Maybe I can be the one to put a stop to all of this.

20

SLEEP ISN'T COMING EASILY TONIGHT, and I'm ashamed to admit that I miss the drugs. The bend in my arm is only just beginning to turn purplish-blue, and I'm finally able to think in coherent sentences, but that also means I can't stop my mind from racing. My conversation with Deb in the courtyard keeps coming back to me in snippets, like I'm the unwilling star of my own movie trailer.

More disturbing—and exciting—is knowing that I was right. MM, Nell's friend and confidante from her journal, is Deb, Evan's long-missing cousin. It brings a shiver to my insides every time I think about how close he was to her this whole time. All the while, she's been right here at Oakside, no more than ten miles from his home. He'd even visited here looking for Dr. Keller because of Adam's blog. He never knew she was here, and she never knew he was looking for her.

I'm just starting to doze into a restless sleep when I hear a familiar hiss.

"Hey, Nell's—I mean, Sophie. You awake?"

"Deb?" I'm so relieved to hear a trusted voice, I nearly cry right there on my pillow.

"Listen up, okay? No juice for you tomorrow. You're going to have your first one-on-one session with Dr. Keller, and you're going to need to be on your best pretend behavior when you see him. You need to act like you're ready to cooperate. It's the only way to keep him out of your head. Which means you'll be able to keep the *thing* from the mirror away. Got it?"

I nod from my pillow, then remember she can't see me. "Hey, Deb? Where the hell are you anyway?"

For the first time, she giggles. It sounds strangely grown-up considering her tiny stature. "I've learned a lot about sneaking around this place over the last few years. There's an air vent and a super lazy nighttime orderly. After our one-on-ones tomorrow, we'll see each other in the rec room. We can talk more then. I have to get back to my room before bed checks. G'night."

I can hear a tiny shuffling sound, and before it fades, I whisper "Deb?"

"Yeah? Make it quick."

"He's never stopped looking for you, you know."

Never has a silence sounded more crowded with unspoken words.

"Evan," I finish, and I hear a tiny gasp before the shuffling resumes, then fades to nothing. And then I'm left to slide into a sleep so shallow it's barely worth the effort.

Days are long at Oakside. At least in my drug-induced haze, I wasn't so achingly aware of the passage of time. Nell's journal probably saved her life. They've offered me no such perks, so I'm left to my thoughts. At least I'm thinking in complete sentences. If I could just have one book to read in between breakfast (the most exhausting part of which is finding a place to dump my orange juice), the daily shower overseen by the orderly with the puckered lips, the morning courtyard visits with Deb, and the afternoon rec center "social time," I might just feel like I could get this itch off of my skin.

Deb is my only saving grace. We have to be careful how much she shares with me, though; it seems there's always someone watching. But I've managed to get some information from her when the inevitable distraction grips our supervising orderly. She knows about the Takers, or at least enough to know that we attract them. And she knows about

Dr. Keller's obsession with the one that used to be Susan.

Mostly I've come to learn that, as alone as I feel in this place, and as empty as it seems to be aside from Deb and myself, we are apparently not alone. The echoing hallways of Oakside are only a phenomenon in our wing. On the other side, the rooms remain full of the neglected patients Adam wrote about in his blog.

Deb sneaked to "the other side" a few times, a phrasing I couldn't help but find absurdly funny (in that sad, not-so-funny way). What she found were rooms packed with two to three patients, all in green scrubs (distinguishing them from our blue ones), and the smell of neglect. There was hardly any risk of Deb getting caught on that side of the facility, mostly, she said, because no orderlies roam those halls. Deb went back only once, mostly for something to do, but she decided it was too depressing to continue after one patient called to her after hearing her in the ducts. The patient told Deb she was cold. Deb said the woman's voice sounded so old, so needy, that it made Deb shake. She went back to her room for the rest of the day, refusing food when it was offered, knowing that if she told the orderlies about the woman, they'd know she had left her room. And it's pretty hard to pass a blanket through a vent in the wall.

• • •

Dr. Keller's clinical office is different from his office-office. The office-office I saw the day I came to collect Nell's box is apparently where all the paperwork is done. This office, he tells me with a conspiratorial wink, is where the *real* work gets done.

"We've only begun to scratch the surface of your psyche, Sophie," he tells me.

It's my first one-on-one session with him. Deb says these happen weekly. He's wearing the Dr. Keller mask I remember from our initial meetings, and I'm glad for it. It makes it easier to loathe him.

"I've been consulting with Gladys. I rely on her for nearly every aspect of my practice. I trust in her judgment explicitly. She used to manage this facility before I took over, you know. It was a necessary evolution for Oakside. One might say a certified doctor has a bit more . . . finesse," he says with a smile that sours my stomach. "And from what she tells me, you're off to a very good start. A very good start indeed," he says to the clipboard in front of him rather than to me.

The more I think about what the Pigeon might have told him—what might be written about me on the clipboard in front of him—the more panicked I become. I can only imagine what I must have revealed during my initial drug haze.

"What, er, what does that mean? A very good start?" I ask,

kicking myself for sounding so skeptical. Deb warned me to be on my best good-patient behavior. The key is to pretend to take my medicine so he can't get inside my head.

He tilts the clipboard, gray eyes sparkling, and looks at me like I'm some sort of delicacy.

"Try not to worry yourself too much with that. Keep doing what you're doing, and we're going to get along just fine," he says, his smooth features easing into a smile that could send me into sugar shock.

Dr. Keller's clinical office is almost entirely white, an anomaly in the all-gray Oakside. The chair he sits in is white mesh with a white base, the table he sits behind is a white sort of Formica. The couch I'm perched on is padded with unforgiving white cushions. The walls, the carpeted floors, even this side of the metal door are all white. In fact, the only non-white part of the whole room is a silk plant standing sentinel-like in the corner across from me. I feel a little like that plant, my blue scrubs and my dyed-red hair subject to acute scrutiny and out of place.

Dr. Keller stands from his chair and walks around his desk, his white lab coat flapping behind his easy strides. To my surprise, he sits on the couch beside me, keeping a respectable distance while leaning toward me.

"Now I want you to relax, Sophie, okay? I'm going to talk

for a little while, and all you have to do is listen. You don't need to say a word. Your only job is to listen to what I say. How does that sound?"

"Sounds pretty easy, I guess." I can't decide where he's going with this, but whatever he's doing, it seems harmless enough. It's not like I really have a choice in the matter, anyway.

"All right, then," he says, sneaking one last glance at the clipboard. "I'm going to tell you a little story. It's not about anyone in particular. It's just a story. Okay?"

"Sure." I shrug.

"The story is of a young woman, about eighteen. She was kind, beautiful. She believed everyone deserved a good life."

"She sounds like a champ," I say, sucking in a tiny breath as I realize what a horrible job I'm doing playing along. But to my surprise, Dr. Keller only agrees.

"She was an extraordinarily good person," he says, his voice taking on a softer tone as affection creeps in. "Wouldn't you think this would make boys flock to be by her side and to call her their girlfriend?"

I nod. Why not? It's a little far-fetched that anyone could be that great, but I'm sort of intrigued to hear the story.

He smiles, and suddenly, his face crumples under the pressure of unexpected emotion.

"Against all reason, she allowed one very unworthy boy to

call her his. He promised her he would always listen, that he would always be there to hold her hand, to appreciate her exquisiteness. That was the day this boy knew he would never be happy unless he could make this perfect girl his wife."

I watch Dr. Keller's manicured hands grip the clipboard that tells *my* story, then go lax, letting it slide to the plush carpet. His hands tremble and shake, his shoulders hunch. His mouth, smiling only moments before, grimaces as if it's taking every last reserve of strength to keep his composure. Pity spills over this man, who's so clearly at odds with himself.

"They planned to go to college together. The boy, he thought he might die of happiness knowing that he had won the heart of this girl. The day before they were to leave for their studies, he prepared a special evening for the two of them. He'd planned to give her a gift, something symbolic that would remind her how much he loved her."

I can feel my chest tightening uncomfortably as he talks. Even though I know what comes next, this story sounds different coming from Dr. Keller than it did coming from Adam. From Adam's lips, Dr. Keller's loss was acknowledged, but that's all. From Dr. Keller, the pain is searing. I can't seem to do anything but listen and feel my insides twist as if someone is ringing them out like a soaked rag.

"She was killed that night," he says.

A gasp escapes me before I can capture it.

"And he knew that he would never be whole again, Sophie."

I shake my head. He's right. How could he ever be the same after that?

Dr. Keller takes my hand so gently, I can barely feel his fingers. "I think you understand me better than anyone, Sophie. You know how lonely it is when you recognize you should have done something to save someone. You know the sting of regret every time your memory replays that moment when you failed them."

That night in the bathroom. The mirror shattered. Nell's wrist bleeding. Her stricken face.

"Regret is horrid. It's maybe the worst thing that a person can feel. It's like a sickness. And so the boy promised he'd find her, even in death."

He inches closer to me on the couch, and I'm so enraptured by his gaze that I can't seem to move away.

"I want to rid the world of that kind of sickness, Sophie. And there are people who can help me to make that happen. People like you."

Suddenly, my chest loosens, and I feel a tickle in the back of my mind.

Evan never stopped looking for you.

I look down, my heart racing with the memory of what I'd told Deb. When I look up again, Dr. Keller's eyes are fixed on me. His hands grip mine so tightly.

"You're lying, Dr. Keller," I say, and his eyes twitch in their sockets, almost imperceptibly.

"I'm sorry?"

"You're lying. You said this story wasn't about anyone in particular. But that's not true."

Dr. Keller releases my fingers and leans back.

"The origin of the story, Ms. David, is less important than how it affects you. Who, for instance, has been abandoned in your life?"

He bends to pick up his fallen clipboard, but his eyes never leave mine. His pupils are the size of donut sprinkles, and gray irises hide any ounce of humanity they showed only seconds earlier. He's trying to hurt me, trying to provoke my guilt about letting Nell down, my emptiness after her death. He wants to break me into pieces, then reconstruct me to suit his singular need.

"Not my life, Doctor. Not *my* loved one."

He narrows his eyes. Nostrils widening like a bull's, he licks his lip, clamps his jaw, then parts his lips long enough to say, "I think we're done for today, Ms. David."

I want to leave but I'm terrified that the minute I stand,

he'll hit me with that clipboard. Or he'll reach for my throat with those manicured hands.

Instead, he makes the first move, standing with a quiet cracking of his joints and walking to the metal door that's sealed us in his clinical office. Reaching inside his lab coat to his waistband, he produces a keycard that hangs on a retractable string from his belt loop. He slides the card through a reader and opens the door, gesturing sharply toward a waiting orderly in the hallway. It's Robbie.

I edge by Dr. Keller, but he places a hand lightly on my shoulder, pulling me back toward him. "By the way, Ms. David," he says. His mouth is only inches from my ear, the heat of his breath is terrifyingly similar to another murmuring I've heard before.

"Gladys tells me you spilled your orange juice the other day, and today she was displeased to find orange stains under your pillow. You really must be more careful."

And with that, he squeezes my shoulder, sending a hot rush of pain through my arm, and hands me off to Robbie, who takes me back to my room.

Orderlies come and go from my room with stiff smiles I suspect are applied for the sole purpose of avoiding conflict. Why they're so careful I can't begin to guess. But I suspect it has something to do with what they think I'm capable of conjuring in front of a mirror. Or maybe it just makes their job easier if they don't engage me.

I, for one, intend to save my "getting worked up" for when I think it will count. And so far, I have yet to see when that might be. All I can do is rely on Deb for my cues, and her only cues thus far have been to play along, particularly with Gladys—the Pigeon. For some reason, Deb seems more terrified of her than all the rest, though I've never asked her why. As for "playing along," I can get behind that for a little while, so long as that doesn't turn into outright compliance. I have no intention of cooperating with this situation long-term. I may not know how I'm going to get out of Oakside yet, but pretending that I like it here definitely won't bring me any closer to freedom.

I had a dream about Evan last night. It wasn't the kind where I woke up sweating and trembling and trying to piece out events in my head, like some jigsaw puzzle. This was straightforward. Maybe it was my subconscious giving me a break from all the mental speculation. In it, Evan's hands were on me. They touched my face first, his fingers running the length of my jaw to my neck, then through my hair. He kissed me, his lips hungry, his tongue tickling mine. He was breathing heavily, and so was I. Then his hands were on my shoulders, pulling me closer to him. He traced my spine, his touch suddenly light, his fingers moving underneath my shirt, exploring places that made my breath start and stop.

I woke up moaning. Then I broke into a cold sweat.

I can't be here forever. I can't be here as long as Nell was. As long as Deb has been. I can't stay here.

This can't be my new life.

21

I THINK IT'S DAY SEVEN, though I can't be sure.

Robbie the orderly comes to retrieve me in the afternoon as usual.

"Rec time," he says flatly.

He steers me down the hallway and around several corners, and I find myself terrified that I'm eventually going to grow used to this—that at some point, I'll know how many turns it is to get to any given room in this place. I need to get out of here. But I'm no closer to figuring out how I'm going to escape.

We turn one more corner and I spot the bright fluorescent glow of the lobby and the adjacent recreation room. Deb is already there, and has been deposited in a corner across from Kenny's old Lego station. My palms sweat at the sight of that table, and I quickly refocus on Deb.

"What's she doing here?" A raspy voice interjects the minute I enter the room.

Robbie checks his watch, then looks to the pucker-mouthed orderly, her heavy ponytail tilting her chin up like a finger pointing accusingly at us both.

"It's four o'clock. Recreation time," he whines, a child reprimanded.

"Don't you pay attention to *anything*? Dr. Keller was explicit in his instruction. They are to be kept separate for the rest of the day today. This one's on punishment," she says, jutting her chin in my direction.

So that's it. I'd wondered how long it would take for the other shoe to drop. I suppose a threat from Dr. Keller couldn't have been my only punishment for defying him.

I steal a glance at Deb, and her eyes ask the question she can't: *Weren't you listening to anything I said?*

I know I should have told her about my encounter with Dr. Keller, but I'd almost convinced myself he was over it. I should have known his memory for pain and vengeance was long and detailed.

"Just get them both back to their rooms," the pucker-mouthed orderly commands, fishing in her pocket and pulling out a box of cigarettes before stomping down the hallway.

Robbie sighs and grabs my arm gruffly.

"Let's go," he says, pulling Deb up by her arm and starting down the hallway with both of us. But a hollow knocking sound makes us all turn to the lobby area.

If I'm startled to see the rather large man in a gray jumpsuit standing at the inside door to the visitor area, Robbie is downright panicked. Suddenly it feels like a hundred years since I've seen anyone who's not wearing blue scrubs or a white orderly's smock.

"No!" Robbie shouts across the room to the man. "No visitors!" he says rudely.

"Pal, I ain't here to visit," the man in the jumpsuit shouts through the glass, hoisting a toolbox so it's level with his stubbled face. "A and J Electric. I'm here to fix your busted keypad."

"Shit," Robbie says through clenched teeth, then looks down at me like he's forgotten he's still gripping my arm.

"Uh, just wait there a few minutes," Robbie shouts again to the electrician.

"Look, kid, I'm already into overtime. If you wanna foot the bill for each second that ticks by, that's fine by me, but it's double-time starting an hour ago," the electrician shouts through the glass.

Robbie takes a few steps in place for lack of direction, then releases his hold, but not before turning his frustration on me.

"Wait here, and *don't* you do a thing. No talking. No looking at each other. Got it? I'm coming right back."

He scuttles to the admittance room and presses the red button to let in the electrician. Then he takes a key from his pocket and twists it in a keyhole on the console, pointing to it and then to us. "It's locked, so don't even think about pushing the button.

"This way," he says to the repairman, searching for his pockets to replace the key.

The electrician follows him at a leisurely pace, but as soon as they turn the corner, I hurry to Deb.

"What happened?" she asks me accusingly.

"Sorry, I guess he got to me."

"No shit, that's why I told you to be on your best behavior," she says. "He's getting crazier by the day, but somehow, he's still great at getting into people's heads."

"I just don't get why he's cracking. I mean, why now?" I ask.

Deb takes another cursory glance around to be sure we're still alone, then leans in. "I heard one of the orderlies talking about it. This velvet rectangular box he used to bring into the mirrored room all the time went missing. I don't know how long it's been gone, but I guess Keller just realized it."

My heart bangs against my chest. "Adam," I say, and her eyes widen.

"Adam, the orderly? The one who ran off with—?"

"Yeah," I nod, my mind racing.

"You know him?"

"We've met, and let's just say he's as eager to bring down Dr. Keller as we are. Maybe more eager. Eager enough to steal something that he thinks might . . . but why . . . what does he think . . . ?" My mind is at war with itself, ideas fighting one another for brain space.

Deb frowns.

"What?" I ask.

"It's nothing. Look, I know your sister liked him, but . . ."

"But?" I prod. We don't have time for delicacy.

"She wasn't around when Dr. Keller and Adam were real buddy-buddy. None of us trusted Adam. Hell, the other orderlies didn't even trust him. Nothing against your sister, Sophie, but she was crazy to run off with him. I mean, how do you know he didn't—?"

"He didn't kill her," I finish, a little too sternly. For the first time, I see a strong resemblance between Deb and Evan. Her shoulders are hunched in exactly the same way Evan's were while we sat in Adam's hideout.

"What do you really know about him, Sophie?"

I take a deep breath and am dismayed that it shakes its way through my lungs.

"I trust my sister," I say with finality, knowing it's not really an answer at all. "So now what?" I ask to change the subject, the initial giddiness of getting to talk to Deb fading. The reality of our hopeless situation casts a dark shadow.

To my surprise, Deb has a quick answer to that question.

"I've been doing a little treasure hunting," she says, her usual conspiratorial smile flickering to her lips.

I open my mouth to ask what she means, but just as I do, her smile vanishes.

A hand lands hard on my shoulder, collapsing me under its weight.

"Robbie may not be an imposing enough figure to obey," the Pigeon says, then lifts me by my armpits and spins me to face her, my nose inches from her beak. "But you'll listen to me when I give you an order," she says, her eyes dancing. She's enjoying scaring me.

And she's right; I am afraid of her.

The Pigeon's thumb burrows into my back as she grips my shoulder to steer me. All I can think is that this is what a mouse must feel like when it's caught by an owl.

She pushes me down a gray corridor I don't think I've

ever seen before, but then I recognize Dr. Keller's office-office, where he gets all of his "paperwork" done. More like where he devises plans for keeping me and Deb in this rat hole while he tries to bring Susan back.

We pass through this hallway and down another that I know I've never seen before. We're getting farther and farther away from any sounds of activity whatsoever. And I can't escape the feeling that nobody will follow us wherever she's taking me.

"Where are we going?"

"Shut up," she commands.

Finally, we round a corridor that leads to a dead end. The only thing that makes this hallway different from the others is a sign pointing to a ladies' restroom. It's not the one with the showers. But I don't know why we're here. She stops and fishes a keycard from her belt loop under her white smock.

"You girls think you can do whatever you want, don't you? No mind for rules. No reason to listen to the likes of us, huh?" The Pigeon glowers. It's clearly not a question meant to be answered. "If you ask me, you've gotten the star treatment for long enough."

"Star treatment? You have to be kidding me!" I can't contain myself any longer, but I immediately regret opening my mouth. Her talon closes tighter over my shoulder, making the tendon in my back pull so hard I cough.

"When I tell you to be quiet, I intend for you to obey. When I was running this place, back talk like that would earn a patient more than some stern words and withholding of children's toys."

Her reference to Kenny's Legos makes me tense against her grip.

"I have a feeling you'll soon be noticing some changes around here. You see, my dear, I could care less about your . . . special abilities. I suspect you view your talents as little more than a burden. I happen to agree with you."

I've never seen agreeability look less agreeable on a person. Her beak-mouth is pinching into a savage smile.

"I view it more as a sickness, something like an infection, one I'm not invested in curing. I'm much more interested in containing it." She shoves me forward and I stumble. Terror seizes my body. Something awful is going to happen. I can feel it with the sixth sense that told me something was wrong on that day when I came to see Kenny and the waiting room was empty.

The Pigeon thrusts her keycard into a reader for the ladies' room.

"Maybe this will make you reconsider the next time you decide you're above the rules," she says before landing a hard shove in the middle of my back.

I stumble forward, recovering only in time to hear the door behind me slam shut, the mechanical lock pinging into place and echoing through the bathroom.

A quick survey reveals little to be frightened of. This bathroom looks like any other I've seen. Five stalls with doors yawning wide open, revealing toilets filled with blue water. The gray tiles below my feet are clean enough—the grout between them only vaguely dingy. The entire room smells like bleach, and for a second, I breathe a sigh of relief. The Pigeon was all talk. She's clearly just locking me away out of sight. She needed a place to scold me, like some sort of crazed babysitter with an over-inflated sense of importance, a power-hungry orderly bent on regaining the authority she once had and obviously wants back.

But when I turn around, I realize I couldn't be more mistaken.

A row of five individual sinks face the stalls. But it's what hangs above those sinks that makes me forget how to breathe. There, spanning the entire length of the wall, is a plank of sparkling, reflective glass. With horrifying clarity, I can see the fear that paints my face as I realize the danger I'm in.

I run to the door and pound my fists as hard as I can on the metal.

"Hey! Hey! Are you crazy? Let me out of here!"

But the thick door swallows the noise I make, returning only my echo.

I turn slowly and face the opposite wall, which is also covered by a full-length mirror. The reflection of my body, small and meek under the loose cotton of my blue scrubs, almost convinces me that I deserve to be locked in an institution. I look the part of an insane person. I close my eyes against my reflection, knowing what will come next, knowing there's not a damn thing I can do about it.

My ears pop, the pressure of the room dissipating. I swallow in vain to recover the sound of the air conditioning's comforting hum, but all that remains is emptiness, the absence of sound.

The murmuring comes first, sliding across the bathroom like a snake, the words urgent but impossible to understand. It fills my ears with its plea for an audience. I fight against hearing it, then concede and try to understand, just like always. And like always, I tremble against it, wanting to do what it wants me to so it will go away.

Then I open my eyes. I watch as my knees buckle. I brace my hands against the back of the door as I shake. My eyes are fixed on the mirror.

"Please, I've learned my lesson. Please, just let me out!"

But no one comes to the door. I've been left alone, and I

have the terrifying sense that the Taker knows, and that it is relishing the time it will have with me.

The wordless murmurings in my ear turn to one strained, sputtering gasp, and I open my eyes wider to catch the faint rippling of my reflection across the bathroom.

"Please," I whisper, no longer believing that anyone will come to my rescue.

The rippling grows stronger, and soon my reflection is disappearing behind an undulating figure that's turning blacker and blacker with each movement.

"Please, don't." But I know it's no use. It won't understand me. Nothing can keep it from trying to take from me what it thinks I have.

A curtain of black, oily hair spills from the glass, obscuring the eyeless face and moving, silent mouth. Long skinny digits follow, twitching on the ends of blackened, rotting hands—a decaying body and halting legs emerge last from the mirror, leaving a layer of oily residue in their wake.

My joints lock into place, freezing me in a stiffened pose, as if they've given up hope before my mind has. My reflection in the mirror is gone. I've already been blotted out of existence. The Taker is laying its claim to my body in an attempt to restore its own.

It lumbers toward me with painful movements, as if every

effort is excruciating. It throws its limbs in wild advance, each step, each sway of its body exaggerated and uneven. It thrusts a shoulder forward, then a hip—giving the impression of moving in stop-motion, like a hiccup on a film reel. But it moves fast. Faster than last time.

"Please" is the only word that seeps through my lips.

It's less than three feet from me. Less than two feet. It's mere inches from me when the gasping in my ear elevates to a near scream, and the dampness on my neck drips to my shirt.

The teeth clack together, and I squeeze my eyes shut. I know I've reached the end now. And the only face that I can conjure is Nell's.

Her green eyes and thick, wavy hair. I remember her hands twisting around my own straight hair, weaving it into braids while it was still damp—the smell of conditioner filling the bathroom. The sound of her voice commands me to lie still as I sleep so I'll have waves like hers when I wake up.

Her voice orders me to hold still. *Wait, it'll all be over soon.*

And then I realize that it isn't Nell's voice at all. It's high and whining, straining with immense effort. An imposter's voice.

"NOOOO!" I scream as loudly as I can, my throat burning

with the effort, my muscles tensed against whatever might come.

All at once, I'm on my back, my head ringing with a tremendous pain, vision fading in and out.

I crawl to my feet and clutch my head until I regain my sight. When I do, I'm staring into the empty bathroom, the smell of bleach strong in my nose, the full-length mirror across the room revealing only a small, terrified version of me and a little dark spot somewhere in the middle.

I spin on my heel and find that I'm inches from a starched white smock. The Pigeon's birdlike face smiles in a way I've never seen and would be happy to never see again.

"Oh dear," she says. "Whatever was I thinking, letting you use the restroom with the mirrors? How utterly foolish."

"You—you—" I stutter, unable to find words to hurl at her.

"Choose your next sentence wisely, dear," she says, cupping my chin in her talon, her thumb and forefinger finding the bone under cartilage. "I think you know that I'm not one to make empty threats."

"Don't you think Dr. Keller would have been disappointed to find his second to last Seer hanging from the ceiling?" I sling at her, hardly believing the words coming from my mouth. I'm not sure I've ever felt closer to death. Saying it aloud only makes it that much more real.

"Don't you dare presume to know what Dr. Keller wants. *He* is hardly in a position to know what that is anymore, let alone you. Besides, the good doctor has entrusted his entire operation to me while he's . . . indisposed. Don't be surprised if we're seeing more of each other from now on."

She releases my chin from her grip with a flick of her wrist, pushing me back on my heels. With her other hand, she grips me by the elbow and drags me behind her as we traverse one long corridor after another. Finally, we arrive in one that looks familiar, and she slides her keycard through a reader above a door handle and swings the door open to reveal the place I've come to recognize as my room.

"Sleep well tonight, little girl. We have a long day ahead of us tomorrow," she says. She pulls the door shut behind her with a metal clank, leaving me to bury my face in a pillow that smells like souring citrus and metal.

I curl myself into a tight ball and refuse to give in to the temptation to whimper. Because I know that if I begin to cry, I'll never stop, and I refuse to give the Pigeon that kind of satisfaction.

A shuffling in the wall above my bed startles me.

"Sophie, are you awake?"

"Deb?" My throat catches.

"Where did she take you?"

My mind pans to the bathroom: the mirror with its rippling image of me, the thing that subsumed that image, the Taker that got so close.

"Sophie? Are you okay?"

I realize I've left Deb in silence. "I'm . . . Deb, we need to be more careful. She's—Gladys, that bird-looking lady. She's out of her mind."

"Trust me, you don't need to tell me that," Deb says almost too quietly for me to hear. "She thinks she's taking over, and honestly, she might be right. Dr. Keller, he's losing it. I've heard them all talking about it. They don't know who it is he's trying to reach, trying to bring back. They don't know all that we know. They have no idea her death sent him down this path, that finding a ghost is the only thing that's kept him going all these years. Obsession is a strong motivator for sure."

We're both silent for a minute, and then Deb's comment makes me remember something the Pigeon said to me.

"Deb?"

"Uh-huh?"

"Do you think we're, I don't know, like, cursed or something? Is that why we see the things we see?"

Deb's quiet for a minute, and then I hear some rustling before she says, "I can't really remember a time when I didn't hear the murmurings. I just remember being relieved it wasn't my dad yelling for me. He used to . . ." She trails off. "He was a really angry guy, you know? Me and my mom . . ."

Deb doesn't finish, but I don't need her to. I keep my mouth shut, not knowing what to say even if I could make the words come. Evan never mentioned this about his uncle. Maybe he didn't know. It didn't sound like his aunt and uncle were all that close to Evan's parents, judging by the way they left town without a word after they sent Deb away.

Deb starts talking again, but my brain is still working through the pain I feel on her behalf.

"When I started seeing the shadows, I hated it, but I guess it didn't surprise me much. I'd already seen some scary things. Then I came here, and for once I didn't feel crazy. It's hard to accept that your whole existence is a curse, you know?" she asks me, and I can't seem to locate an answer.

Deb has been in this place for longer than Nell and I combined. A lot longer. It should have occurred to me before now, but it didn't. Maybe that was a reality too painful to form into a solid thought. But now my brain gnaws on the information like a bone.

"Before I came here, I didn't know anyone else like me," she whispers.

And there it is. That forced independence—a need to rely

on only oneself. The spark that ignites people like Deb. Like Nell. And perhaps Adam. Maybe.

But me? I'm not so sure.

"But there's more. Something I didn't get a chance to tell you in the rec room," Deb says after another long silence. She's moved on, and out of respect, I fold up the conversation and stash it away in my brain. Or maybe I just don't want to think about it anymore.

"Yeah?"

"Yeah. I found something. Well, some*place*. Near my room. I'm pretty sure they'd kill me if they found out I knew about it. I didn't get very far exploring, though. They should be taking us to the courtyard tomorrow. I'll tell you more then. I've got to get back to my bed."

With that, her voice ceases. And silence follows.

A slow ache creeps over my forehead, resting in my temples. My brain plays a reel-to-reel of the childhood I imagine Deb and Evan shared: They play "pretend" games, which were only pretend to Evan. I overlay the images with my memories of Nell, and the things I started to hear and see only after it was too late to tell her she was right, that she hadn't imagined the voices, the visions, and that she didn't need to protect me from them anymore.

Protection.

I picture Evan's arms, his strong body, shielding me from the Taker he hasn't seen but believes is there. He believes me. If only I could tell him how close he was to finding Deb—how right he was to beg me not to come here alone. I would give anything to feel his arms around me now.

My heart doesn't stop racing all night. My restless sleep is tormented by nightmares of things rotting and blackened.

22

THE NEXT MORNING ARRIVES TOO fast, which makes me even more irritated to see Robbie the orderly, who wheels my breakfast in on a rickety metal cart.

"Bon appétit," he taunts, leaving the tray on the bed and backing himself and the cart out the door—shutting me in.

Today's breakfast is nearly the same as other mornings, though it appears they're experimenting with styles of eggs. Joining the bread (this time untoasted) and fruit cocktail are two glossy sunny-side-up eggs, staring at me like unblinking eyeballs. I take a few bites of the runny egg whites and swallow my fake pills, then eat the fruit from the syrup of the cocktail.

I get more creative with the orange juice this time,

breaking the yellow yolk in the eggs and smearing it on the plate, then pouring some of the juice in with the yellow paste. I sop up some of the mess with the untoasted bread, then pour some of the orange juice into the cocktail syrup. There's still about a quarter of the glass left when I hear the pinging of the lock slip. Once again it's Robbie, who immediately eyes the juice still left in my glass.

"Down the hatch," he orders, looking tired even though it's first thing in the morning and the start of his shift. Something tells me Robbie hates this time of day more than anything. This happens to be my new favorite time of day, tormenting the only orderly I seem to have any effect on in this place.

"I have to use the bathroom," I say, and when he tightens his lips and crosses his hands over his chest, I obligingly dump the remainder of the orange juice into my mouth and slam the plastic cup back onto the tray,

"You know the way. Make it quick," he orders.

I hustle to the end of the hallway and around the corner. The minute the bathroom door shuts behind me, I spit the juice into the toilet and flush just in time to hear the door open. The pucker-lipped orderly with the heavy ponytail looks me up and down as I emerge from the stall, cinching the drawstring on my pants to complete the ruse.

I splash my hands under the sink and wipe the water on

my pants while she nudges me down the hallway toward the the courtyard.

It's chilly outside this morning too, but I am focused on seeing Deb. Her revelation from the air vent kept me up half the night. Whatever it is she found could finally be a lead for getting the hell out of here. Between cycles of nightmares, my brain swirled with snippets of conversation from my session with Dr. Keller, trying to tie that with what Deb said about Susan's missing bracelet. And for the first time in days, I reflected on entries from Adam's blog.

It takes something else, too. Some sort of object.

Suddenly the significance of that statement takes on a new weight. I'm all but convinced Adam stole the bracelet from Dr. Keller before running away from Oakside with Nell. What I don't know is why. That's what I'm hoping Deb can help me figure out. Maybe that's what she was trying to tell me yesterday.

The pucker-lipped orderly deposits me in the courtyard and accepts a cigarette from Robbie's pack before finding her place in the sun with a couple of other staffers. A quick scan of the space reveals I'm the only patient out here.

I march up to Robbie. He's the only one I think I have even a chance of getting an answer from.

"Where's Deb?" I ask, my voice shaking.

"Who?" he asks.

"She means her little friend. The mousy blonde with the googly eyes," the pucker-lipped orderly says, the lines around her mouth deepening as she releases a crackling chuckle, which triggers a wet, phlegmy cough. I stifle my rage at seeing Pucker-Mouth laughing at Deb's expense, and refocus my gaze on Robbie while the rest of them look at me like a specimen in a dish.

"Do you know where she is?" I ask with as much humility as I can muster.

But Robbie just shrugs and says, "Look, kid, they don't tell me anything around here. I just bring you breakfast and make sure you drink the juice."

He receives a swift slap in his gut from Pucker-Mouth. Then she moves her stare to me, resting her eyes on mine as the lines return to her face, and her lips set in a deep frown.

"Gladys says Dr. Keller doesn't want you two spending so much time together anymore."

"Why not?" I ask, then remember one of the first things Deb told me. "Aren't you interested in, you know, seeing if we can get anything to happen?"

I say this while twinkling my fingers in the air, hoping I convey the possibility of some sort of magic, but I only receive a deeper frown in response.

"Sweetie, if we want you guys to make something happen, trust me, we have ways," she says, giving in to another phlegm-filled laughing/coughing fit.

I back away and find the bench where I had my first face-to-face conversation with Deb. I pull my knees to my chest and rest my chin on them in the same way she sat. I tell myself over and over that she's just in her room, that they're not doing anything to her, that they only want to keep us apart. I am resolute in my attempt *not* to think about the bathroom with the mirrors where the Pigeon took me. I am resolute and unsuccessful.

After the orderlies have finished their inane conversation and I've chilled myself to the bone in the shade of the building, Robbie guides me back to my room.

"What are they doing to me today?" I ask him, a little of my former panic seeping back in. The thought of more drugs, more tests, more clipboards, makes me queasy all over again.

He gives me the same tired look he gave me at breakfast and slams the door.

I imagine that doesn't sound as final as I think it does, and I slip underneath the scratchy covers, curling myself into a ball until the warmth returns to my body. I wait for what feels like hours—my heart speeding with each set of approaching footsteps and subsiding only when those footsteps continue past my door without stopping. Have they all made a pact to torment me today—to keep me guessing as to what they have in store?

I can't stop thinking about what they might be doing to Deb. Is it possible they figured out whatever secret she discovered?

I'm pretty sure they'd kill me if they found out I knew about it.

I slow my heart and hug my legs, seeking the warmth that just won't seem to stay.

After who knows how much time has passed, a set of squeaking shoes stops at my room, and a metal latch slips in its bolt, cracking the door open to reveal a tight bun.

The Pigeon stares at me like I'm her dinner.

"Time for a little recreation," she says, and I slide obligingly from my cot and follow her out of the room, brushing fresh gooseflesh from my arms.

The lobby is dim with the growing dusk, and my stomach drops like it does every time I see the sliding glass doors. Freedom is only feet away and totally unattainable.

I turn to the Pigeon and immediately regret it. A slippery smile peels across her face, and I know she enjoys tormenting me. She likes taunting me with a glimpse of the parking lot, and the road that could lead me to a gas station, a neighboring house, a phone. To rescue.

"Make yourself comfortable, dear," she tells me, motioning toward the far corner of the room where Kenny used to sit. "There's a whole bucket of Legos over there that no one's using anymore."

A hot anger spills through me, and I clench my fists to keep my hands from shaking.

I start walking to the opposite side of the room, when from the corner of my eye, I spot a blue-cotton-clad knee poking out behind the chair at the table where Kenny used to sit.

"Deb? Oh my God!"

I rush to her side and take inventory as quickly as possible. Deb's lids droop over her downcast, glazed eyes. She sits cross-legged, slumped with her back to the wall. Her hair is stringy and loose around her slack face. A cotton ball is stuck to the inside of her elbow, pinched by a strip of white medical tape. Her hands are limp at her sides, palms upturned, fingers curled but loose and unable to grasp my hand when I try to hold hers. In her lap is a yellow bag of unopened peanut M&M's.

"What did you do to her?" I demand of the Pigeon, but she's not paying attention to me.

She strides to the pucker-mouthed orderly, who is settled behind the admitting desk with a magazine.

"What is she doing here? Dr. Keller's instructions could

not have been clearer. You were to return her to her room immediately following her session."

The pucker-mouthed orderly leans away from the Pigeon and takes in Deb with one quick up-and-down evaluation, then turns back to the Pigeon.

"Look at her! What do you think she's capable of right now? Honestly, Gladys, you're starting to get as nuts as he—"

"You can stop right there," the Pigeon warns, and Pucker-Mouth leans even farther away. "You forget your place. We wouldn't want you saying anything that might get you a reprimand, now would we? I think we both know how sensitive Dr. Keller is these days to orderlies who betray his trust."

I take this opportunity to reach out to Deb again. I squeeze her hand to try to get her attention.

"Deb, I know you're in there. Whatever they did to you, you've fought against worse. Deb?"

But it's no use. Her mouth hangs slack, her dry lips parted on an unhinged jaw. A tiny trail of spittle slips from the corner of her mouth.

"Deb, you just hang in there, okay?" I tell her, wiping the drool from her pant leg with the end of my shirt. But as I begin to blot away the moisture, I notice something rigid tucked into her sock.

I glance over my shoulder. The Pigeon is still berating

Pucker-Mouth. Turning back to Deb, I place myself in front of her and keep my hands out of view. Lifting her pant leg, I find a stiff rectangular card with a magnetic strip tucked deep into the folds of her scrunched socks. It's identical to the cards I've watched the orderlies pull from cords on their belt loops and drag through readers on nearly every door here at Oakside. I search her eyes for any sort of hint about how she got it, but I receive only a dull stare in response. In one swift motion, I slide the keycard from her sock and into my own, covering it quickly with my pant leg.

Pucker-Mouth's voice rises defensively, and I glance over my shoulder again to reassure myself that they're still too preoccupied to be paying attention to us. This time, when I turn back to Deb, her eyes find mine with tremendous difficulty; they look heavy and slow.

"Deb? Can you hear me? Do you understand me?" I squeeze her ankle in hopes of jogging some sort of response from her.

Her mouth closes, then opens, then closes again. She's trying to say something. Her breath sounds tight in her throat, and comes out in tiny, mouselike squeaks. I lean closer, and at last, I make out two repeating words.

"Linen closet."

I pull away, shaking my head. "I don't understand."

But her lips shape "linen closet" over and over.

Suddenly, I feel an iron grip on my shoulder.

"That's enough. No more social time for you," the Pigeon says, dragging me to a standing position.

She pulls me toward the hallway. Then Robbie's voice calls from the lobby.

"Gladys, you need to get over here!"

"Handle it, Robbie, I'm busy!" she scolds.

"But Gladys, I . . . I don't know what to—"

"Not *now*, Robbie!"

It all seems to happen at once.

I hear a dull banging that sounds like it's coming from the end of a long tunnel. But when I turn back toward the lobby, I see the shadows of two figures, one of whom is flailing from behind the glass doors. It's growing dark outside, which makes it difficult to see who it is. But then the doors part, and a frightened-looking Robbie emerges from the Plexiglas room with the door controls. All at once, Evan and Aunt Becca are standing in the lobby, their eyes searching for the nearest person in white, which unfortunately for them and for him happens to be Robbie.

"Where is she? Where's Sophie?"

"Please, I need to see my niece!"

"Visiting hours are over. You'll have to come back tomorrow," Robbie insists, his voice cracking.

"Please, my sister and I are very worried. You haven't let us see her since we admitted her, and we're rethinking—"

"Where is she?" Evan demands, fists clenched.

"Sir, please, you're going to have to calm down," Robbie pleads.

"Where is . . . oh God . . ." Evan gasps.

The Pigeon's remarkably strong arm slips across the front of my shoulders while her palm clamps over my mouth with so much force that I nearly bite my own lips. I shake off my shock, and adrenaline shoots through my veins. I pull against the Pigeon's grip with everything I have. But at the moment, she seems to have more strength, and my struggles are in vain. She tries to jerk me around the corner, but I manage to keep my feet planted in the hall.

Evan ducks out of view and then starts shouting.

"Oh my God . . . it's Deb. Deb? Deb! It's me. It's Evan. Do you recognize me?"

I try to scream but the Pigeon's hand stifles the sound before it can leave my mouth.

"Evan, are you sure?" my Aunt Becca says.

"Please, this is highly inappropriate. You really have to leave. This is against policy," Pucker-Mouth demands, the strain in her voice on the verge of panic.

"What did you bastards do to her? What's wrong with her?"

"Sir, if you'll just follow me outside, I can explain," Robbie says, fear popping in his voice like tiny sparklers.

"Please," Aunt Becca repeats. "I just need to see my niece. We'll leave tonight. We'll come back tomorrow during normal visiting hours. I just need to see her tonight. *We* need to see her. To make sure she's okay. Then we'll go and come back tomorrow per regulations."

Good ol' Aunt Becca. Always the diplomat.

I feel the Pigeon lean toward my ear.

"You're going to go out there, and you're going to put on a nice little show for us, or your friend Deb's going to develop a permanent drooling problem. Do we understand each other?"

She pinches the muscle on top of my shoulder as punctuation, and I nod, blinking back tears.

"Good. Now get rid of that look on your face, and let's go."

She marches me to the lobby, releasing my shoulder just in time for Aunt Becca's worried gaze to find me.

"Sophie!"

She nearly knocks me over with a hug so tight, she cuts off my air. I've never in my life been happier to suffocate.

I try to open my mouth, try to say something, but I can't set aside the knot that's formed in my throat. Instead, I just squeeze her back, trying to make my hands do the talking my mouth can't.

I smell a sweet musk and feel the shadow of Evan close to us, and when I pick my head up from Aunt Becca's shoulder, I see his faded football jersey, still stained with grass. Even after re-creating him in my nightly dreams, nothing compares to the real thing. He looks better than I've ever imagined him.

Aunt Becca holds me at arm's length and examines me. It takes every ounce of willpower to not burst into tears. Evan watches me, then turns to Deb in the far corner of the room, then turns back to me again. I give him the faintest nod, and he returns it. In that one exchange, I feel sane for the first time in over a week.

"Sophie, are you—?"

"I'm fine, Aunt Becca," I lie.

Evan stiffens beside Aunt Becca, and I twitch my head to create a tiny shake, warning him not to pursue it. He seems to get the hint, because his shoulders settle back to a level below his chin.

"They treat us well here at Oakside Behavioral Institute," I say, hoping they both catch on to the formality of my speech and the un-Sophie-like delivery. "They're giving me the help I need."

I'm forcing a calm over myself, and I'm surprised to find it's actually working. My voice betrays only a hint of strain, the quavering only recognizable to the closest observer, which frankly could be anyone in this room except for Robbie. He and Pucker-Mouth stand near Deb, watching in silence. I can feel the Pigeon's stare on my back. I know the second she gave the command, Robbie and Pucker-Mouth would cart Deb away for another heavy dose of drugs and a visit to the mirrored room.

"Your mom and I . . . ," Aunt Becca starts to say, her voice catching in her throat. She swallows and tries again, Evan's hand providing support on her shoulder. "We've been so worried about you."

Her voice collapses under its own weight. In those few words, I understand everything. That they're sorry. That they made a mistake in letting Dr. Keller keep me here. That they're trying to get me out. In Evan's touch on her shoulder, I see that he's told them at least some of what we know. I see that he's forgiven how I betrayed his trust by coming here without him. As with Aunt Becca and my mom, he's only focused on getting me out, and getting Deb out. And that makes me realize that I have this one chance to communicate with them. And it doesn't take me long to figure out what I need to say and to whom.

I lock eyes with Evan to make sure he understands the significance of what I'm going to say, and when he leans slightly forward, I say, "Dr. Keller is just like family. Like a long-lost father. He's so . . . *charming.*"

Evan pulls back from me and furrows his brow, as though he's trying to unlock my meaning. All at once, the lines disappear from his forehead, and he says, "I'm so glad to hear that. I can think of a few charms he has right off the top of my head."

"All right, I think that's enough visiting for tonight, everyone," the Pigeon interjects in her most hospitable but firm tone.

Aunt Becca opens her mouth to object, so I say something first.

"I'm okay, Aunt Becca. Really. Just go home and take care of Mom, all right? I'll see you during visiting hours."

She frowns and says, "Your mom's fine. We just—we should have been—I wish I'd—"

I put my hand in Aunt Becca's and squeeze. "I know. It's okay. Just tell her I'm fine."

She draws me in to give me another lung-collapsing squeeze, and I let her. I feel Evan's hand reach for mine, and we lace our fingers together. I fight another wave of sobs and pull away from them both using my very last reserve of strength.

The Pigeon guides me away as Robbie and Pucker-Mouth

usher Aunt Becca and Evan out the sliding glass doors to the parking lot.

When we arrive at my bedroom door, the Pigeon nudges me inside and stands in the doorway, the light from the hallway casting her long shadow on the wall behind my bed.

"Don't count on visiting hours anytime soon," she says.

Without retorting, I let her feel her moment of victory before she closes the door.

Because I know three things she doesn't. I know that Evan understood the message I gave him right there in front of her. I know that Deb found something in the linen closet near her room.

And I know I have the keycard to get in.

23

I DON'T HAVE A CLOCK in my room, but it's not hard to tell when the shift change takes place at night. The diligent squeaking of shoes during the daytime gives way to stuttering, sporadic footsteps that pass the threshold of my door much less frequently. The monotony of this place might threaten to dull my senses if not for my new plan—conceived thanks to Deb's help.

I wait for what feels like decades until the stumbling of lazy feet squeaks past my door at what I estimate to be thirty-minute intervals. Except for once—when I feigned sleep—nobody has bothered to check on me since the Pigeon left. As I expect, I hear dragging feet stop before my door and a lock slip from its place. The door sighs open, and the light from the hallway seeps through the sheet I've used to cover my face and head. After a brief pause, the door closes, shutting out the light.

I wait for the footsteps to fade around the corner, then launch out of bed and drag my pillow beneath my sheets, balling the tail of the fitted sheet underneath it and curving it into the rough shape of a sleeping Oakside detainee.

Slipping Deb's pilfered keycard from my sock, I pass it through the reader and watch as a green light above the door handle flashes three times before releasing the lock with a tiny ping.

I crack the door and look to my left, then my right, then my left again before I inch into the hallway. Heading toward the shower room, I stop myself, take another deep breath, then peer around that corner, finding the hallway beyond empty.

I duck into the corridor and hurry on tiptoe toward the showers. Around the corner on my right is the linen closet—the same room from which Pucker-Mouth pulled a new set of scrubs for me the day I spilled orange juice all over myself. It's directly across from Deb's bedroom, and I have a feeling they'll be checking on her pretty frequently tonight. And I know why that might be the case. The peanut M&M's mean she had a session with Dr. Keller, which means they might have found out about whatever it was she was going to tell me today. Still, after the risk she took trying to tell me her secret, there's no way I'm going to let her discovery be in vain. This might be our only shot at getting *both* of us out of here.

I inch my head around the corner, and duck just in time to catch a glimpse of a tight topknot lean from Deb's doorway. I hold my breath, knowing there's no chance I'll make it around the next corner, let alone back to my room, before the Pigeon sees me fleeing. I strain my ears and listen for the squeaking of rubber soles, but as each lub of my heart pounds against my chest, I hear nothing to indicate the Pigeon's movement.

At last, the footsteps head down the hallway in the opposite direction and fade away. I stealthily peek around the corner again, and after ensuring it's clear, I move on the balls of my feet toward the linen closet. I glance at Deb's door and fight the urge to check in on her first. I know I might only get one shot at this, and I need to stick to the plan. I swipe the card through its reader, but my movement is jerky, and a red light followed by a buzzing scolds me that I've done it wrong. I hold my breath and look over my shoulder at a thankfully empty hallway. I slide the keycard slower, steadying it with both hands. This time I'm rewarded with a flickering green light. I push the handle down and disappear behind the door, letting it settle closed behind me as I lean against it to catch the breath I forgot I'd been holding.

"Okay, Deb. I'm here," I whisper to the room. "Now tell me what you found."

I thought my room was small, but this closet is only about seven square feet in size, and with the shelving, there is barely enough room for me to turn around. Cracks of light from the hallway seep in around the door frame. I quickly spot the blue stacks of scrubs. The opposite wall has similar sets, only these are mint green.

For the other patients. The real patients. The ones being neglected at the expense of Dr. Keller's obsession and his orderlies' allegiance to him. I think back to what Deb told me about her excursion to the other side of Oakside, and about the woman in the overcrowded and under-visited room. More than ever, I want to shut this place down. But none of that's going to happen while Deb and I are trapped here. Even if Evan understood my message, and even if he's able to come through, that's only half of the plan. The other half will be up to me when the time comes.

I scan the room with what I hope are fresh eyes, terrified to turn on a light for fear of it shining underneath the door. Instead, I wait for my eyes to adjust to the dark and imagine I'm Deb on a similar mission just a night earlier.

On the wall opposite me is a heavy-looking wire shelf filled floor to ceiling with towels and blankets, each embroidered with the Oakside insignia, just like the blanket Evan and I found in the old house in Jerome.

I follow the shelf to the ceiling, finding nothing out of the ordinary. Then I trace the stacks of blankets to the gray linoleum floor. It practically yawns at its own boredom. As I peer a little closer at the floor, I think I see a groove in the seam of the linoleum. I stand over it and quickly find a perpendicular seam joining its corner, then another at the end of that seam. The last side of the roughly two-foot-by-two-foot-square in the floor is a crease in the linoleum.

I walk all around the square on the floor, bending to trace my fingers in the grooves. I feel a tiny breeze of air from the cracks, and my heart thuds behind my ribs. I press my fingers into the cracks, trying to pull the edge toward me, but it won't budge. I push from the same place, but the floor will not give. I stand in the center of the square on the floor, but nothing moves, not the floor and not me.

I stand outside of the square of linoleum and frown at it. Then, for lack of trying everything else, I run the keycard along the edge of each side of the square. And when I get to the edge closest to my feet, I see a faint green circle illuminate from beneath the floor, and a muffled click tells me I've succeeded. The floor pops up, a lip of the square slanting upward toward me, and a dusty wooden staircase illuminates itself below me.

"A basement?" I question.

I'm no architect, but I know enough about Arizona buildings to know that it's not common to have a basement here. Some of the newer houses have them, but that's only because housing development companies can charge more for a house with a basement. Typically, the clay-laden ground is too hard to dig that deeply. This already feels wrong.

"A secret basement. What else are you hiding, Dr. Keller?"

I take one more breath before lowering myself into the stairwell and closing the trapdoor behind me.

The wooden stairs creek under my weight, and I clamber quickly to the bottom, eager to make the noise stop. What I find ahead leaves me far from comforted.

I've only seen a mausoleum once in my life, but once was enough. It was right after my grandmother's funeral, and I was maybe four years old. The image of that place is seared into my memory like a scar. I recall an endless row of little doors leading to the resting places of so many people, all for someone's mother or brother or uncle—or sister.

The entire place had been made of concrete, floor to ceiling, except for those little doors. So everything had echoed.

My shoes with their squeaking patent leather, my mom's heels with their click-click-clicking as she took her long, glamorous strides. Nell with her rubber soles that chirped in time with her tiny sobs, knowing that she'd never see Nana again.

Everything was amplified in that place, and sound pinged from one end of the mausoleum to the other. That is, until the sound approached one of those doors. Every time we passed by one of them, sound seemed to disintegrate. I always got a chill thinking about that later. It was as if the doors, and whatever was behind them, had somehow swallowed the sound.

Oakside's secret basement looks just like that mausoleum.

The walls and floor are concrete. The only non-concrete part of the whole basement seems to be the doors and the stairs to each tiny storage room—and those are made of rotting wood. Little black numerals, like house addresses, are nailed to the tops of the doors, each number indicating a range of years. Oakside's lifespan is noted in five-year increments beginning with 1955 all the way up to the present day. The door at the end of the corridor is labeled with the most recent years.

A groaning sound above me snaps my attention from the door.

A giant pipe runs the length of the low ceiling, painted white like the ceiling and the walls down here. Only they're not really white anymore, not after years of grime and decay.

I thought Oakside was a hole. Its basement makes the rest of the facility look like a palace. I am quickly regretting descending those stairs. Dust covers every surface. More to the point, it covers the floor, and on that floor are exactly zero sets of footprints. If Deb made it to the basement, she would have left a mark of some sort, which leads me to believe that when she said she didn't get very far, she meant she got as far as discovering the door, maybe the stairwell, but that's it. I suddenly feel more alone than ever.

But the memory of Deb's face as she sat slumped in the lobby's recreation area renews my courage, or at least what I'm trying to convince myself is courage. If she thought this place might hold answers, I want to know why.

Standing in front of the door at the end of the corridor, I see that it's adorned with the same keycard reader as every other door in Oakside, and not a rusted padlock like the rest of the storage doors.

"Great," I whisper.

I only have the one keycard. I shrug and slide it through the reader. My effort is returned with a brief green flash, followed by a click.

"Well, what do you know," I say to the lock, half expecting it to respond.

Turning the industrial metal handle affixed to the rotting wood, I give it one more command. "Show me what Deb didn't get a chance to see."

Freed from its tether, the door opens. I should be excited, but I'm unsettled, afraid of what I might find.

The storage closet is dark and probably six feet high, tall enough to admit me or Deb with ease, but squat enough to make anyone else stoop low. It's impossible to tell how far back it goes. Not far, I would imagine, probably no more than eight feet. But I'd feel better if I knew where it ended.

I'm surprised to find only a few boxes—moldy cardboard folding in on itself with age and wear. Two rotting steps precede the door. I climb them reluctantly and enter the musty-smelling closet. Big black letters announce a few boxes are TAXES, and the one on the floor beside those is labeled MISC. I decide to search that one first, and though I don't know what I expected to find, I am at once disappointed and relieved to find it filled with more blue scrubs, mostly in extra large.

I peek into the boxes marked TAXES and find nothing of interest, mostly receipts and government forms. But my toe hits another box—one I hadn't seen at first, and when I slide it closer to me, there's no label marking its contents.

As I unfold the top flaps, I find an assortment of files and folders, scraps of paper, a laminated tag. I pick up the tag first. It's a photograph of a somber-looking Adam dressed in stiff white. The photo was snapped against a gray background, making his dark features even darker by contrast. Below his photo is his name, *Adam Newfeld, Orderly.*

I don't have to search through the box much before I find a thick folder, a burgundy accordion thing bound with elastic and sealed with a gummy adhesive stamped CONFIDENTIAL. The cover of the folder, I see once I hold it to the faint light by the storage door, reads *David, Nell.*

"Nell," I repeat to the folder, as though I could conjure her just by staring at her name. And when I unbind the folder, I'm startled to find that in a way, I do: a Polaroid of her falls from the top of the stack of papers I've unearthed.

I draw in a sharp breath at the sight of the photo, realizing this is the most recent picture I've seen of her, maybe the last one ever taken. My stomach turns at the image of her face, thin and stark against one of Oakside's smooth gray walls. Nell's cheekbones, normally plumped by a sly smile, are sharp and crude. Her sunken eyes are nearly buried in dark circles, and her hair, normally full of body, looks lank and is splayed across her shoulders. For the first time, I understand why the sight of her makes my stomach ache so much—I was afraid of her.

For some reason, I remember something Adam had said that day in Jerome, about when Seers begin to experience what it is that changes them forever, setting them apart from everyone in the worst way.

There's no connection to age, not that I know of.

I believed him then, though I didn't know why. And now, looking at Nell's picture, I'm reminded of another time she looked more like this than I'd like to admit. It was after our grandmother died. That day in the mausoleum.

Nell had been close to our Nana, closer than I ever was. I was too young to really understand that sort of closeness. But Nell's additional year of maturity gave her a special relationship with our only living grandparent. When Nana died, Nell withdrew for weeks. She wouldn't play with me, would barely speak to anyone. And she'd looked, I don't know, almost like her soul had withdrawn from her body, as if trying to take a break from the pain it felt inside of her. And when she seemed to get better, that's when she started hearing things.

And then so did I. After everything began happening to Nell.

"The pain makes it happen," I whisper, only a little aware of my own voice. I've finally figured out what makes a Seer begin to hear the Takers. Just like a Taker is born of pain, its soul split, a Seer is born of pain, too. Or rather, they're born with the ability, like a predisposition, but only when they experience the type of pain a Taker has experienced do they begin to hear the Taker's whispers.

It's a commonality that bonds them, the very same connection that dooms them both.

With some effort, and several shuddering breaths, I set the picture of my sister on the floor beside me and begin sifting through the rest of the papers from the folder. My hands shake with the need to learn more.

I find what look to be sheets torn from a yellow legal pad, the handwriting neatly slanted. The headings on each page are all the same, with dates spanning every couple of days from the day after Nell was admitted to the day before she ran. And next to each date are the letters *J. K., MD.*

Dr. Jeremy Keller.

"I've got your notes, you sick freak," I say, and spread the first sheet over my knee like a treasure map, skimming the superficial observations for something of relevance. It doesn't take me long to find it.

Patient exhibits signs of paranoia and hallucinatory qualities, manifesting in auditory and visual symptoms. Further observation is necessary; candidacy for Test Evocation promising.

"Test evocation," I say under my breath, my blood pulsing hard through my veins. The bastard was already sniffing her out for guinea pig status.

The next few pages hold more of the same kinds of observations.

Patient David, Nell, is of optimal age for maximum impact.

Exhibits positive response to individual therapeutic sessions. Vulnerability to abandonment, doubts of sanity, insecurity with relations to immediate family.

Employee Y initiated to begin multidimensional observation and engagement. Preliminary findings promising.

"Employee Y," I whisper, rereading it. I'm having trouble deciphering the tilted handwriting, but I can't find any other interpretation. Someone was watching Nell outside of her sessions. Someone besides Dr. Keller.

"The Pigeon," I realize with disgust. Of course. Who else would it be but his willing sidekick—the same person who's poised and ready to take over Oakside the minute Dr. Keller succumbs to his own obsession?

But the thought of the Pigeon gaining Nell's trust is baffling. Of course, I wasn't in Nell's position. I wonder how alone she felt and desperate she must have been for a friend. I fight back a fresh wave of nausea, thinking about how I nearly succumbed to the same desperation during one or two encounters with Dr. Keller after my drug-induced haze.

I try to distract myself by flipping through more of the pages, but most of it is paperwork I don't understand, official-looking documents, contracts of some kind, and admittance forms signed in handwriting all too familiar to me—Mom's.

Seeing her name in this place, surrounded by the mold and grime of this basement, feels strange, like she might as well be living in another dimension. Then again, that isn't too far off the mark.

Yet a tiny flame of hope flickers inside of me as I remember Aunt Becca's panicked words from earlier this evening.

She's fine. We just . . . we should have been . . .

I let that vague reassurance serve as fuel as I continue to sift through the unmarked box.

Frustrated with the contents of the accordion folder, I set it aside, carefully replacing Nell's Polaroid face down between the sheets of paper, unhappy to put her back there but unable to have her look at me anymore. Besides, that wasn't really her anyway. Not the way I remember her.

The only other item in the box is a thin folder with two metal prongs at the top attaching more legal pad pages in a crinkly stack. Leafing through, I see that the handwriting is different, tilting not to the right but straight up and down or slightly to the left. The edges of the letters look sharper. There are smudges of ink at various places on the page.

I understand immediately. "A lefty," I mutter. Nell was a lefty. She couldn't go a day without licking a finger and rubbing away the ink from the knuckle of her pinky. She was always too intent on the poetry she was writing to remember to lift her hand away from the page, so as not to smear the words.

The headings of these notes are in a similar format to Dr. Keller's, with a date at the top, and *Patient David, Nell.*

"Employee Y," I hiss through gritted teeth. I've found the Pigeon's notes.

But as I skim the first entry, dated a couple of months after Nell's admittance, something about the way the notes are written doesn't feel like the Pigeon. I would have expected sharp, almost brittle observations. I'd imagine she'd relished watching Nell fight demons she had convinced herself were only in her head.

Instead, the first entry is short, almost guarded:

Patient is in a severe state of trauma. Physical signs of stress present. Notably withdrawn, suffering from sleep deprivation. Possible reduction in medication suggested. Appears distracted. Startles at visual stimuli. Receptive to interpersonal interaction.

It's almost as though I'm reading notes from someone who *should* have been treating Nell. Dr. Keller's notes felt . . . hungry. These are sympathetic, almost protective. I flip the page and continue reading.

Patient recalled a memory today, possibly the initial signs of Seer tendency. Popping sensation in the auditory realm and vague vocal stimuli. Further assessment required. Possible phenomena evident in sibling. Further research needed. Second request for reduction in medication.

As I continue to leaf through the pages, it seems that the entries get shorter, and somehow more guarded as they go on, as if major details are being withheld.

Patient experienced breakthrough today. Meeting strongly suggested. Notes insufficient.

"Meeting with whom?" I ask, but I know the answer the moment the question leaves my lips. Dr. Keller, of course. These notes were meant for him.

I rest the folder on my lap and rub the dust from my eyes, which only seems to make them water more. I had no idea what I'd find down here, but being this close to Nell's last days, I'm overwhelmed by just how alone she was.

As I smear the wetness away from my eyes, I become aware of something poking into my thigh through my blue scrubs. I lift the notes from the folder and peer underneath them. Another Polaroid sticks out—this one again of Nell, but it looks like it was taken without her knowing. She is hunched against a wall, her slim legs drawn up with her knees under her chin. She's biting her bottom lip, and that one motion seems to draw the rest of her face downward. Her eyes are half-closed, but alert—hysterical. It barely looks like my sister. I think back to the notes in their crooked handwriting: *notably withdrawn, suffering from sleep deprivation. Further observation required.*

"Oh God." This was the Pigeon's idea of observation? To dope her up and follow her around with a camera? But as I lift the Polaroid to fling it away in disgust, I'm surprised to find two more pictures stuck to the back of its glossy film.

The first is a snapshot of two faces close to the lens. The photo's blurry, but I recognize them immediately. To the right is my sister, smiling the way she used to, so hard that her neck strains and practically all her teeth show. She's the one holding the camera. The other face is Adam's. I'm struck by how his dark features seem somehow lighter. His stiff white uniform collar stands against his neck, but his shoulders are low, his chin dipped toward Nell's face. Under any other circumstances, they might have looked like a cute couple messing around with a camera in the park instead of the sterile desert courtyard of a psych ward. For just a second, I suppose that maybe my sister was not so alone after all. She had Adam, the one person who knew what was really going on at Oakside and fought to get her away from it, even if that put him in danger too.

I'm still holding onto this thought when I peel the photograph away to reveal the one stuck to its back.

This image is of Adam. He's in his starched orderly whites, his mouth open in protest. The corners of his lips are turned down, his hand extended to the lens as though reaching for it. A blurred finger sneaks into the frame, and I can just barely make out the tarnished sheen of silver that matches my own. Nell was taking the picture.

My eyes fall to Adam's extended hand—his left hand—and I see a dark blotch of blue ink along the side, stretching from his pinky finger to the bottom of his palm. My stomach sinks. In the picture, Adam is clutching a legal pad.

I drop the Polaroid as if it burns.

"It was you," I say to the image of Adam now lying on the floor of the storage closet. "You're Employee Y!"

Suddenly, Adam's voice reverberates through my mind.

He was made head psychiatrist at Oakside, and he made me his orderly, his right hand, in a way. By then, he knew I could detect a Seer as well as he could.

Then Deb's voice interrupts my memory.

She wasn't around when Dr. Keller and Adam were real buddy-buddy. None of us trusted him.

Adam never hid the fact that he and Dr. Keller used to be close. He was an *Insider* in every way. But what if I've been reading him wrong this whole time? What if he has been working for Dr. Keller all along, trying to lure another Seer to this place in order to pick up where they left off with Nell? I read back over his notes.

Possible phenomena evident in sibling. Further research needed.

Could it be that I've fallen into a trap? Stumbled into whatever it was Nell was so desperate to keep me away from? Could I have really been that stupid?

All at once, the basement goes dark, the lights extinguishing with a disturbing hiss and sizzle.

It's just a power outage. Nothing to worry about. At least that's what I repeat over and over to myself. But as the seconds tick by with no light and I sink further into darkness, I come to the reluctant conclusion that I'm going to have to make my way out of this basement by feel. I'm already worried one of the orderlies has decided to check my room ahead of schedule.

"Just find the stairs, find the door, get back to your room, and then you can figure out what the hell to do," I coach myself, as if saying it aloud will convince me. *It's an old building. I'm sure the power goes out all the time.*

But nothing about this theory eases my feeling of dread.

I poke one foot from the storage closet and find the step down. Planting my foot, I ease out of my crouch, the thick manila folder containing Nell's records falling to the floor of the closet, a double-slapping sound resonating in the wake of the fall. I find my footing and lean against the wall to keep my balance and get my bearings. Once out of the closet, I strain my eyes. It's a futile effort, but I can't help it. The dark is thick, and my only choice is to run my hand along the wall of the little mortuary doors until I find the railing to the stairs.

The wood is cold and damp to the touch, like everything else in the basement, and I try not to knock into the door handles. I'm terrified of waking the basement creature my mind has managed to conjure. After what feels like hours, I finally find the metal railing and the first step leading out of the basement. I run up the stairs, no longer caring how much noise I make, relieved to be past the worst part. I'm nearly to the top when I remember the keycard.

"Shit," I whisper.

I lift my right foot to grope the only place I could have stuffed it—into a sock. It's not there. I check my left sock, already certain I didn't put the keycard there, either. In fact, I didn't *put* it anywhere. I was holding it when I opened the door to the storage closet.

What did I do with it after that?

I've already been down here too long, and I'm sure I'm going to miss the next bed check.

Then I remember the accordion file hitting the floor and the slapping sound it made. The keycard must have been in my lap along with the folder.

The thought of retracing my steps back to the closet makes my stomach plummet. I take a chance and try pushing upward on the door, hoping beyond reason that it will open without its key. The trapdoor refuses to budge.

I descend the stairs once again, determined to move as quickly as possible in the dark.

"Just go down the stairs, down the hallway, grab the keycard and run," I tell myself, like it's the easiest thing in the world.

I plod my way back down the stairs and through the corridor—it actually is sort of easy. I find the closet still open, realizing that, by some dumb stroke of luck, I'd forgotten to close it behind me. My God, what if I'd closed the door with the keycard still inside?

I sink to my knees, searching for the accordion folder that is no doubt covering the key. My hands quickly fall on the file's banded cover, and just as I lift it and feel the coolness of the keycard beneath it, my ears pop, as if the air pressure has left the room.

It takes me only a second to realize what's happening, and terror takes hold.

It's faint at first, but the rustling sounds creep to my ear slowly, then rush past me like a vicious wind, sending a shudder through me.

The murmuring.

It's indecipherable but terrifying. My ear is hot. Someone is breathing too close. It's horribly familiar, and though there are no mirrors nearby, I know what it wants. It wants me to lean in close and listen. The unfinished soul. The Taker.

The murmuring continues, warm and wet, against my ear.

And then something happens that's never happened before.

I can hear what the voice is saying.

"Let me in."

I try to scream, but nothing escapes my throat. All I can do is listen.

"Let me in."

This time I respond. Not in words. In action.

My hand tightens around the keycard and I run. I run so fast down the two steps of the storage closet that I nearly fall, catching myself with wobbling ankles. My hand that isn't clutching the keycard drags along the doors to my right, jangling the handles as I go.

"No," I whisper between heaving breaths. "No!"

It doesn't need a mirror to get to me anymore, and it's found a way to make me hear its words. I pound up the flight of stairs, nearly running headfirst into the trapdoor. I bring a shaking hand to open it. But the card reader is nowhere to be found.

"Come on. Come on!" I gasp at my shaking hand or the trapdoor or the keycard, I have no idea. But my thumb finally finds the slot, and I slide the card through the reader and launch through the trapdoor. The force bangs the door on its hinge and bounces it back on my head.

I have no time to register the pain before I pull my legs up onto the linoleum floor of the linen closet and drop the door closed behind me, catching it just before it slams. A red light glows faintly under the floor before flickering out, reassuring me that the door is sealed.

I hold my hand to my chest in an effort to keep my heart from lurching out of it, then use my remaining strength to stand. Sliding the keycard through the pad to the linen closet, I poke my head into the hallway and find it blissfully empty. I slither through the door and let it shut behind me—praying I've sealed the Taker inside—and angle my body around the first corner, then the next. I slide the card through the reader leading to my room and quickly shut the door behind me, leaning on it to catch my breath. I pop the card back into my scrunched sock and pull the pillow and the sheet back into place, replacing the lump under my blanket with the person who should actually be there.

My entire body is screaming for sleep, though my eyes remain wide and searching in the dark of my room. Because

I can't decide what's worse: the evil I've unleashed in the basement, whose words are all at once horrifyingly clear, or the evil I've unleashed by convincing Evan to find Adam and bring him back to Oakside—an Adam I seem to have horribly misjudged.

24

I WAKE UP BECAUSE I can't breathe. Because something is *preventing* me from breathing.

I open my eyes, but the blackness of the room reveals nothing. My mouth is covered and my shoulders are pinned.

But not my legs.

I thrust my knee toward my head and make contact with what feels like a stack of ribs, and a muffled groan follows. I scramble out from under the weight that's temporarily lifted and pull in one frantic breath before the weight finds me again. It's an enormous hand that clamps its fingers tightly together to obscure any sound I might try to make. It smells like burnt coffee.

My flailing arms are once again pinned, this time with my arms wrenched behind my back.

"Stop. Sophie, stop! Stop struggling," the voice in my ear whispers. The voice sounds familiar, but I can't place it in my panic.

I try to scream, try to make the adrenaline that's shooting through my body do something productive, *anything*, but all I'm able to do is struggle against a strength that far exceeds mine.

"Come on. Let's go," the voice whispers, and pats one of my ankles, then the other, fingers searching out the keycard I shoved into my sock.

"Thought so," the voice says in a low tone, deep and cavernous.

A green light flickers and a tiny metal ping follows. As light pours into my room from the hallway, I squint against the pain behind my eyes while they struggle to transition. When the white light clears, I squirm enough to see the profile of Adam.

His enormous hands restrain me expertly.

I try to scream again, but his hand mashes against my lips and I think my jaw might come unhinged.

"Don't make a sound. Not a sound, understand?" he whispers into my ear.

I do what he tells me, mostly because I couldn't make a sound even if I wanted to. I'm picked up and carried into the next corridor, the one leading toward the lobby.

And the exit.

My thrashing heart slows for a moment as I consider the possibility that I'm going to be rescued, that I was right in sending Evan to track down Adam again, and that maybe there's an explanation for the papers that I found in the basement—the ones revealing him as Employee Y, who had pretended to get close to Nell only to carry information back to Dr. Keller. Sure, this isn't exactly the way I saw it happening—Adam restraining me and practically shoving me out the front door—but any way I can escape Oakside is good by me, so long as he has a plan for Deb, too.

The lobby and the double-sliding doors come into view, but Adam takes us down a different corridor, which feels eerily familiar. *Why?* Something feels like it's rotting in my stomach. Wherever Adam's taking me, it isn't good.

He shuffles me down another corridor, then around a corner, and down another hallway. I can hear far-off laughter and the phlegmy coughs of what sounds like Robbie and Pucker-Mouth, but they might as well be a million miles away for all the good they can do me right now. Besides, at this point, I can only assume they're on the same side as Adam, and that everyone is playing for Team Keller. I'm seriously outnumbered.

Adam stops in front of a metal door, and thank God for

that because my jaw feels like it's about to crack under the pressure of his hand. But my relief melts into horror when I see that instead of a keycard reader, there's a glowing keypad, beckoning for a code it seems Adam still remembers.

He punches the one and the two zeros before I pounce, bringing my bare heel down across the bridge of his sneaker, probably hurting me more than it hurts him. But it's enough to make him loosen his grip over my mouth for just a second, as I widen my jaw and bite the fleshy insides of his long fingers.

Adam cries out, and I taste freedom. All of my limbs unencumbered, I make it halfway down the hall before I'm yanked backward by my wrist, my shoulder wrenching in its socket.

"No!" I manage to shout before his hand clamps over my mouth again.

"Stop fighting me!" he growls through gritted teeth.

"Who's out there!" I hear Robbie's voice followed by footsteps.

I struggle to scream.

"Damnit, now look what you've done!" he scolds me.

He reenters the first three numbers of the code, then quickly follows with the five, the eight, and the last five, releasing the lock. He shoves me into the room and follows, slamming the door shut, then I watch in stunned silence as his fingers deftly punch a different code, to which the computerized locking mechanism responds with:

"Code change initiated."

"What? Wait, no!" I scream, springing toward him. But he's too fast for me. With one of his long arms, he keeps me out of swiping distance and, blocking the keypad from my view, punches five new numbers, earning the computer's confirmation.

"New code activated."

A second later, I hear rubber soles squeaking to a stop outside the door, fingers trying and retrying to key in the old code that now refuses to open the door.

"Please help me!"

Adam turns to me, his dark features crumpling in disbelief.

"Are you insane?" he asks me.

"Is that a serious question?"

We exchange looks of matching confusion, and for a moment, I wonder if Adam really thinks he's helping me. One glance at the wall of mirrors tells me all I need to know.

Adam means to kill both of us.

A sickening déjà vu passes through me like a ghost. I stare at Adam, but all I can see when I look at him is a bulbous, shaved head and darting blue eyes that are so wide, they have lost their ability to see clearly.

There's a flurry of commotion on the other side of the door. Voices yell over one another. Orders are barked three at a time. Then, rising above the chaos, I hear a familiar voice.

"Sophie? Are you okay? Are you in there?"

"Evan! Help me! This room is full of mirrors. He's going to kill us!"

"Oh my God, Sophie, punch in the code like you did last time!" Deb's voice guides me from the other side of the door.

"He changed the code. I can't get out. Someone help!"

"Adam, what are you doing? Get out of there! This wasn't part of the plan!" Evan shouts, but Adam only shakes his head, his face sagging. I recognize that defeat from my last visit to this room. He's trying to end it. Just like Kenny did.

"Adam! Come on, let's go!" Evan shouts.

"None of you are going anywhere. The minute Adam comes out, you're all headed straight for the sheriff. Breaking and entering. Trespassing. Do you have any idea how much trouble you're in right now?" the Pigeon threatens them. But I can tell she's relishing the chaos.

"Lady, do you think I give a shit about the sheriff right now? Get them out of there before that . . . that *thing* comes for them!" Evan screams.

"I know what I'm doing," Adam says in a voice I can hear but I doubt anyone on the other side of the door can.

To my surprise, someone does. And he responds.

"Adam? Adam, come out of there. Bring the girl. You don't need to do this."

It's Dr. Keller. I almost don't recognize his voice. The last time I saw him, he was terrorizing me outside of his clinical office. Now his voice sounds almost . . . fatherly.

"I can't do that, Jeremy. I know you don't understand. But I have to do this," Adam says, his jaw twitching under his skin. "This ends tonight."

Adam turns to me, his eyes pulling on mine, and he nods, almost imperceptibly. "You know what to do. I know you do."

He presses something cool into my hand. It's sharp, but fragile, and snakes in my palm.

"I need you to trust me. If you don't believe me, believe what your sister did. Believe your heart. You know I'm not here to hurt you."

Then he takes another step closer.

"You know we can end this."

My ears pop, the sound vacuums from the room, and I'm left with nothing. The wordless murmuring floats to me from across the room as though on a fog. It fills the void of noise left by the vacuum. It tickles my ear, enticing me to listen, dampening my skin with its hot breath.

Sound comes roaring back on the end of a long, agonized

gasp. I hear pounding, pleading from behind the metal door.

"Adam, let her out!" Deb shouts.

"Adam, you don't need to do this, son. You know you've always been like my own flesh and blood."

But Adam only shakes his head, his eyes anguished. "You never believed that. You only wanted me for what I could do. You never came looking for me. You never tried to find me after I left. You only wanted me when you realized what I took."

My hand squeezes Adam's gift, the metal pressing into my palm.

There's a long pause, then Dr. Keller sputters back to life. "That's—that's not true. I love you."

"You love your obsession," Adam says with finality, his face strangely calm in the midst of such a painful exchange. When I follow his gaze toward the mirror, I understand why.

His reflection and mine have begun to merge, overlapping and creating a distorted image of our bodies. Then something flickers behind it, and I lose all track of what everyone's hollering from the other side of the door. Because the reflection is losing itself, becoming something else. Something black and rotting.

I see the mouth first, lips splitting over long yellow teeth that are too large for its skeletal head. Oily hair parts to reveal a decaying mess of a face, two gaping holes stare from

where eyes should be. Spindly fingers reach through the glass, seeming to part it like liquid.

Adam ushers me behind him, forcing me to peer through the space between his elbow and his hip. I follow the Taker's movements, compelled to watch.

Its mouth moves rapidly, chewing silent words. Its legs jerk from the mirror, gaining momentum on the linoleum of the room. It lumbers toward Adam and me, its movement tight, like it's trying to crawl from the confines of its own rotting body.

"Adam!" A voice pleads from the hallway.

But he doesn't say anything. He only wraps an arm behind him to keep me close.

"Just trust your heart, Sophie," he whispers, and I swallow hard, not sure I trust anything anymore.

The Taker is only three feet from us now. As it approaches, it stops, tilts its head from one side to another. It's weighing its options. It's deciding which of us to go after first.

There's a renewed pounding on the door, voices crawling over one another, intermittently drowned out by the force of their fists banging on the door they no longer have the combination for.

The odor of the room changes. The air is thick with the smell of waste. I watch the Taker's long fingers dance at the ends of thin planks that might have once been palms. Its mouth is moving faster and faster. Its breathing is raspy.

Then, in one quick movement, the Taker swipes its sinewy arm, throwing Adam to the other side of the room as if he is no heavier than a crumpled piece of paper.

"NO!" he screams as he flies through the air, arms and legs scrambling. He hits the wall, smacking his head against the sheetrock, and slumps down in a heap on the dull gray floor. He doesn't make another sound.

The Taker focuses its eyeless gaze on me. Its stench clogs my senses, making me dizzy. The murmuring is still awash in my ears, sloshing like some sort of tidal wave. But now I hear the words clearly, just as I had in the basement.

"Let me in," it says, over and over, soothing, like a lullaby. "Let me in."

"I-I don't want to," I cry, whimpering like a child.

"Let me in, and it won't hurt anymore. The pain will all go away. Let me in."

"No, I can't."

"Let me in. Do it now. You'll be with her again. She misses you. Let me in."

"Sophie, don't listen. Don't let it in." Adam's voice sounds as though he's at the end of a long tunnel. He's slouched in the corner, struggling to get to his feet.

"Don't let it in, Sophie. Don't give in. Use what I gave you!"

I hear a rattling breath, and the Taker directs its eyeless stare at Adam in what looks to be a warning. Adam lies still on the floor.

The Taker turns back to me, its mouth moving rhythmically over its hideous yellow teeth. I want to back up. I want to fight it. But I can't seem to move. I can only stand still and watch it come for me. Three feet away. Two feet. One. It's nearly on top of me. The smell is horrible, but I can't make it stop.

"Let me in. Let me in."

"Sophie, let me in!"

I can't tell the difference between the voices anymore. The Taker. Evan. Dr. Keller. They all sound the same. Everything sounds like it's under water. Toneless and muffled. I only want to sleep. To give in to the pain. To release it all and be done for good.

I just want to see Nell again. Just one more time.

"She misses you. You can go to her. Just let me in."

She misses me. And I miss her. I miss her so badly that my chest feels like it might cave in. I can see her now, a terry-cloth towel wrapped around her shoulders, a hair clip fastening the towel around her neck. Nell holds a hairbrush in her hand, her fingers making a cutting motion like imaginary scissors.

Come on LS, it's your turn, she says to me. She's motioning to me to take a seat on the stool she's set up. We're playing beauty salon, and it's my turn to be the customer.

"It's your turn. Let me in."

I want to see Nell. Just once more. I want to tell her how sorry I am that I let her down. I shouldn't have been afraid. I should have been as brave as she was.

A metal door handle rattles.

"Sophie, let us in. Adam, for God's sake!" Deb screams.

"Sophie, open your hand!" Adam pleads.

"Let me in. It's the only way."

Now I feel the heat on my ear. It's telling me how to let go, how I can see Nell again. My toes tingle, like the feeling they get before my feet start to fall asleep. Pins and needles. Flat pine needles in primary colors. All I want to do is sleep and never wake up.

"Wait, no!" I hear a deep voice say. It's trying to wake me, but I don't want to wake up.

"You want me, wait!" it says, and I don't understand.

"Sophie!" Evan calls.

Something roars in the Taker, something prehistoric. Its mouth clacks in front of me, so wide it looks like it could swallow me whole.

Screaming, I startle to my senses and take cover behind a gurney beside the door, but the Taker lifts it up and throws it against the mirror, shattering the glass. My heart throbs, my mind conjuring the memory of a sink dripping with Nell's blood, the fleeting image of something unnatural reflected in those fragments of glass as they fell from the bathroom wall. Something that Nell tried to stop me from seeing.

"Sophie, look out!"

I'm suddenly aware of Adam again. He lunges forward to push me out of the Taker's way. My head hits the corner of the countertop that juts from the wall. My ears ring and the rushing waves of the murmurings cease.

The Taker swipes its long arm at me but Adam deflects it, this time bracing himself against the impact. Now he's directly in front of its face, its mouth still hanging wide open, its yellow teeth bared like a vicious animal.

"Adam!" I cry out, but he holds his hand out to me without turning around. I see now that he's purposely placed himself directly in front of the Taker's eyeless gape.

"You want me instead," he tells the Taker in a voice so steady and calm, I can't believe I've heard him right.

"Adam, no, what are you—?"

He puts his hand out to quiet me again and leans his head in toward the Taker's. The Taker's mouth suddenly clamps shut, and this time, its teeth come together in the most hideous grin I have ever seen, its cracked lips curling under to make space for it.

Adam never breaks his focus, never once flinches as the Taker leans in and whispers in his ear. As his eyes close, Adam rises up onto a single toe, and I watch in utter horror as that toe leads him up the wall and onto the ceiling, the rest of his body hanging like a caterpillar from its cocoon.

"No!" I cry out, but it's too late.

Adam has already let the Taker in.

It whispers once more into his ear, but by then, Adam is already gone. His black eyes wander to mine just as the last of his life begins to leave him, and the Taker leans in to find that part of itself it can never have.

But this time is different. Adam doesn't turn to me and utter a parting message like Kenny did. Instead, he points to my fist, which I'd forgotten I was clenching. I open my palm and dangle a long braid of gold—tiny charms in the shape of a shamrock, a shoe, a treasure chest, a puppy. Twinkling with the sweat from my hand is the bracelet that had at one time meant something to a young Dr. Keller and his young Susan.

Holding this symbol of Dr. Keller's love, I imagine the pain that he felt upon losing Susan, the pain Susan felt when her life was taken from her, her soul ripped in two through no fault of her own. I allow myself to feel the pain of their separate but connected losses, each equally irretrievable. I envision it so vividly, I'm practically there with them, on some anonymous street corner, a knife between them, a gift ungiven.

The Taker drops its eyeless gape from Adam and focuses on the bracelet dangling from my fingertips. And in that second, Adam squeezes his eyes shut, and with what looks to be his last ounce of strength, he screams.

"O-FOUR-THIRTEEN-THIRTEEN!"

The room falls utterly silent. I can only hear the pounding of my own heart in my ears. Then comes beeping followed by a ping.

The door whooshes open. Dr. Keller is in the doorway, his skin white and filmy with sweat, his lab coat and clothes looking somehow bigger on him. His lip trembles, searching for something to say. His head sways on his neck. His hands shake.

Dr. Keller is transfixed by the Taker, its rotting body twitching in place, its hungry mouth clearly at a loss for whom to attack first.

"Susan," Dr. Keller whispers, his face twists in horror at what he sees, and the Taker cocks its head so far to the side that it's nearly sideways.

"That's not Susan, and you know it," Adam says, his voice

cracking under the strain of staying conscious and alive.

"Susan, I know you're in there somewhere," Dr. Keller croaks through tears. His face is folded into a million creases. His fingers spread and flex, curling into little balls, glistening with the same perspiration that slicks his pasty face.

"She's not," Adam says.

The Taker turns to Dr. Keller and tilts its head, taking one jerking step toward him, then two more.

Suddenly, Dr. Keller's face shifts, and his pleading turns to horror.

The Taker leans toward him, and I remember the bracelet.

Without thinking, I place myself between Dr. Keller and the Taker, fighting the urge to listen to what the rapidly moving mouth has to say. I reach out for its waving fingers. Taking each end of the bracelet, I encircle the rotting blackness of what might have once been a wrist.

The Taker stops jerking its arms and legs. It spreads its cracked lips, teeth clicking, and looks down at the bracelet, letting its mouth fall open like a lever releasing itself.

The sound splits the room in half. It's like a roar, so horrendous that I scream along with it. The Taker crumbles to pieces like ash falling from a flaming piece of tinder. The remnants fill the room with the putrid smell of decay, then disintegrate into a pile of fine black dust.

Then the dust disappears into the gray linoleum like it was never there. In its place, all that remains is a green Lego. And resting atop that green Lego, wrapped around one of the nubs like a horseshoe around a stick, is a gleaming silver ring that matches the one on my own finger. The only trace of the charm bracelet is the tarnished leaf of a tiny gold shamrock.

The rest of the night is one I know I'll barely remember even as it's happening. A cloud has already started to gather over it, obscuring the events and blurring the details. Only the loudest voices, the boldest colors, the strangest actions are left in my memory.

Adam falls from the ceiling and collapses into a heap. He's revived by none other than Dr. Keller, who cries for him the way I can only imagine a father might cry for a child.

The Pigeon attempts to pull Dr. Keller from Adam's side and is rewarded with a slap to the face, one that leaves her cheek spotted bright pink.

Adam recovers in time to see the police arrive, nearly a dozen tan uniforms with holstered guns in black cradles at their hips. Handcuffs are produced, and people in white—not the trespassers of the night—are taken to cars with flashing lights that crowd the normally empty parking lot.

Dr. Keller's perfect hands are bound behind him in silver

bracelets. So are the Pigeon's, in her tightly wound topknot; and Pucker-Mouth's, with her phlegmy cough; and Robbie's, with his face pinched in worry about what will become of him.

Tired-looking people of all ages, all levels of disorientation—all in mint-green scrubs—are led away with blankets wrapped around their shoulders like confused superheroes.

Evan's arms, strong and stable, encircle me.

Deb's eyes, amber and wide and alive with fire, watch all of it.

Mom and Aunt Becca, their matching curls and red-rimmed green eyes, search me out in the waiting room.

The smell of conditioner.

Adam stands beside me in the lobby, answering question after question from the sheriff, the health department, social services.

Adam tells them all he can without telling them what he knows they won't understand.

His coal-black eyes meet mine, and I understand. He's sorry he scared me. He's sorry I thought he would betray me.

When no one else is listening, when everyone's preoccupied with their notes and comforting those who've been scarred and scared, Adam says, "I loved her more than I've ever loved anyone. I thought I could save her."

I shake my head at his confession and tell him, "You gave her more than any of us could. You did save her. You saved her from loneliness."

We made promises—to call the next morning, to talk more, to see one another's faces the first thing the following day.

Those of us who were left were given rides home in cars that weren't our own. Red and blue lights flashed spastically against the asphalt until we arrived at our respective homes.

And then there was sleep. In the same bed with Mom and Aunt Becca. The smell of conditioner on either side of my head lulling me into a fitful, but otherwise lovely sleep. Because every time I woke up, one of them was there staring at me, making sure I was okay, making sure I wasn't going anywhere. Making sure I didn't feel alone.

25

THE WEATHER IS STILL RELATIVELY cool. It's ninety degrees, not bad for April in Phoenix. But the air feels stiff as a linen shirt dried in the sun. I can tell our mild days are numbered as we creep into the long summer.

"So, how does it feel to be the smartest girl to ever pick up a book?" Evan teases me as we walk around the block. We got home from school twenty minutes ago, and we've been circling the neighborhood in a bid to squeeze out a little more time together.

It's been three months since classes started up again for the semester. This is his way of congratulating me on my position as Mrs. Dodd's teaching assistant for next year, which means I'll be spending my first period helping other students analyze Kafka instead of taking some lame elective. I can still hardly believe she asked me of all people. One of these days, she's going to figure out I don't actually have any idea what I'm talking about. Of course, that's precisely the quality she says makes me the best person for the job. As she puts it, so long as I don't think I have all the answers, I'll continue to ask the right questions. I'm positive that my face turned a hideous shade of crimson when she said that, but it still felt pretty good to hear it.

"I hope you'll make time for the little people," Evan says, teasing me. But I detect a note of insecurity.

"Please, like you're going to have a spare minute for me with all the time you'll be spending on the field."

I'm not the only one who received exciting news this week. Evan made varsity, and he'll be practicing two times a day in preparation for fall. Apparently, Coach Tarza likes to get an early start.

"Tell you what," I continue, "if I start spending every free minute buried in a pile of books, you officially have permission to yank me away and make me watch a horror movie marathon." We both grow quiet with a shared memory of the first time I mentioned my love for horror movies—right before he tried to take me to Jerome for our first date.

"So," Evan says cautiously. "No more follow-up visits I take it?" Evan means the police. This is new territory for both of us, talking about my last night in Oakside, and everything that happened afterward.

"Nope, not for a couple of weeks. I guess it's finally over," I say, knowing I don't sound the least bit convincing.

After that night, Oakside hit the news in a big way. National news, as it turns out. Corrupt and neglectful mental institutions make for great headlines. And this, for better or worse, made the police investigation of what happened there the night we killed Susan's Taker even more invasive. The police brought every one of us in for questioning. Evan, Deb, Adam, and I were all hoping to spend more time together, but that wasn't exactly the way we'd planned it. We all played dumb, of course. Deb and I told the police that we were drugged at Oakside, and that we were subjected to vague and confusing tests with no clear purpose. We followed Adam's lead in sharing just enough to answer their questions, but not sharing so much that it would lead to *more* questions.

The police made subsequent visits so they could complete their reports. Just when I would think the nightmare was over, more police would show up, or call. Cops. Detectives. Medical professionals. They all wanted to know about the tests, the drugs. They asked me about the basement. I told them it was all a blur. I couldn't tell them the truth—that some nights I don't sleep, so sure that I'm going to close my eyes and feel my ears pop before I hear that horrible whisper.

Then, two weeks ago, the calls and visits from the police stopped. Not coincidentally, I'm sure, this cessation of interest coincided with Oakside's disappearance from the media. After the national news mania died down, the local news buried the story under a more sensational money laundering scandal connected to some city administrator. And when the cops finally stopped asking questions, my head finally stopped hurting.

My heart still has a ways to go.

"Hey, where'd you go?" Evan asks me, his face pinched in now-familiar concern.

"Sorry. Just remembering," I say.

That happens a lot these days.

"How's your mom doing?" Evan asks after a long period of silence.

"Good. She's good." And for the first time in a really long time, I actually believe it. Mom's been going to an AA meeting at least once a week, sometimes more if she feels like she needs it. Evan knows this. We pretty much see each other every day, and when our paths don't cross at school, we spend hours on the phone in the evenings. It's strange; our relationship started with many unexpected intimacies, but we've had to fill in a lot of the gaps and start from scratch.

Well, maybe not from scratch. That would be impossible. But we rewound a bit, went on actual dates instead of excursions to mental institutions and far-away cities. Instead, we go to the movies now. Or the mall.

Not all parts of our relationship have slowed down, though. All those connections we had in the beginning, all the making out—there are some things you just can't slow once they've started. Feeling the warmth of Evan's lips on mine, his calloused hands on my skin, his breath—I couldn't have stopped that if I'd wanted to. I feel an actual tug inside of me when I haven't seen him in a day. It's almost painful, but in the best way. And all of that pales in comparison to knowing I can talk to him about anything and he won't think I'm a freak. He's already seen all of my secrets.

"I've got a session tonight," I say, glad I don't have to say more.

We've started going to therapy—Mom, Aunt Becca, and me.

"That's good," he says, and we leave it at that. He's right, it is good.

I think it might actually be helping, too. The therapy. I'm less angry these days with Mom and Aunt Becca. And I don't hunch my shoulders in fear as much as I used to. Sometimes my ears pop because my sinuses get stuffed up. But then there are other times that they pop, and the murmuring returns. I still see things that others don't know are there. I am still leery of mirrors. I don't like to look into them for too long. I know that this will never go away. Cursed or not, this is who I am. I will always be a Seer. Only now, I know that I'm not alone. And now I know how to control it.

"Deb and I go tonight too," Evan says, and I nod.

He goes with Deb, mostly for moral support. In a lot of ways, she's been through more than any of us have. A lot more. Evan never knew about his uncle's abuse. He thinks his aunt must have known but was too afraid to say anything. I can only guess that's where the therapy is starting. They'll get to the Oakside stuff later. When she's ready. After all, a regular psychiatrist probably isn't going to be well-versed in the world of Takers and Seers.

Deb lives with Evan and his parents now. The courts miraculously allowed it, although I'm sure the fact that her parents turned her over to Oakside, an institution that the media successfully (and accurately) demonized, probably didn't hurt Evan's parents' petition for custody. That and Deb's plea to the court to be allowed to live with the only people she had ever really considered family.

Deb's put on a little weight since she moved in with them,

and the space around her enormous amber eyes has plumped out, so she resembles Evan more than ever.

I watch Evan now as we round the corner toward my house.

"What?" He looks embarrassed.

"What are you thinking about?"

"Gatorade," he says wistfully.

"Be serious," I give him a little shove. "You looked far away."

He scoops me close and presses me to him. "There. Can't get much closer than that."

He's right.

"Well, speak of the devil," Evan says as my house comes into view.

A tall figure leans against Evan's car where he left it parked at the curb. A much smaller figure leans in a similar fashion beside the tall one.

As we approach, Adam pushes himself away from Evan's white Probe and walks over, nodding formally like he's some sort of guard in charge of my safety.

Which I suppose isn't too far off the mark.

"Hi, Sophie," Adam says, his voice warm and rich, like freshly steeped coffee. He rests a giant hand on my shoulder, then pries his gaze from me and extends his other hand to

Evan. Evan told me that as soon as he figured out what I was trying to tell him in Oakside, he'd sped to Jerome in search of Adam and nearly missed him. Adam was making good on his threat to find a new hiding place. A few more minutes, and he would have been gone. I still get panicky when I think about what that could have meant.

Evan and Adam look at each other now, exchanging sad but meaningful smiles. They look like war buddies.

Again, not too far off the mark. This is how they typically greet each other. Guys are strange.

"I was taking the bus home from class and found a familiar face," Adam says, peering down at Deb. "She said she was coming to meet you, Evan. I just wanted to be sure Deb got here safely."

"Thanks, man," he says to Adam, then turns to Deb. "Hey, Squirt," Evan smiles easily and puts his arm around her in a brotherly squeeze. She protests against it, but I know she loves it.

We all stand awkwardly together beside Evan's car for a minute, a circle of battle survivors. We're all still a little bruised. Some scars are more visible than others. Adam is still impossibly thin, though he has stopped living like a hermit. In fact, he might be more well-adjusted than the rest of us. He's renting an apartment downtown—one with actual running water and free coffee in the lobby every morning—and he has been accepted into the psychology program of his top-pick local university. He told me about it a few weeks ago, and I proceeded to brag about it to everyone: Evan, Deb, Mom, Aunt Becca. What I didn't tell them was that one of Nell's poems was why he applied: In the poem, she credited Adam for making her believe there was a purpose in her life. He helped her recognize that her life was worth living. It was that poem, he told me, that made him realize that he could inspire others. He intends to do more of that.

Once he's earned his doctorate, Adam wants to open his own practice. And then he'll do what Dr. Keller had promised him they'd do many years ago, only this time, Adam will do it for real. He will find Seers (he knows they're out there from his blog, which he started up again a few months ago. He even started letting them post comments), and he will help them understand what they're going through. He'll make sure they're not alone and help them realize there are ways to cope. Being a Seer isn't always a curse, and it doesn't always have to end hanging upside down by a toe.

I wear Nell's ring above mine these days. Hers seems to keep mine more securely in place on my finger.

"Evan," Deb tugs lightly on his sleeve. "I've got to get to my appointment."

She gives me and Adam a quick hug, then turns to me.

"Movie marathon Friday night?"

"Wouldn't miss it," I say.

She smiles, gives me one more hug, then playfully punches her cousin in the shoulder before disappearing into the backseat.

"You want a ride home, man?" Evan offers to Adam.

Adam nods. "That'd be great. Thank you, Evan."

"Dude, you can, like, start calling me bro or something."

Adam's face creases into a smile. His teeth are broad and a little crooked along the bottom row. A tiny dimple forms in the corner of his mouth. I decide that dimple will now be the first thing I see when I picture Adam.

Then he climbs into the passenger seat of Evan's car, readjusting his long legs to fit.

"Call me later?" I ask Evan, knowing I sound a little needy, but I'm okay letting him know I need him now.

"Count on it," he says, and pulls me to him, pressing his lips against mine. They linger like the scent of him. I let my lips graze over his until I'm dizzy with the contentedness of being in the arms of someone who loves every part of me, even the scary parts. I watch them drive away in Evan's old white Ford, and I turn slowly toward my house.

Just before pulling my key from my bag, I take a moment

and breathe deeply, letting the spring air in my lungs push against my ribs, then slowly exhale. I realize it's the first time in close to a year that I've been able to take a deep breath. It feels so good I almost cry.

Mom's sitting at the dining room table when I walk in. It's still weird to see her out of bed and dressed in the middle of the day. But weird in a good way.

"How was school?"

She's a little unpracticed. It's like she has to remind herself how to ask the normal "mom questions."

"Fine," I say, deciding to save my teaching assistantship news for later. She'll like hearing about it over dinner. It feels good to want to tell her that kind of stuff again.

"That's good," she says, gripping a mug of tea between her palms. She's concentrating on the rich brown liquid. Then the wood of the table. Then the carpet.

It's going to take a while. She said in therapy that she still can't look at me without seeing Nell. I'm working on not holding that against her.

"I'll be in my—I'll be back there," I say, not sure I should tell her whose room I'll be in.

I turn to leave, but as I do, Mom's fingers brush mine. She stands from the table and pulls me into a hug so tight, it knocks the wind out of me.

"Honey."

I swallow the thickness from my throat and put my arms around her waist. I press my ear to her chest and listen to her heart thump. It sounds like *honey, honey, honey.*

When she finally lets me go, it's like neither of us knows what to do from there. Mom's the first to leave, deciding her tea needs to be reheated. I tell her I'll see her at dinner. I smile to myself when I picture her excitement at hearing I'll be Mrs. Dodd's aide.

In my room, I change out of my school clothes and pull on Evan's practice jersey and a pair of shorts. I crack the door to Nell's bedroom and flop down on her bed, reaching beneath the mattress, feeling around for the journal I've been reading for nearly half a year.

Pulling the composition book from its place, I open it slowly, ceremoniously, and allow my eyes to fall across the page of Nell's swirling letters. These are the words she left behind. The words Adam carried with him when he took her away from Oakside, and later left for me to find.

I run my finger across the impressions of her script, and let the gleam of her ring and mine catch a sliver of light. For just a moment, they look joined as one band, reinforced. Stronger. I take another deep breath.

And I read the words Nell wrote that inspired her to live—

the same words that inspire those who loved her to go on living after she died. Her poetry isn't a code to decipher anymore, but a language for her and me to share, even if she's no longer here to speak it.

He says there's a chance.
I say, What's the point?
He points to me.

ACKNOWLEDGMENTS

I feel so fortunate to have as many people to thank for their support as I have for this novel. Every author should be so lucky.

I am so grateful for my incredible editor, Annette Pollert. Thank you for your enthusiasm, warmth, and expertise throughout the whole process. When I dreamt of publishing, I always pictured an editor exactly like you. A million thanks to the entire team at Simon Pulse for your dedication to *The Murmurings*. Thank you: Bethany Buck, Mara Anastas, Jennifer Klonsky, Michael Strother, Lucille Rettino, Julie Christopher, Carolyn Swerdloff, Paul Crichton, Aaron Murray, Amy Bartram, Beth Adelman, Jenica Nasworthy, Jessica Handelman, Craig Adams, Mary Marotta, Christina Pecorale, Mary Faria, Brian Kelleher, Jim Conlin, Theresa Brumm, and Victor Iannone. Your eyes, minds, and hearts have made this novel possible.

To my brilliant agent, Steven Chudney—endless thanks for believing in me from the start. Your insights, intuition, and tireless efforts make me a better writer. No author could wish for a better advocate.

Professors, teachers, and mentors along the way, I am so grateful for your guidance. A very special thanks to Kathryn Reiss, Elmaz Abinader, Cornelia Nixon, Victor LaValle, Stephanie Young, and Yiyun Li. My experience at Mills College continues to sustain and nourish me.

Much, much love to my extraordinary writing group: Lizzie Brock, Laura Joyce Davis, Nina LaCour, and Teresa K. Miller. Thank you for your close readings and encouragement, and thank you for renewing and inspiring me every month. You mean so very much to me. Additional thanks to early readers Nate Davis and Liz Vachon.

To Frank Bumstead—did you think I'd forget? Thank you for making sure I didn't have any excuse to shy away from my dreams.

Mom and Dad, thank you from my very core. You never once told me it wasn't possible. Never once did you let on that writing might not be the most prudent endeavor. That seed has rooted me deeply, and has kept me upright when insecurity threatened to tip me over. To my brother, Matt; to Nikki, Rick, Jan, Bethany, Grandma Ruthie (of blessed memory), and Grandpa Phil: Thank you for your unceasing support and encouragement. I am humbled by your generosity of spirit, and so very lucky to call you family.

To my son, Simon, for the doors you've opened, even

though you don't have the dexterity to do that yet. I promise to dedicate my life to making sure you know how much you are loved.

For my husband, Matt: For making sure writing is always there, around every corner, never too far from my side. For insisting I never, ever let it slip away, and for catching it when it falls out of my hand. For believing when I don't. For listening when it hurts and when it's exciting and when I hate and love and fear it. For sushi and inspiration, for late night musings, for taking it seriously but always knowing when to laugh. For standing by my side. For facing it with me. For loving every crazy ounce of me. I love you, always.